Damn The Dead

Arcadia Book 1

Phillip Tomasso

Praise for Phillip Tomasso

"VACCINATION is a thrill a minute. Narrated in a gritty noir voice, Phillip Tomasso drags you into a zombie outbreak face first and doesn't let you go until you've ripped your fingernails off clawing for help. Smart, intense and damn right frightening, VACCINATION is a must for any zombie fan."– Max Booth III, author of Toxicity

"It's hard not to get emotionally attached to the small group of survivors and root for them despite their personal flaws. It's pretty much impossible to describe the end without giving away too much. I'll just say that it was a great twist. Whether you are new to zombie fiction or have been a fan for years, I'd tell you to check this one out. It's a great read." – Ian McLellan, Zombie-Guide.com

"Tomasso created a Zombie book that seems all too possible! This book kept me wired tight from the beginning until the very end. If you like awesome adventure, and vivid storytelling, then you will LOVE Vaccination! 5 BIG Stars!" – Cedric Nye, author of The Road to Hell is Paved with Zombies

"There's a bit of a cliff hanger at the end of the book, which left me wanting more. I'm anxiously awaiting the publication of the second book. If you're looking for a great zombie book, then I highly recommend you grab a copy of Vaccination. Props to Phillip Tomasso for writing this fantastic zombie novel!" – J. Cornnell Michels, author of Jordan's Brains

"Tomasso explores a humanity left dormant in the infected with graceful elegance. While we get glimpses into that unexpected possibility throughout the book, I would have loved digging deeper down that rabbit hole and see what he would have gifted us with. Simply put, however, VACCINATION is on fire!" — The Bookie Monster

This one is for my kids,
Phillip, Grant and Raeleigh

PART I

The Mountains

Chapter 1

It started with the flu.

That's what Charlene's dad explained, three years ago. He worked at 9-1-1, was taking emergency calls when the apocalypse began. Strong Memorial Hospital's research team supplied the country with vaccinations. Contaminated serum was accidentally used and the mistake wasn't caught until far too late. Those injected became messed up creatures. Chase McKinney called them zombies because they reminded him of monsters from old movies and crazy, popular television shows.

Char had been fourteen then. As much as she wished, she could never forget any of it. She remembered it all. Worse, she couldn't escape the horrors when she slept and her dreams were plagued with nightmares. The events that unfolded in her mind while asleep had really happened and were not obscured while in some hypnagogic state. She was forced to relive the haunting torments night after night. The only silver lining, she didn't sleep much. If she was lucky enough to find somewhere safe to lay down for a bit, she rarely slipped into a deep enough rest to reach a state of R.E.M. While perpetually exhausted, she was just slightly more than thankful.

Charlene McKinney —goes by Char— hunkered down behind grey rocks and thick brush, and eyed a tractor trailer packed full with supplies. This meant they had access to gasoline, too.

Her father, Chase, had died trying to deliver a band of survivors across the Mexican border. His thoughts centered on economy. The third world country was too poor to inoculate their citizens, and the walls built by the US would prevent most infected from crossing south over the border. He was confident that Mexico would prove to be a sanctuary.

Her father had been right. Mostly.

She spent a year in Mexico. The constant dry weather and ninety degree heat felt crippling. Finding water —drinkable water— was nearly a daily struggle. She stayed on her own, not wanting or trusting others. Zombies were bad, but what she learned while her father was still alive was that the non-infected were oftentimes far more dangerous and deadly.

She supposed she looked a lot like her mom, but the best she could remember, only thinner, more muscular and wiry, maybe. She kept her chocolate brown hair in a tight pony. Chopping it short made the most sense. She just couldn't bring herself to do it. It was the small bit of vanity she held onto, and it hopefully drew attention from a knife scar that ran across her lower left jaw line.

"Char? You in there?"

She snapped her head to the right.

"We going to do this or what?"

It was early September, or mid-October. Monday or Thursday. Char had planned to keep months and days straight in her head. It seemed important, but it wasn't long until she lost track. This bothered her. She'd close her eyes and try to count days off in her head, but to no avail. In Mexico, seasons didn't change. One day had melted into the next.

When she left Mexico, she encountered Tony Dibella. She'd spotted him, alone, walking down the center of a road in Texas. Armed with a bow and quiver full of arrows, he looked worn out, close to collapsing. She followed for several miles. The man pushed himself, stumbling now and again, but never stopping. At one point he paused for water from the canteen clipped to the side of his belt. He took a long swallow and then said, "Be better to have someone walk with me instead of just following me."

She stayed hidden, watching. Okay, he knew she was there, following him. It didn't mean it was safe to reveal her location.

After a while of patiently waiting, he threw his hands in the air and continued on his way.

Just before nightfall he'd wound his way off the streets and into a thin forest that ran between the road and an interstate highway. Char watched, keeping her distance, as he climbed up a tree and sat on a branch. He armed his bow with an arrow and waited. She supposed he reminded her of her father. They were about the same age. This guy was bigger, though. She couldn't tell if it was muscle or not with his clothing and gear. His hair was a bit long in back, and the rest tucked under a Texas baseball cap. Unshaven for perhaps a week or two, his beard was scraggly and grey around the chin.

She knew he hunted dinner. She watched as a squirrel wisped by the tree. The man loosed the arrow and dropped the tree-scurrying rodent with silent skill. The small fire he built was used to cook the meat once he'd skinned the animal.

"There is no way I am going to be able to eat this whole meal by myself," the man said. He sat on a dead log beside his fire. The squirrel was on a stick, being roasted like a marshmallow at a campout. The bow and quiver full of arrows sat directly beside him.

She hated to admit it, but she thought she might be starving. Her stomach gurgled like an office water jug. She clapped a hand over her belly, feeling certain the rumble would give her away.

"I know you must be hungry." He wasn't going to give up.

She knew she should just keep moving. If she had no plan to join this man, then stalking him made absolutely no sense.

Then he took the squirrel off the spit. "I'm going to eat this and then hightail it out of here. The smell is going bring out the dead. If you want some, this is the last time I am offering and once I go on the move again, I am going to consider you hostile. Fair?"

With the gig up, her hunger winning out, she stood up and slowly emerged from out of the shadows. She kept her longsword up in a double-fisted grip. He didn't even reach for his bow, but instead, offered her peeled squirrel meat on a makeshift dinner plate. "I'm Tony. Headed north. What about you?"

She thought about giving her full name, but decided against it. "I'm Char. I've been on my own for the better part of three years. Last time I saw my fath—"

He held up a hand. "I only have one rule. No history. We've all gone through shit. No sense dwelling on it. You're Char, and like I said, I'm Tony. We good with that, with just moving forward?"

It's simple, but it's how the friendship started.

"My plan is pretty easy. Stay to the high ground, use back roads. Less chance of running into. . . populated areas. That work all right for you?"

"Sounds like a good plan," she said. They even shook on it.

"Then here, help yourself to some dinner."

# # #

While they had been on the road for months, at one point few days ago, Tony announced they were either in Virginia or West Virginia and amidst the Blue Ridge Mountains. The Shenandoah River flowed close by. He'd gone camping with his parents at the national park while growing up. Tony promised apple orchards, fishing, and plenty of wildlife to hunt.

They wouldn't starve.

"We need to focus," Tony said.

The horses were tied to a tree trunk behind them. They were atop a narrow ridge looking down on a paved road. The scent of sap and weeds made her eyes itchy and watery. "I'm focused."

"You weren't." He ran a thumb over the fletching on an arrow and squinted as he stared toward the trailer. "We've followed them this far. Undetected, best I can tell. No one else is following them, or us. They look like they might be settling in for the evening."

"They have to be exhausted," she said. She knew *she* was. Her butt was sore. They'd been riding hard all day in an attempt to keep up with the tractor trailer. Thankfully the rig stayed in low gears to better climb and maneuver the narrow road. There might be medical supplies, bandages, ointments, and aspirin. Wishful thinking led her to hope for toothpaste, shampoo, and soaps.

Luxury items on any survivors' list, no doubt. Char knew what else was locked inside that trailer. She just refused to think about it.

"That's what I'm hoping. We'll keep an eye on them. Wait until they fall asleep —until we're sure they're asleep— and then move in. We have to do this fast. Get in, grab the reins, and go." Tony pursed his lips. She knew he was merely talking out loud to soundboard his idea. The plan didn't need to be said, it was that obvious. He might have needed to convince himself that it was *indeed* the right plan. Char had no problems with that, waiting until everyone was asleep, since it made the most sense.

"With the six of them, one or two will keep watch. A shipment like that, there is no way they can afford to sleep at the same time," she said. Two men had ridden inside the cab. The four others followed near and far on horseback, armed with assault rifles.

"You ever work a security job?" Tony slid off the bank and pressed his back against dirt and loose gravel.

"I'm seventeen. I was just barely a freshman in high school when this started. My life experiences are a little limited." She knew Tony knew that she'd never worked security —or any job for that matter. He liked to talk. Ask questions. It made him happy or something. Just staring at him with an, *Are you kidding me face,* just made him pouty. There was always a time for that. This wasn't one of them.

"I worked as a rent-a-cop for a few years. It was for a health insurance company. The guard station connected underground parking with the building. I worked midnights. When I got there, the only other people in the building was the guard I relieved and the I.T. guys. They made sure the computers and databases didn't crash, lose power, or that kind of thing. Six floors, all mine. Know what I did from midnight until eight in the morning?"

"Slept?"

He nodded and laughed again. "Like a baby."

"We wouldn't do that."

"We wouldn't, but I can't see us in possession of *that* kind of cargo." He laughed.

"Yet," she said. The possibilities of what might be inside that trailer were endless. Since Tony had taken care of some basic needs, like food and shelter, she couldn't help but hope to find staples like shampoo and soap, toothpaste and deodorant. Just the idea of a chance to find dental floss made her almost giddy.

"While we wait for them to settle in and fall asleep, guess what you're going to do?"

She sighed. She didn't need to be a mind reader. "First watch."

He clapped her on the back. "First watch. Use the binoculars, all right? I want to keep an eye on our friends. If anything looks funny or dangerous. . ."

She hated when he treated her like a kid. It wasn't on purpose. Her father did it to her all the time, too. At least then, she'd been a kid. That was no longer the case. "I know, Tony. I just let you sleep and handle the situation on my own. We're good. Now, get some rest. You definitely need your beauty sleep."

He didn't laugh, but knew he wasn't mad either. "I'll take first watch, but I expect you to get some sleep, and I mean it. You need some rest. We don't want to stage an ambush and look more like the zombies around us, do we?"

Tony knew she didn't sleep well, either. "You know how I feel about that word."

Unlike her father, Tony didn't like the word zombies. He preferred to call them the *infected,* because they were people once, and he believed there were still souls inside. Messed up and sick, but souls just the same. It didn't stop him from killing the creatures. He was just sometimes more thoughtful about it.

"Infected," she said.

He nodded with approval. "Two hours."

"Not a minute longer."

"I'll use the stars as my clock." Char pointed at the sky. "As soon as the Big Dipper arcs across the center of the sky."

"Smart ass." He sucked in a deep breath, held it a moment, and then exhaled as he spun around and took another look at the trailer a few hundred feet below them. When satisfied, he pushed away from the bank and removed a sleeping bag off his horse, which had been tethered to a nearby tree. Char watched him get settled in. He placed his bow and quiver beside the bag and took off his baseball hat. "Two hours," he said. He set the hat over his face as if it were a Stetson.

"Sweet dreams." Char lifted the binoculars off her chest and got comfortable in the dirt and loose gravel on the ridge. Without night vision, the binocs would only benefit her so long, despite however many stars lit the night sky.

The danger wasn't just below them.

It was all around.

The infected had a habit of showing up when you least expected them. If they weren't in moaning packs, they could go undetected until too late. Char hadn't survived this long being careless. She split her time between watching the trailer below and the forest around them.

She did not like the idea of waiting. They needed to overtake the men below and get the trailer from them. There was no telling what could happen if they missed this chance. It really came down to stealing it now, or possibly never.

Possibly never was not acceptable. Tony wouldn't allow it, and neither would she.

If anything, they'd die trying. That's just what it came down to at this point. Walking away was not an option.

# # #

Char and Tony stood across from each other, hidden behind trees. They were still several yards from what they had come to consider as the enemy's camp. They'd made sure there was no movement for nearly an hour before moving this close.

"Two on watch?" Tony said.

The moonlight helped. The bright orb sat in a cloudless sky. With no street or city lights to interfere, the stars finally had a chance to illuminate the heavens. The billions of stars resembled a blanket of light, were milky, and still, and silent against a Catalina blue sky. "One ahead of the trailer. The other is just behind where the others are asleep."

"I was worried they'd unhitched the horses. Animals are not going to be well rested having been tethered together like that all night. Idiots," he said, "that's not going to help us much. We want to hightail it out of there, and the things are going to be panting and shit. Not good."

"You should have told them earlier, explained that in order for the horses to rest properly, they need to be unhitched." Char rolled her eyes.

"You go on ahead. Find the guy out front. I'm going to handle the one back there. We'll take care of the other four together. It's not perfect, but I think it's our best plan right now."

"I'm good with it." She had her machete out.

"You be safe. I'm serious."

Char nodded. "You, too."

She moved slowly but with purpose. The only sound she heard was her own footfalls and tried to step as quietly as possible, breathing shallow breaths. Tiny plumes escaped her lips and nostrils and then were gone. She went cautiously from tree to tree for cover, knowing the man on horseback was not *too* far ahead. Forest animals were silent. Her presence a deterrent from their nighttime chatter. Their silence was also a revelation. It warned the enemy that something approached. At a minimum, the man would be on guard, hopefully straining to see into the thicket for the infected and not at all on the lookout for a machete wielding young lady.

Hopefully.

The man's horse was tied to a tree. The man was not there. Char stood still, kept her back pressed against the bark. She looked left and right. The moon and stars helped pierce the darkness. The canopy above still prevented an excess of light from filtering through. Her eyes were well adjusted to the dimness encompassing the forest.

The horse snorted and shook its head, rattling the reins. It sounded like thunder in the silence. She watched the animal, wondering where the rider might be. The terrain was far more rocky in this direction. She stepped up to a boulder, lowered her chest down onto it and tried to see what lay beyond. With still no sign of the man with the assault rifle, she crawled up and over. Her eyes never stopped roaming left and right. He had to be somewhere close by.

Perhaps Tony had been right, and he was somewhere asleep.

She gripped the machete with both hands, held the blade out in front of her and walked toward the horse. She didn't want to risk getting too close and spooking the animal. While she walked, she hoped Tony was alright. His man was closer to the other four. If there was much of a scuffle, it would alert the sleeping men. The thing about Tony, he would use an arrow and could make the kill silently from fifty yards out. He'd been teaching her how to use the bow, but they just hadn't yet come across another she could keep.

Char did not think the man would wander far from his horse unless he found a safe place to catch some zzz's. She stood still and just listened. Her heart pounded inside her chest.

A tree branch snapped.

Char spun around. She saw the butt of the rifle coming at her face and ducked. It caught the side of her head. She went down, not from the blow, but from losing her balance. Her left foot slid on loose stones. Her elbow took the brunt of the fall. Pain shot through her arm. A tingling sensation raced down to her wrist, and then up to her shoulder.

There was no time to coddle the injury.

She rolled to the right, off her arm. It was fast, but not quick enough. The man delivered a kick. His boot caught her on the side and she gasped as her lungs fought to inhale oxygen. She feared at least one rib might have broken. Her hands were empty.

Where was the machete?

The man made no noise. He survived the infected this long by learning to keep quiet, too. It didn't stop the attack. He kept at her, kicking her in the back and sides over and over. She kept rolling, trying to get out of reach, looking for a chance to get back on her feet. It wasn't working. The beating was relentless and she knew the pain would overtake her. The last thing she wanted was to lose consciousness. She'd be as good as dead.

Stay still.

Play dead.

He wasn't a bear. She didn't think she could do it. Her grunts and cries could not be contained.

"Shut up," he said. It came out like a snarl. His words a whisper that escaped between bared, clenched teeth, but he'd stopped.

Char stayed on her stomach, knees drawn and arms protectively wrapped around her head. Breathing was difficult. She sucked in air; each breath sent pain radiating through her. There was no means of comfort. She didn't dare move.

She didn't dare move, until she was certain she knew how to gain an upper hand.

"Where did you come from? Wha. . .are you a girl?"

She heard it then. It was in his voice. He went from angry to something else. The slur of his words was not lost on her. The excitement in his second question was telling. The man's beard was thick and black. It was the only clear feature she could make out in the darkness. The rest of his face was cast in shadow.

"I said, where did you come from?"

She whimpered. A small cry slipped out. Her head throbbed. The butt of the assault rifle broke skin. Warm blood spilled from the gash, a pungent odor of copper filled her nose. The scent trapped in the tight space; her head on the earth, her arms around her head.

"Who else is with you?"

The longsword was useless with no way to unsheathe it from her curled-up position on the ground. The knife on her hip was the best choice. It was a serrated ten-inch blade, but she couldn't reach for it, not with it strapped on the same side where the man was who stood looming over her.

"I'm not here to play games." It was back. The lust in his tone of voice. It filled her ears and sparked her memory. Mexico had been a horrible country. The uninfected far worse than the walking dead. No mistaking that both were hungry for flesh.

Char learned quickly to best avoid getting into sticky situations —when possible.

"Maybe you need to be taught a lesson?"

At least one rib had to be broken. She knew if she tried to move, to straighten out, her insides would violently protest.

She heard his belt buckle jingle loose.

A foot pressed against her side.

She cried out in pain.

He rolled her over.

She kept her knees up to her chest. Blood and tears mixed on her face.

"You need to shut up," he said. She couldn't see his face. The available light was above and behind him and he was merely a shadow before her. His breathing was fast, labored. He was working himself up, eager.

She bit her lip. "Sorry."

"That's better," he said. The man dropped to his knees. He grabbed her legs and pulled them apart.

She offered no resistance other than a timid cry and turned her head to the side.

When he climbed on top of her, Char did not hesitate.

When she'd been kicked over onto her back, her hand unstrapped the knife. She had it in her hand.

She punched the knife deep into his side and dragged it up to his first rib.

He fell off her. The blade protruded from under his arm. He writhed, kicking his legs.

Char forced herself up onto her knees, pushed herself up onto one, and then stood. The man screamed.

Standing felt better than being balled up on the ground.

Breathing was not any easier.

The man continued screaming, rolling back and forth, covering himself in blood and dirt. "I'm going to die."

Char ignored her pain as she took a few steps and stood over the man. She raised her foot in the air and brought the heel down on his skull. "You need to be quiet," she said.

This was not a good person.

She was not a murderer.

He had planned to rape her, she had no doubt. He would have killed her after, or worse, kept her around, just barely alive but useful for days, and then killed her. Either way, he'd of taken her life.

She looked around, but the thicket and darkness that surrounded them made it hard to find her machete. There wasn't time to search, not with him making so much noise.

Her mind spun as her brain was pumped full of endorphins. She knew her pulse was fast. She thought about drawing her sword, but instead, forced herself to kneel down next to him. He couldn't keep still.

Being that he was alive, he was still a threat.

She wouldn't let her guard down.

Not around this one.

Char pried his hand off the knife with one hand, and grabbed onto the handle with the other. There was a wet *sloshing* sound when she yanked out the blade, and the man let out a curdling cry that pierced her ears. She thought she smelled the contents of food in various stages of digestion emitted from the long, wide wound, and nearly vomited.

In one fluid motion, she reached across his chest and slid the blade across his throat.

That stopped the cry, mid-scream.

He lay still, finally.

A moonbeam shown on his face. Blood filled and gurgled out of the corners of his mouth. He attempted to cough, to breathe, and to hang onto life. His eyes were locked on her. Rapid blinking ensued as the life behind the retina slowly clouded over, leaving a vacant look in his expression.

The blood still oozed from his neck.

It bubbled inside his mouth.

She watched him until she was certain he was dead.

It was when she smelled urine and feces that she knew it was safe to get up.

Char went back to the horse. It snorted, as giant eyes strained to watch her every movement. Like her, the animal did not trust people. She unbuckled the belt on the belly of the horse. She didn't want to leave him tied to a tree. The man's death cries gave away their location. He would become an instant meal for not just potential infected, but also dangerous wildlife in the area. The mountains were filled with black bear, mountain lions, coyotes, and wolves. She removed the nylon halter and head collar as she pet his nose and whispered into his ear that everything would be okay.

Chapter 2

Char tried to follow the exact path she used back toward the ridge. She kept low, bent forward, and moved fast. There was no hiding the sense of dread that seemed to follow close behind. Something had to have taken notice during her struggle with that man. Something had to have heard them and was on the way to investigate further. It would not surprise her if a herd of infected were close behind.

It felt good having the machete back in her hands. She'd felt naked without it. It was her favorite weapon. She remembered dressing like her father. They'd uncovered an armory of sorts and stocked up on knives, both strapping a longsword into a scabbard about their waists, and a machete sheathed on their backs. They wore knives on their hips and secured to their thighs.

That was years ago. When the world was full of infected.

The world was *still* full of the infected; it just seemed like less, as if they'd died off, starved as a living food source ran dry. It was a war. The last three and a half years were full of battles she'd remember forever, but would always try to forget.

She would never forget her dad.

"You make any *more* noise, and *I'll* have to kill you."

Tony. He'd startled her, but she recognized the voice instantaneously.

Char hadn't realized she'd stopped moving, and that she stood still in a clearing. The lack of tree canopy above had her spotlighted.

"You okay? Your head. . .you're bleeding."

"Got a little rough. I'm fine, and he's dead," she said. She spoke without emotion. There was no need to admit the rush that came with killing the man. He'd been evil and didn't belong. That guy would not have added anything to this new world except a promise to deliver more pain, more suffering. She did what needed doing. It didn't make her feel better about having killed. Nothing would. It was her sin. One of many, and she'd carry it with her forever.

"I hit mine. He took off on his horse. Ran south." Tony stared at Char just a little longer than he should have.

Char knew Tony was upset about losing an arrow. "You think he's dead?"

"Dying, that's for sure. I followed for a bit. Horse was far too spooked, ran like lightning down the trail and I couldn't keep up. The guy was slumped forward, barely hanging on." Tony reached forward and brushed hair off her forehead where it stuck to the gash on her skin.

She knew he wanted to ask if she was okay and knew he wouldn't. He knew better. Neither of them was okay. They'd both suffered terrible losses and were desperate and depressed, but surviving. So there was no point in asking each other if they were okay; the answer was both assumed and accepted. What they knew was that the other did care, and that when it came down to it, that was what mattered.

"And the sleeping babies?"

"Still asleep." Tony pointed.

Char couldn't see the targets, but knew they must be close. It was a good thing he'd spotted her. Had she started running again, she may have trotted right into the enemy's makeshift camp.

"I was just coming to make sure you were all set," he said.

"I am. All set. How do you want to handle this?" Char slid her machete back into the sheath on her back. She winced and regretted the show of weakness.

"Char?"

"Might have busted a rib or two," she said. Nothing could be done for broken ribs. They just needed time to heal. The bones would mend on their own with rest and nourishment, the two things she knew she'd never have. "It's good. I'm okay."

She rolled her shoulder around; it didn't eliminate pain, but added to the discomfort.

"They're in sleeping bags, feet to feet. Like a cross. I have an idea to do this quick and quiet. I just want you down close in case something goes wrong. If you can. Are you up to it?"

"Absolutely. I've got this."

Char followed Tony. They made their way across tall weeds and around trees. He was smooth and moved soundlessly. They stopped at a giant rock not twenty yards from where the men slept.

"Guns by their heads," Tony said.

"See 'em." She shouldered up to Tony. "The plan?"

"It's simple. Get by the trailer. Stay hidden. I'm going to try and hit all four. Kill shots. I want you to run in, grab up the rifles and ride that thing out of here. You said you can drive a stick shift, right?"

"I can. I learned in Mexico. Seemed like all the cars out there were stick."

"They get a lot of older US models. Okay, good."

"What about—"

"We'll take care of that after, once we have some distance."

Char nodded, knowing he was right. "And what about you?"

"I'm going to run back up and grab our horses."

"What about the two over there?"

He pursed his lips thoughtfully. "I want our horses."

She knew what he meant. "Okay, but I'm going to free those two, then."

"That's fine," he said, "just be quick about it."

"You be quick. We'll, what —meet down the road?"

"Exactly." Tony reached back and removed four arrows from his quiver. "Now get in place."

If anything went wrong, it would be in close quarters. She armed herself with the knives, wishing she'd cleaned the blood off the blade from her last kill. She ran to the side of the trailer, squatted by the sets of tires and listened for signs of movement from within the cargo. There was none.

Tony was well hidden behind the rock. Even in the moonlight she couldn't see him. The only reason she knew he was there was because, well, she knew he was there.

She squatted by the wheel, staying low to the ground. Pain ricocheted inside her body, setting nerve endings on fire. She cringed and bent forward. Black stars passed in front of her eyeballs.

Her stomach lurched.

She fought it, refusing to vomit, and worried she might have a concussion. The temple struck by the butt of the rifle throbbed, a steady beat like a bass woofer booming inside her skull.

The air silently split as an arrow shot forward. It was no kill shot. The arrow protruded from the one man's gut. The guy sat up, both hands around the point of entry, fingers encircling the shaft. The broadhead arrow tip resembled a pyramid, razor sharp on all three sides.

The man's mouth opened and Char was certain the sneak attack was over. Once he screamed, it would become a free-for-all. She was just about to run forward, knives tightly gripped, when a second arrow struck. The broadhead perfectly placed —it smashed through the open mouth. Even in the dark she could see the tip sticking out of the back of his neck before his body fell back onto the sleeping bag.

Another stirred, but didn't wake up.

Ever.

An arrow slammed into the center of his chest at an angle and it looked like it shot up under his ribs and into the heart.

Two down.

The men stirred. "What the fuck?"

Char was ready to attack, but waited. She didn't want to race in and accidentally take an arrow not meant for her.

She waited.

The man pulled back the sleeping bag and switched on a light. A flashlight.

They had batteries?

The beam traced the others beside him.

"Ah shit, no, man!" He jumped to his feet, waking the other guy.

"What's going on?"

"They're dead. Fucking arrows."

Thankfully the flashlight shown on the two dead men.

What are you waiting for, Tony? she thought. She couldn't just stand there and do nothing. The waking men were frightened, still disoriented from sleep. They'd overcome that fast.

The guy with the flashlight reached down for his rifle.

Something was wrong. Tony wouldn't let these guys get up.

She charged forward, ran fast. Their eyes would not be adjusted to the darkness yet. She used it to her advantage and hoped to strike quick, adding to their confusion.

She jumped over the man still struggling to wake up and landed directly in front of the guy with the flashlight and rifle. He'd fumbled with both, trying to ready his weapon without losing his control over the light. Perfect.

She plunged both knives like daggers into his chest, pulled them out, and slammed them back in. There was no getting used to the feel of a blade popping through skin and sawing against bones. The sensation vibrated through her palms.

Once her blades were free, she dashed forward as he dropped to his knees.

He released the flashlight.

She hit the woods, spun around, and dropped into the high grass. Her fists were by her face, white knuckle grip on the knife handles. She breathed fast, hard, and watched as the last man in the group of six reached for the flashlight. He seemed oblivious to the extent of the attack.

Just as she thought, Tony must be in serious trouble, the flashlight fell to the ground again.

The beam of light shown past the sleeping bags and under the trailer.

Then was blocked.

The man fell forward. His head a foot from the flashlight. His eyes were open. Blood poured from the man's temple, pooled on the side of his nose, and then dripped steadily off the bridge.

Charlene thought she could see the shaft of an arrow sticking out from his temple.

Tony.

The plan. Throw the guns onto the trailer, free the horses, and high tail it down the road.

"Get my arrows. I'm going back for our horses." He was a shadow. He stood by the trailer. She saw him now. No features, just his outline.

"Tony, what happened?"

"Infected. Three. They came out of nowhere."

She waited. Silent.

"They didn't touch me."

She exhaled. "Go get the horses."

"Roger," he said.

Char emerged from the woods and stopped at each corpse. She placed a foot on the chest of each man and with two hands, yanked the arrows free. Penetrating a target with a broadhead was bad, it did lethal damage. Trying to remove the arrow just made a bloody mess. It would almost be easier and cleaner just to push them through and pull them out from the other side. She'd suggested that once. Tony said blood and guts ruined the turkey feather fletching.

With the guns and Tony's arrows loaded into the rig, Char climbed in. "Okay. Okay. I've got this."

She placed the rifles and arrows on the passenger seat and thought back to driving cars in Mexico. This was a bit different from a five-speed. She depressed the clutch and shifted into gear. The rig snap-hissed, and groaned. The steady chug of the running motor vibrated under her seat. The trailer was huge, heavy. She had no idea how fast she'd be able to travel pulling a full load.

Before long, she saw Tony. He was on one horse, the other in tow. When he came to a stop, she pushed the clutch and hit the brake. "What's up?" she said, and could not help thinking Tony resembled a cowboy.

Tony trotted close to the rig. "I'm going to hitch your horse to the back of the trailer."

"Will he be alright back there?"

"He'll follow along just fine. Just give me a second. Keep an eye out. We're making a lot of noise on the trail."

"No kidding," she said. Tony disappeared with the horse.

She heard him talking, holding a calming conversation. She couldn't hear what he said but felt thankful. If they would of had more time she'd have done the same. Hopefully, there would still be time.

All she could hope was that they weren't too late. . .and that her friends were still alive.

"We're all set," Tony said. He had his reins wrapped around the horn on his saddle.

"You hear anything?"

Tony shook his head. "But don't worry."

Char wanted to smash the lock, climb into the back of the trailer, and go through the stacked supplies now. She didn't want to wait. Tony would argue against it. The important thing was to stick with the plan. Confiscate the trailer, take it as far off the trail as possible, and find somewhere safe before climbing inside and searching the contents.

She was worried, but said, "I'm not. Let's go."

Go where, was the unasked question. They had what they wanted. The man that escaped on horse could prove to be a problem. If he wasn't dead, he might reach Broadhurst. If he reached Broadhurst, their head start was cut in half.

He'd have come after them anyway, once he realized his shipment didn't make it to wherever it had been headed.

That could have taken days, or as long as a week, quite possibly.

They had to assume the man did not die, and that he would make it back to their camp and would be able to tell Broadhurst that Char and Tony ambushed the convoy.

Chapter 3

Tony led Char off the main road. The trees were still sparse, but the trail was no longer paved. They were on an incline, as well. The engine whined, exhaled, and grunted. They moved along, but the going was slow.

She braked. The rig hissed. Cutting the engine, she realized rocks should be wedged under the tires to prevent the trailer from rolling backward.

Tony eventually realized he was on his own and turned his horse around. He came at her galloping and stopped alongside the rig. "What's wrong?"

"I can't keep going."

Tony knew what she meant. It wasn't about feeling tired. "We've only been riding for an hour, maybe less. We haven't put much distance behind us."

"We put enough." She didn't want to say it. Didn't think she needed to. "We have to check."

Tony stared at her for a full minute. The silence just lingered between them. She knew he was afraid to look and he was afraid not too. "Okay. Let's look."

She jumped down from the rig. She wondered where Broadhurst was getting diesel fuel. The man was resourceful. That much credit was deserved.

Walking toward the back of the trailer, Char kept an eye on the surrounding forest. The dead were not as prevalent in the mountains. Maybe it was because of the damp autumn weather, she knew the things hated rain.

Tony searched on the ground for a rock. "This looks big enough," he said. He walked to the back of the trailer and smashed the rock against the padlock.

Char pet her horse, attempting to keep him calm. "Shh, shh."

Tony pounded the rock against the lock over and over until it broke. He removed the halves and lifted the latch.

"What are you waiting for?" she said.

"Get your sword out. We really have no idea what's inside."

"Before we started following them, we saw them load the trailer."

"Take out your sword. Please."

She reached across her waist and pulled the sword from the scabbard. Gripping the hilt with both hands, the blade pointing toward the sky, she nodded. "Okay. I'm ready."

Tony yanked on the doors. Rusted hinges screamed in protest. "It's pitch black in there."

Char looked around. This would be the perfect time for the infected to attack, while they were distracted. The hairs on the back of her neck rose. She hated the feeling. She remembered watching a movie with her father after her younger brother had fallen asleep. A captain miscounted the number of passengers on his boat, and after a diving excursion, left the area for the night, leaving a couple stranded in the middle of the ocean. They spent the night trying to stay afloat and alive. The couple kept expecting to be attacked. They knew they'd never see it coming. Before help arrived, they were both eaten by sharks. What stuck with her most after seeing the film was the fear and tension that grew the entire time they spent treading water and just waiting for the inevitable.

"I'll go in," Char said.

"I will," Tony said.

She shook her head. "Stand back," she said.

Char replaced her sword. She unsheathed the machete and stepped into Tony's cupped hands as he hoisted her up and into the back of the trailer. Confronted with fifty-three feet of darkness,

Char wasted no time. She used her feet to kick at the items stacked on either side of the narrow aisle. "Hello? It's okay now. It's me. It's Char," she said. She knew not to yell. She talked loud enough to be heard. While she expected her voice to echo, it only fell flat.

"Anything?"

"No. Not yet," she said.

Char did not think the infected were piled in the trailer. If anything, the danger was outside surrounding Tony, surrounding both of them, but in here, she was safe. She replaced her machete and used her free hands to help search.

Something moved. It was slight. A shuffling.

Standing still, she was unsure where the sound came from. Regardless, it was a good sign. A great sign. "I'm coming. You're okay. You will be okay!"

She could not believe she'd left that flashlight at the enemy's campsite. It was probably still on the sleeping bag, a dying beam shooting a now dim yellowing light toward the trees. With renewed vigor, Char climbed up and onto stacks of boxes. A tower tilted, wobbled, and crashed.

"Char?"

"I'm okay," she called out. She pushed items out of the way, confident the sound came from the very back of the trailer. She just wanted some light. She smelled cardboard and urine. "Sam? Grace?"

"You got them?" Tony said.

"They're back here. I'm almost to them." Her hands worked as her eyes. She felt in front of her as she crawled over boxes on her knees. They had been tied and bagged and riding in the back of this trailer the entire time. It was hot inside the box, the air stagnant and rank.

Char reached the back of the trailer. Her palms planted against the inside wall. She worried she'd made her way past them and remained still as she called out their names once more.

Something wiggled below her. She felt around. There was a break in the tower stacks. She lowered herself down between them and she stepped on something squishy. A muffled cry erupted.

Using the boxes, Char lifted herself up. She had landed on at least one of them.

It hadn't been that long ago, while on the way from Texas to the mountains, that Tony and Char met up with two other people. One was Sam Gerringer. He was just a year or two older than Char was, but acted ten years younger. He reminded Char of an undisciplined, but thankfully, potty-trained, puppy. He was the exact opposite of Tony, with curly blond hair and red acne on his cheeks. He had big blue eyes and wore jeans and an Aztec-style parka.

The three had then found Grace Mattison on the roof of a backyard shed surrounded by the infected screaming for help. While the screams brought potential help, it was also like a dinner bell for the monsters. . .

"It's me. I'm here, guys. I'm going to get you out of there." Char used the toe of her boot and felt around for a place to stand. She lowered herself to the trailer's floor. Ignoring the pungent odor of urine, Char got onto her knees. She used her knife to saw through rope around ankles, straddled legs, and severed more secured rope around the middles, and finally cut through a third section that was tied across necks. They were in bags. There must have been air holes or Sam and Grace would be dead.

She tore at the plastic and was now sitting between the two.

"Oh, man," Sam said, sitting up. He pulled the bag away from his face as he got to his feet and shook the bag off the rest of his body.

Char assisted Grace out of her bag.

"She's not moving," she said. Char damned the darkness as she lowered her ear to where Grace's mouth should be. She listened. "She's breathing—barely. Help me get her out of here."

"Where are we?"

"Sam, I need you to help me." She squatted, moving behind Grace's head. "I'll get her under the arms."

Boxes crashed down around them.

"What was that?" Char said.

"I'm clearing a path," Sam said. There was more grunting and shifting of boxes. Something glass smashed open.

"Char!"

"We're good, Tony. We're coming out."

"Hurry. Something's in the forest and is coming this way!"

"We have to get out of here," she said.

"I know. I heard him."

"Grace?" Char said, as she struggled to maneuver over fallen boxes with Grace in her arms. "Are you helping at all?"

"I have her legs."

It didn't feel like it. "You go first," she said, not wishing to walk backwards.

"Char!"

"We're coming!" Her foot landed on the edge of a box. She slipped and lost her balance. The tumble was awkward with her arms tucked under Grace. She landed on a knee and toppled down on her side.

"You okay?"

"Hold on," Char said. She used the muscles in her legs and back to get back up while lifting Grace with her. "I'm fine. I'm good. Let's go."

Sam walked backward, stepping carefully. The center of the trailer was a clear path. Char's eyes were adjusting to the darkness inside the trailer; she could see out of the back end where the doors were open and Tony stood ready for battle.

"We should set her down," Char said.

"Why?"

"Set her down, Sam. She's safer in here. We'll close the doors. Tony needs our help."

# # #

"What have we got?" Char jumped down from the back of the trailer and stood on Tony's right.

"Hey, man," Tony said, offering a hand up to assist Sam clambering out of the trailer.

"Thanks for the rescue."

He cocked a thumb toward Char. "She made me. Where's Grace?"

"She's not alert. We're keeping her inside the trailer," Char said. "Close these doors, she'll be safer in there."

"I've got movement all over the place. Nothing is coming out of the trees, though; it's almost like they're spooked," Tony said.

"Maybe it's not the infected?"

"Take a whiff," Tony said.

The three of them sniffed the air and Char said, "It's them. The infected."

"I think we might be better off just getting out of here," Tony said, grabbing one of the opened doors and swinging it closed. "Sam, get the other one."

"No. We can't. Grace is lying unconscious in there, and she's right in the center of the trailer. With all the rocks out here, we could jar loose a stack of supplies, and she'll be crushed," Char said.

"I could ride in back with her," Sam said.

"It's too late to discuss it anymore," Tony said. "Here they come."

Chapter 4

The infected were too numerous to count as they stumbled out of the forest. Thankfully, it had been some time since any fast ones has been spotted. Char figured the fast eventually become the slow if they survived long enough. Time and being undernourished took a toll on them. Once the rigor mortis set in, they could barely walk. She didn't know if that eventually killed them for good, but it made fighting them much easier.

The freshly bitten were still fast. The ones that fed often, fast.

It didn't mean three against a horde was a fair match-up.

"There's too many," Sam said. "I don't have a weapon."

Char gave him the sword, and she removed her machete, ready for a war. While the infected may be fewer in numbers and slower than when first turned, they were still cunning. It was as if once adjusted, they regained some brain function. It wasn't that they became smart, or smarter, as much as they became instinctive. They learned, and used that new knowledge to hunt flesh more efficiently, more effectively. That was what made even the slow and starving infected so dangerous; the surprises they sprang.

There were no answers. Whatever the virus stemmed from, it seemed to mutate. Her father had tried to find answers, and he died while still searching.

Char ran at the closest infected and chopped through the air. The machete sliced through the rotted skin around the thing's neck. She sawed the blade as she pulled it away, and black blood spilled from the severed arteries that in someone normal, supplied oxygenated blood to the brain. The spine, not as brittle as expected, kept the head in place. Damage was inflicted, and the impact drove the infected to the ground. She set a booted foot onto his shoulder, slammed the machete into the back of the neck, and pulled it out in one swift motion.

She heard battle cries from around her.

Her peripheral picked up Sam just as he swung the sword like a baseball bat. Without a whetting stone, she was forced to improvise when it came time to keep the steel sharpened. Satisfaction filled her as she saw an infected sliced into half. Sam kicked the creature in the chest, knocking the torso off the lower half of the body.

The sun was rising. Daylight would aid the fight some. Steam, like clouds, swam through the mountains on a chilling morning airstream; Char wielded the machete in one hand and a serrated hunting knife in the other, as she was about to charge a group of infected that ambled forward clustered close together. She counted four heads. Two men in front, the women behind them. The bobbing heads of the men allowed Char to notice bite marks on the women's faces. They looked raw and oozed pus.

Something about that was wrong.

The men stepped aside, slow, sluggish. The women ran at Char.

"They're fast!" She crossed her arms out in front of her. The blades clanked as she turned them into one X-shaped weapon. She set the crux of the blades to one infected's throat and uncrossed her arms. The makeshift hedge clippers cut through skin, meat, and bone. The head toppled backward but did not fall off the neck, its threat minimized.

The second infected woman was about to wrap arms around Char just as Char fell purposely to the ground. She backslid between its legs, rolled onto her belly, and cut through both Achilles tendons. Springing to her feet, Char swung, and severed the infected's head. The black blood was not as dark, not as crusty. The thing actually bled.

She spun around and lacerated the first man. Her machete slid across its belly, doubling him over. She drove the knife into the ear of the second man. It was stuck in his skull. She let the handle go, and gripped the machete with both hands. She brought the blade up and swung down, finishing the first man with a swift motion that decapitated him in a clean slice.

Char retrieved her knife from the skull of the other man and stood looking at the bodies scattered along the road.

They had managed a win; it was a small victory, but a victory, nonetheless. She would take it. "You guys alright?"

Sam was bent over, one hand on a knee, the other on the sword's handle. He breathed heavy, deep breaths. He did not answer, but nodded his head.

"Handful of fast ones," Tony said. "I didn't expect that."

"Crafty bastards," Sam said. "Crafty little bastards. Let's get Grace into the cab. I can ride either your horse, Char, or drive the truck. Makes no difference to me."

"Can you drive a stick shift? It has like a hundred gears," Char said.

"No. I cannot." Sam bit into his upper lip as he shook his head.

"That could be a problem," she said.

Tony threw open the back doors while Sam climbed up and into the trailer. "Grace?"

"She okay?" Tony said.

"She's still out of it," Sam said. "I don't like this. She needs a doctor. I don't know what's wrong with her."

"Did they hurt her?"

"Roughed us up, but that was all. Bagged us, tied us up, and tossed us in back of this trailer."

"She's got to be dehydrated, hungry. She could be in shock," Tony said.

"Shock. That's bad right?"

"If it's medical shock, but if it's acute shock, she'll be okay. We just have to get her someplace safe, warm. She's going to be alright," Tony said. Char thought Tony's explanation sounded convincing, but maybe because she knew it was what Sam needed to hear.

They maneuvered her body out of the trailer, placed her in the passenger seat of the rig, and seat belted her in place.

Tony didn't hesitate. He removed the reins from the back of the truck and climbed onto the saddle of his horse. It neighed and twisted its head. Its breath was visible as it plumed from giant nostrils.

Char pet her horse's mane. "It's okay, baby. It's okay. Sammy is going to take good care of you."

She held the reins, keeping her horse calm and steady as Sam mounted her.

"Where are we headed?" Char said.

"Somewhere far from here. We need to find some other roads, get some twists and turns behind us. We don't want Broadhurst finding us too easily, now do we?"

"No. We don't," Char said. She patted the horse's neck and quickly nuzzled her face against his. She scratched him lightly under the chin. "My baby," she said, in a baby voice.

"You spoil him," Sam said.

"And you'd better, as well. I love this horse!" She ruffled his mane and patted his muscular neck. She wished she'd had an apple or carrot. There was little she loved as much as hand feeding her horse. "You take care of Dispatch—promise."

"Promise."

#

Char followed behind her friends in the eighteen wheeler. Tony and Sam rode nearly side by side at a steady gallop, with Tony just slightly ahead. She kept the rig in one gear as her eyes searched the woods that lined the narrow mountain road. She knew they were always susceptible to an attack. Letting one's guard down was beyond foolish, it could prove deadly. It was up to each of them to do their part. From up inside the cab, she felt like she could see clearer, further than her friends on horseback.

The sun's rays burned away the rolling steam. It looked like the beginning of a beautiful autumn day. Despite the anarchy that surrounded her life, she took in the foliage, appreciating the red scarred and brilliant orange flamed leaves that decorated tree branches.

Char didn't like time alone, and even though Grace sat buckled beside her, she wasn't conscious. Char thought about how the days were long and full. They took turns sleeping, someone always on guard. They spent hours of daylight looking for food; hunting and fishing. Most nights they set new snares to catch rabbits, opossum, or anything unlucky enough to walk into the trap. Life was about surviving, and surviving was about having enough to eat so as to keep healthy. Since they reached the Blue Ridge Mountains, it had become easier. Not easy, just easier. She wanted Grace to wake up so she wasn't forced to spend so much time thinking.

It all changed about a month back when they crossed paths with Frank Broadhurst. . .

Chapter 5

One month ago . . . Parrottsville, TN — Cherokee National Forest

Char winced. Every step she took felt like stepping on broken glass. It didn't matter that they walked on plush, high grass. The backpacks they carried were full, stuffed with extra clothing and supplies looted from abandoned locations they came across. Hers was solid, the zipper seam strained with the constant threat of buckling. It was midday, and she coughed continuously.

"You just going to keep doing that?" Sam said.

"Doing what?"

"Hacking a lung."

She cringed. "We need to find water. My throat is too dry. I can't help it if I am having a hard time swallowing."

"We're all thirsty," Sam said.

He was right. She knew she shouldn't be whining. It had only been twenty or so hours since they last had water. The heat and humidity was the problem. It sapped her strength, and she was sure they felt the same.

Tony was stopped along a wire fence.

Grace, a few feet behind him, did a slow three-sixty, cautiously scanning everything with a furrowed brow. She kept one hand on her hip, the other on the handle of an aluminum baseball bat. Closer in age to Tony than to Sam, Grace was anything but motherly. You couldn't make it during times like this by being too empathetic, sympathetic, or soft.

Grace wore a dark bandana on her head as if it were a hat. It was tied with the small knot resting just above the back of her neck. The man's white dress shirt was buttoned over a navy blue tank top. What Char focused on was always the leather biker vest, leather pants, and black biker boots. Grace was taller than Char was, but not by much. Maybe she was five-six, five-seven at the most. Her dark skin was shiny with sweat. She ran the back of her wrist across her forehead and the once white shirt cuff mopped away the dripping beads.

"What are we doing here?" Sam ran up to the fence. It was low, three feet high with a set of wires routed from post to post outlining a good sized piece of property. "This electrified?"

"Once," Tony said. "Can't imagine it is now."

Sam tentatively tried to slap at the wire with the tips of his fingers, but kept pulling his hand back before any actual wire to skin contact. As much as Tony begged to keep back stories to a minimum, Sam talked to them nearly every night. There wasn't much they didn't know about him. He'd lived with his parents and two younger sisters, and younger twin brothers. He'd just returned to Oklahoma University for his sophomore year, majoring in Computer Science. He thought it would be amazing going to college a few states south of home, of Chicago. Their tiny house was packed full of kids and chaos. It turned out he hated it. He missed being home, and surprisingly, missed his little annoying siblings.

When the apocalypse hit, he was in his dorm still drunk from the night before, and had skipped class and ignored his cell phone. In doing so, he'd miss calls from his mother, from his brothers, and from his sisters telling them that dad was acting funny and that they'd locked him in the basement. Of course by the time he woke up and listened to his messages it was eight or nine hours later. None of them answered when he'd tried calling back. He never talked to or seen any of them since.

Char grabbed the wire with both hands. "You know what, Sammy? If the fence was still electrified and you touched it even a little, you'd get electrocuted. Zapped. Fences like this probably had enough juice to cook you from the inside out. Huh, Tony?"

Tony ducked down and climbed between the wires. Once on the other side, he held the top wire up for Grace and the others. "She is right, Sam. If you really think that wire might be live, how should you have handled it?"

"Throw something at it."

Tony just raised his eyebrows. "So why didn't you do that this time?"

"If you thought it could be live, why didn't you stop me?" Sam said.

"It's a fence to keep horses inside the perimeter. It'll zap you; Char's right. Won't be much worse than that. Figured if it was live, I was willing to risk it," he said.

"Risk me getting shocked? That's not right. Why would you do that? What if I had a bad heart?"

"Do you?" Char asked.

Sam clapped a hand to his chest and shook his head. "No, but you didn't know that. I could have had one, a murmur or a pulse, a pup—"

"Palpitation," Grace said.

Sam pointed at Grace. "That's it. A pupitation."

"Palpitation."

"That. I could have had that and touched the wire, and bam, no more Sam!"

"I touched it already," Tony said.

"You what?"

"I already touched it. I knew it wasn't live."

Sam, for once, was silent. He looked from Tony to Grace to Char. "But you didn't know Tony had already touched it, or that it wasn't live. You wrapped your hands around the wire."

Char shrugged. "I figured it wasn't live. How many places have we been to with power?"

"Since the four of us have been together?" Sam said.

Grace looked tired of the conversation. "What are we doing here? Seems like you knew where we were headed the whole time."

"Passed by here once or twice. It's like a dude ranch. It's been like fifteen or twenty years since I've been out here. Used to come with my folks. It's called the Meadow Creek Mountain Ranch, or Creek Meadow Mountain Ranch. Signs around front on the main lodge. They have these cool little cabins you rent, and stables with horses. We stopped to look around once. My mother loved it. Wanted us to stay. I remember my little sister and I took off running. We went right for the stable to see the horses. I think we were all a little disappointed when dad said we weren't going to be staying there. He liked it a little more backwoods than cabins and lodges. Right now though, I appreciate the time we spent sleeping in tents, learning to trap and skin animals, and how to pick out the edible berries and mushrooms when they grow side by side with stuff that will kill you in minutes."

"I don't see any stable," Sam said, "or a lodge, or cabins."

"We're in the field, Sammy," Char said and huffed, to show she was annoyed. "Do you think there are still horses?"

"I doubt it," he said.

"Then why are we here?"

"There should be a well with a pump. Old fashioned running water," Tony said, "and if we're at all lucky, somewhere nice to set up camp for a bit. See what's what. Ahead of us are the mountains. Blue Ridge. We're going to cross out of Tennessee, and at that point kiss the warm weather away. See if we can dig up useful supplies like parkas, backpacks, tools."

"Horses *would* be cool," Char said. She wasn't going to mention the bottoms of her feet.

"You know it," Sam said.

# # #

Char used a pitchfork to toss hay around inside an empty stall. The stable did not contain a single horse. There were saddles, reins, bits, and riding whips.

Her brother, Cash, would have loved coming to a ranch like this. He would have been fourteen now if he were still alive. It was his death, even more than their father's death that plagued her dreams with nightmares. He was not bitten by a zombie, the infected. They never got close to him. No. His death was far more tragic. While she had been in charge of keeping an eye on him, a gunfight broke out. There were soldiers, Coast Guard, and other survivors, and it was all about moving a boat. Things escalated quickly. When it all went down, she'd been unable to protect him.

Her father never blamed her. She always thought she could see it in his eyes, though. Soundless accusations that felt as real and painful as a punch.

"Hey, daydreamer."

Char lifted the pitchfork, ready to use the long and sharp tines as a weapon. "Tony, you startled me."

He never should have been able to startle her. It meant that she hadn't been paying attention to her surroundings. You didn't stay alive by daydreaming. That was wasting time. Fantasy worlds did not exist, and having thoughts like that would turn a person soft. There was no room on her body, in her mind, for soft. She was solid, a rock.

Tony sauntered up to the stall. He crossed his arms and rested them on the wood gate. "If you're all done with your chores, ma'am, there's somethin' I'd like to show ya."

She laughed. His southern accent was right-on. He already sounded like a man born and raised in Texas, but the added hillbilly drawl just added to routine. "Cows done been milked already, I 'spose if you be needen' to show me somethin', then let's go have a looksee."

"Looksee? Is that Little House on the Prairie-like?"

"Depends," Char said.

"Depends on what?"

"What is Little House on the Prairie?"

Tony shook his head. He grabbed a length of coiled rope and ran his arm through the center like he was sliding into a jacket. The rope rested on his shoulder. "Grab some more rope. Follow me," he said as he walked out of the stables.

Tony did not look back, but forged forward. Char walked close behind and slowed to smile at Grace who sat squat in front of the water pump. Sam worked the arm up and down. Clean, clear water spilled from the spigot, slowly filling the basin in front of Grace.

"Where you guys going?" Sam said.

Char just shrugged and hurried to catch up to Tony.

They crossed a field and stopped when they came to the wire fence outlining the back edge of the property. "There," he said.

Two horses meandered about eating grass.

She tightened her grip on the rope. "Think they're from this ranch?"

"I'm betting they are. Probably ran away when things were chaotic, but this is home for them. Could be more around, too. Figured, if we can get close, not spook them, maybe we can use them. Take a load off your feet. I know they've been hurting you. We can take turns riding or something."

She loved the idea and smiled to show how she felt. "We're going to have horses?"

# # #

They cooked rabbit on spits over a small fire. The horses were safe in the stables. Char had spent several hours cleaning them up and brushing them down. She was anxious to ride them. Tony advised giving it a day or two to let them get acclimated to being domesticated once again. Made sense. While she sat around the fire, all she could think about was having a horse. She knew which one she wanted, the black one with patches of white. She decided to name him Dispatch, in memory of her father. Tony didn't have an interest in naming his horse. He made no bones about his attachment issues.

"Dinner smells good," Grace said. "Those snares worked real well, Tony."

"They do, luckily. As long as we can bait them, we shouldn't have a problem." Tony turned the spits. "I've always enjoyed rabbit. A little gamey, sure, but as long as you expect that when you bite in you're not shocked."

Sam laughed. "You're a good cook. I'll give you that."

Char heard neighing from the stables. "You think they're okay by themselves in there?"

"Might not be thrilled about being penned up. Could take them a while to get used to it. Have to remember," Tony said, "they've been running free for years. Imagine how you'd feel if you were suddenly locked up and confined to something not much larger than a prison cell?"

"I'd hate it," Char said. "No way I'd let someone lock me up."

# # #

Someone shook her by the shoulders.

Char opened her eyes, and her mouth, ready to scream.

"Shh." Tony had a finger pressed to his lips. "Listen."

She had been sound asleep. She could not recall a nightmare. If there hadn't been one, it would be the first time in, she wasn't sure how long, that she'd slept so peacefully. It might have something to do with the horses. They made her hopeful, which was an emotion in and of itself that she could not truly recall feeling. "What is it?"

"People. Outside the ranch."

"Where are Grace and Sam?" Char knew the two of them had a thing. They made for an awkward couple. It wasn't like there were singles mingles they could attend. The two barely spoke to each other during the day; public displays of affection were non-existent. When it came time to settle in for a night, they were inseparable. Char was happy for them and that they'd found each other; found something in each other to love and cling to. She wasn't sure she'd ever meet anyone and fall in love. It wasn't likely. She knew she was more like Tony. She had attachment issues, too.

"One of the other cabins." Tony moved away from the bed, toward the window. He stood with his back to the wall and parted curtains with the back of his hand. "Too dark. There has to be at least three, maybe as many as six."

Char stayed still a moment, listening. The voices were low, but audible. "They're going to know someone's here." She thought about the pit used to cook the rabbits. The fire had been extinguished, but even a hack of a tracker would know it had been recently used. Maybe it had been the fire and the aroma of rabbit that brought them to the location in the first place. It was possible, which was why they tried to move from wherever they were after cooking a meal. The fire, the smoke, the smells, it always attracted something. Tony had also warned that in the Blue Ridge Mountains the infected and raiders weren't all there was to contend with. There were bears and mountain lions, as well.

Tony kept a finger by his lips.

Whoever was outside was close to their cabin. Char could feel her heart beat. It thudded hard inside her ribcage. She knew her breathing had changed to quick, shallow breaths. Beads of sweat formed on her forehead. One rolled down the bridge of her nose. "What do we do?"

Tony shot her a look, as if asking if she didn't understand the gesture he'd been making with his finger.

Their bug out bags leaned by the wall next to the door, the only obvious way out of the cabin, Char rolled quietly out of bed. She stayed low to the floor. On all fours, she crawled toward the door.

Tony knelt by the window, still keeping the curtains slightly parted. Thanks to a cloudless night, moonbeams filtered into the room and sprayed across the area rug in a long and thin ray of light. "I count seven," he said, "At least one is a woman."

His whispering sounded like thunder booming in the enveloping silence.

Char stood up and put her machete harness on over her head and shoulders. She belted the sword in place around her wrist. "Let's go get 'em."

Tony got to his feet, and in two strides he crossed the room. He retrieved his bow and quiver, and placed his mouth near her ear. "I am going to try to open the window. I might be able to drop half of them before they even realize something is wrong. You—"

They heard the bang of a door being busted open.

Grace screamed.

"No time," Char said.

Tony grabbed her arm. "I saw assault rifles. We need to be smart about this."

Char shrugged her arm free. "We're not staying here. We have to go help."

Tony went back to the window. With the noise coming from outside, he pushed open the window, certain the sound made would be well masked. He parted the curtain, and knelt as he nocked an arrow in place. "Stay, Charlene. Wait until I say go," he said.

Char heard Tony's words just as she slid out of the cabin onto the small front porch. When they made it through this, she planned to kick Tony's ass. He knew better than to call her by her full name. He was not her father. She had not been Charlene in over three years.

Char forgot her shoes. The bottoms of her bare feet protested, sending waves of pain up her calves through raw nerve endings. She held her machete out in front of her, considering the weapon an addition of her being and more than some prosthetic extension of her limbs. Staying with her back to the front of the cabin, she slinked across the porch to the side of the structure. She stood still, listening.

Nothing.

There was not even the sound of a struggle any longer. Char assumed Grace and Sam were two cabins down. Why they didn't just stay in the one directly next door confused her. She was certain however, that one was vacant.

She bent forward and ran from her cabin to the vacant one. On that porch, she mimicked her movements, staying close and in the shadows as she moved toward the opposite end. The moon lit the rear of the locations. Keeping well hidden by darkness on the porches was not going to be difficult.

Char had been right. Sam and Grace were in the third cabin down from where she and Tony had been sleeping. From it, she heard muffled voices. Several people were inside the cabin. Were all the people Tony had seen inside, though? That was the question.

Where was Tony? Waiting with his bow by an open window was not going to help the situation. They needed to surprise the raiders and attack together.

Her chest felt tight, and for a moment she closed her eyes and focused on her breathing. Adrenaline and fear pulsed through her body, racing through her veins and arteries.

Rapid gunfire erupted. Char held her breath. She felt tears brim in front of her eyes, but she stood statue-still, waiting. Before long she heard one of the men speak: "What are we going to do with them, Broadhurst?"

"They're coming with us." It must have been Broadhurst answering the question.

"Both of them? We really only need the woman," the first man said.

Char tried to imagine what was going on inside the cabin. Were Grace and Sam forced to kneel at gunpoint? Were they bound and gagged? Were they dead?

They couldn't be dead. Either of them. That didn't make sense, not if one of the guy's was asking if they were taking both Grace and Sam. The fact that he was asking such a question indicated both of her friends were alive, and probably all right. Probably.

"Don't move."

Char gasped.

"Shh!"

It was Tony. He was all stealth, and had managed to get up alongside her without her having noticed. "They're going to take them."

"Shh."

Char bit her lip. He was driving her crazy. They needed to work out a plan. If they went at the raiders half-cocked, they'd get hurt or killed.

Boot footfalls on wood.

Char turned her head. The cabin was feet away, but she could not make out anything on its porch. Someone was on it though, and that someone more than likely had an assault rifle, but he couldn't see her and Tony cowering in shadows.

"Get up. On your feet!" The orders came from inside the cabin.

Char stayed still. They didn't have long. Their time to act, to re-act, was now. Options would become more limited.

"Take him out," she said to Tony, knowing even in the dark he was an excellent archer.

"Who's there?"

Char heard Tony sigh. Obviously her plan did not match his.

She heard it, though. The arrow hissed as it cut through still air and flew past her face. There was a fraction of a second before the sound of a body collapsing onto the porch was heard next.

"Run," Tony said.

They darted off the porch and into the tall grass.

"The fence," Char said. It had to be close.

The reached it, went under, and continued running. Thoughts swam inside Char's mind. She knew they were now in danger.

Yelling and shouted commands came from behind her.

They would not be able to see Char and Tony as they searched for somewhere to hide. The problem was that there were no trees in the field.

"Drop down," Tony said.

They got low in the grass, and faced the cabins. The cabin was a black silhouette with the moonlight behind it.

"I want that arrow back," Tony said.

From where they were, they were close enough to see the shadows of men searching in and around the other cabins. They hurried, and barked out questions, comments and complaints.

Char said, "We need to—"

"Shh," Tony said.

She was getting sick of his shushing her, calling her Charlene, worrying about an arrow. "We have to rescue them," she said, determined to be heard.

"Stay quiet. I won't warn you again," Tony said. He spoke so softly, she wasn't sure if he'd actually spoken. "This is not the time."

They could have been there hiding in the tall grass for a half hour or two hours. Char couldn't tell. The moon seemed to have moved across the sky. Or maybe it hadn't.

Eventually, the raiders reunited back at the third cabin. Four people with assault rifles surrounded the cabin. Eventually, still silhouetted by the moon's light, Char saw Grace and Sam. They had their fingers laced and hands on their heads as they were lead between the cabins and out of sight.

"What do we do now?" she said.

"We sit still. We wait."

"Wait?" Char said. "For what?"

The others around the cabin did not immediately leave. They made like they had followed along after everyone else, but they never left. The shadows they cast were visible now and again.

Time ticked by.

Hours.

The ground felt cold under her belly.

"Do you think they checked our cabin? My shoes are in there," she said.

Tony remained quiet.

Grace and Sam were gone. "How are we going to find them?"

"We'll find them," Tony said. "Tracking that many people will be as easy as following railroad tracks. Don't worry. We're going to get them back."

Chapter 6

"Anna?"

Char looked at Grace. The woman struggled against the seat belt; her eyes were open wide. It was as if she wasn't seeing, though. The laceration across her forehead looked deep. Thankfully it was no longer bleeding. It might be what caused her to lose consciousness. A concussion needed medical attention. Char had no idea what to do to help.

"Anna!"

Char reached out a hand and gently placed it on the woman's arm. "Grace. You're okay. It's okay." She was not sure who Anna was, nor was she sure she'd ask. People's pasts were haunting.

"No!" Grace kept her mouth open long after the word was screamed.

Char needed to get Tony and Sam's attention. They were too far ahead. The last thing she wanted to do was pull the cord to activate the rig's horn, the blast would give away their location to anything even remotely close. It wasn't like she was in a compact car where the honk sounded more like a feeble sneeze. She decided to apply the clutch and brakes. They were smart guys; they would realize she had stopped. They'd turn around and head back.

"Grace," she said, as the rig stopped. The motor let out hisses and moans. It exhaled a puff of smoke out of the pipe over the cab's roof, as if a dragon were settling down for the day.

Grace held onto a startled expression. Her hands shot forward and braced on the dash as she looked left and right. "Where are we?"

"You're safe. We've got you. We saved you from those people," Char said. She tried to speak softly. She had no idea what horrors Grace endured. She shuddered just thinking about the endless list of possibilities. It was surely the kind of things that nightmares were bred from.

"Charlene," Grace said. Normally she'd have protested. This time she let it go. Grace was working to get her bearings in check. It was okay, forgivable.

"I'm here."

"Sam? Where is he?"

"He's safe, riding horseback with Tony." She looked out the front window. She had expected to see Tony and Sam returning. There was no sign of them yet. She didn't think they were that far ahead. "We're far, far away from those bad people."

"They were bad people," Grace said. Her voice fell flat. Her eyes lowered, looking down at nothing, maybe the gearshift.

Char found it hard to swallow. "Who. . .who is Anna?"

Grace's head snapped up. She locked eyes with Char.

Char knew better than to have asked. "I'm sorry. It's none of my business."

"She was my baby. Anna was my daughter."

There was really no need to say more. Char had lost her family, friends, to the infected, to battles against crazy people she'd come to know as raiders. If Anna wasn't here, it didn't require much imagination to figure out how it ended. The only difference might be some specifics.

Grace's expression softened. She took her hands away from the dash and folded them in her lap. "Anna was just ten years old. An itty-bitty thing. She looked so much like her father, I always tried not to hold that against her. He was such a son of a bitch that man, but he was handsome. I won't lie. One of the first things that attracted me to him was his looks. He had these big broad shoulders and arms that looked more like marble than muscle. He was tall and dark, and had a deep raspy voice. The kind of voice that, when he whispered —it melted your heart. I don't know if it was infatuation, or plain and simple lust. We were no good together. He drank too much, and I guess I did, too. Our arguments oftentimes became physical. He could have killed me if he wanted to, a single punch would have shut my lights forever. No. He never hit me. I guess what I mean when I say that our arguments became physical, is that I used to beat the shit out of him. Hit him till my hands hurt too bad to hit him anymore, and then I'd find something else to use to hit him with," she said, smiling. She was actually giggling, as if the idea of abuse was funny. It wasn't. She worried something might still be wrong with Grace. The woman needed help, a doctor.

Char felt uncomfortable and kept looking out the front windshield. They sat in the middle of nowhere, alone and vulnerable. She wanted Grace to share, to open up, to get it out, but what she didn't want was for a horde of zombies to surround them because she wasn't able to pay attention. Nor did she want raiders attacking or Broadhurst finding them. "Are you okay if I keep driving?"

Grace seemed not to hear. She just stared ahead; her hands fidgeted together in her lap. "No, we were not good together. Too much alike, I think. That saying about opposites attract? I think opposites attracting is less dangerous than similar people being together. I don't even know if that makes any sense."

It wasn't a question. Grace did not seem to be talking to Char as much as she just seemed to be talking. There was a vacancy in Grace's eyes that was unsettling. It had to do with opening doors to the past. The haunts freed. Char decided to shift into gear and try to catch up to Tony and Sam. She felt extremely isolated, and that scared her.

"He stayed three months after finding out I was carrying his child. I think staying even that long nearly killed him. Don't get me wrong. He was excited about the idea of becoming a father. At least he let me believe he was, but I heard the rumbles from friends. He wasn't being faithful to me. I'd put weight on, the way a pregnant woman will. He swore it had nothing to do with the weight. Said he just couldn't perform with me, knowing it was his baby inside. Said something about that it just did something to him. He considered me a mother —not like he thought of me as his own mom. Nothing Oedipus-like. I suppose I understood. At the very least, I tried to understand, but one night he came home, had to be four in the morning, and he just smelled like liquor and sex. I knew he was out disrespecting me, but did he have to come home flaunting it? It was more than I could take, more than any woman should have to take, if you ask me. I just let him apologize, and let him beg and plead with me to forgive him. I remember just smiling at him. Smiling and nodding. All the while he just kept talking. I don't know how many times he told me he loved me, or how many times he told me all the other women meant nothing to him. All the other women, seriously? But I didn't say a word. I just kept giving him that smile—you know that smile, like I am sympathetic to his situation, and I get it that he had no other choice but to sleep with any woman that would have him? For some reason that calmed him down. He climbed into bed and passed out. That's when I went and got his baseball bat that he kept with his softball team stuff, and I kicked that mother fucker's ass with it. Broke ribs and bruised every part of his body. Every inch of his skin had to have been a terrible shade of black and blue."

When Grace laughed, Char wanted to cup her hands over her ears.

The light at the end of the tunnel was on horseback, just ahead of them. Tony slowed his horse, and Char lowered the driver side window.

"You guys okay? We were just about to turn around," Tony said. He kept looking up at Char and then back to the road as it unfolded.

"Grace is awake. Something's wrong. We're going to have to stop soon; now if possible."

"We'll see if we can find a good place to pull off the road," he said.

Char put up the window. Grace did not seem to notice the interruption.

"Needless to say, he didn't stay after that. Didn't press charges or anything, but he didn't stay. Instead of just punishing me by leaving, he punished Anna. He wanted nothing to do with her. Never tried to contact her, or me, for that matter. It was his loss. He missed out on being a father to one of the most wonderful little girls in the entire world," Grace said. She made no move to wipe away tears that rolled down her cheeks, cutting through dirt and leaving clean streaks.

"I think they found a place for us to pull off the road," Char said. She hoped Grace heard and understood her. She did not want to hear any more about Anna's father. She did not think she could take it much more. As horrible a story as it was, it was still from a time when things were *normal*.

"We were on a city bus, headed downtown to do some shopping. The school year had started, and wouldn't you know, Anna had a growth spurt, outgrowing everything I'd just bought her? I worked as a legal secretary, making shit for a wage. The lawyers made the big bucks. You know who did all the work, though? Us secretaries, the paralegals, but we were paid only a little better than fast-food workers. I could have had me a job at a McDonald's with half the stress and aggravation. Instead, I wanted more of a career, something that Anna could be proud of. It makes a difference. Someone ever asked her what her mother did for a living, she could tell them I worked at a big, fancy law firm, and not flipping burgers or sitting fries into a deep fryer. There ain't nothing wrong with a job like McDonalds. That's honest work. I just wanted more, even if it was just the perception of more. Because, like I told you, the money I made, it was only a fraction better than the pay I'd have received from a place like McDonalds. I chose to do all this work, long days, late evenings, all so the lawyers I supported could sign their names on the bottom of the research I'd conducted, the papers I'd constructed." Grace waved a dismissive hand in the air as if wiping a memory clear.

Tony and Sam were off their horses, waving Char their way. On the left side she saw what looked like a flat field. It seemed like a perfect place to pull over. She switched gears and used her directional. Tony shook his head.

"I had a bit of money saved. Wanted to use it for Christmas shopping. That was a big holiday in my family. Growing up, we never had much. My mother raised seven of us on her own. We didn't have a pot to piss in, but come Christmas there was always a gift under the tree. For each of us. Some years it was just one gift a piece. Some years there was more. Usually though, it was just one.

It didn't matter what was enclosed in that wrapping paper. The care my mother took with each gift, I figured she spent hours just doing the wrapping. She made sure the corners were perfectly creased and folded and taped down. She used bows and ribbons. I almost hated opening them. Almost." Grace laughed. At least the memories that must have been flashing inside her mind made her happy. "But just like my brothers and sisters, when it was my turn to open my gift, I tore into that paper like there was no tomorrow."

Char stopped the truck. She knew not to shut down the engine. The nights got cold. She had no idea how hard it would be to start in the morning.

Her stomach growled.

She was hungry.

She remembered something. The back of the rig, the trailer. It was packed full with food. Drinks. They were going to feast. She reached for the door handle.

Grace grabbed her arm.

Char looked into Grace's eyes. They silently begged Char to stay, to listen.

There was a knock on the door.

Char lowered the window. "We'll be right out. Give us a minute."

"You guys okay?" Tony said.

Char nodded. "We just need a minute. Girl talk," she said.

Tony walked away.

Char looked back at Grace. She hated to do it. She asked, "What happened on the bus, Grace?"

# # #

"Can I play with your phone?" Anna sat on the bench next to her mother.

"Wait until we get onto the bus, dear," Grace said. There were two other people waiting with them. A teenaged boy wore oversized headphones, the adapter plugged into a phone he held in both hands an inch from his face. The brim of his baseball cap was tilted upward and worn to the side. Even though it was Saturday morning, the other person, an elderly woman, was dressed in a pant suit and carried a briefcase. Grace had worked countless Saturdays over the years and sympathized.

It wasn't long before the bus came. It slowed to a stop in front of the bus sign, and the doors swooshed open. "Have your pass?" Grace said.

Anna held up her bus pass. "Right here, momma."

Grace tapped her finger lovingly onto the tip of Anna's nose. "Well then, our chariot awaits."

"We have a chariot?"

Grace laughed. They stood up. She was so tempted to lift Anna into her arms. She knew better. The conflict at home stemmed from granting bits and pieces toward Anna's independence. Anna tried to set rules. Grace figured she would at least hear them out. If they were unreasonable, she would pull rank and play the "I'm-your-mother" card.

There was to be no more hand holding. No kisses hello or goodbye unless no one was around to witness the displays of affection. Under no circumstances was Grace to carry Anna anywhere, except maybe up to bed when she fell asleep on the sofa in front of the television. Grace knew it was a phase. She'd gone through it with her own mother. It passed. Eventually. That was what Grace held onto, the hope that Anna would forget such silliness and welcome hugs and smooches again one day soon.

Until then, Grace agreed to abide by the rules. She would not force physical affection onto her daughter, as painstaking a task as it might prove to be.

"What are they doing?" Anna said, and pointed toward the back of the bus.

Grace shook her head and made a tsk, tsk sound. "Misbehaving."

Three teens were on their feet. They all wore jeans that sagged below the ass. The only way the pants stayed in place was if the kids stood bow-legged, making their thighs work as a belt. One wore a filthy white tank-top. It looked like blood covered the cotton, and their baseball caps were cocked to the side. The rope chain jewelry around their necks could not be real; no child could have the money to afford that much gold.

The yelling they did became loud, dangerous. Grace placed a hand across her stomach as if it could stop the sinking feeling she felt. She glanced over her shoulder and saw they were on State Street, still several blocks from their stop. "We're getting off at the next stop, honey."

"Are we there?"

"Just about." It was better to get out of a situation before it exploded and there was no chance to escape. Violence has always been bad in the city, ruthless and relentless. The last several days, however, the news had been filled with reports of vicious attacks. Unruly groups beating and even killing innocent people on the streets.

One of the teens ran forward—or stumbled forward really. It was the boy in the tank-top.

He fell in front of Grace and Anna.

It was blood on his shirt. Bright, red blood that still looked wet and fresh.

Grace covered Anna's eyes. She wanted to say something, to scold the child for acting like an animal, but didn't. The last thing she wanted was to draw attention. She sat motionless in her seat, watching, the way the other people on the bus were doing. No one wanted to get involved.

The boy tried to scramble to his feet.

His face was cut. The cheek under his left eye flapped open. His eyes were opened so wide they bulged from the socket, as if threatening to pop from his skull.

He placed a hand on Grace's knee for support.

She kicked at him, a reflex. "Get away from me!"

A man screamed for help from the back of the bus. Grace turned her head in time to see one of the other teens raise a baseball bat.

There was a woman who looked dead. Her skin was grey, eyes bloodshot red. Her mouth was open, but her jaw hung too low, as if dislocated and only hanging onto the face by cartilage.

If that boy struck the girl with the bat, Grace was not sure she could sit idle any longer.

She just wanted off the bus.

"Keep your eyes closed, baby," she said.

The teen did not swing the bat. Instead, he shoved the barrel end into the girl's mouth and drove her backward. She fell onto a man's lap. The man tried to remove himself from the area, pushing and scratching to get her off him.

The boy with the bat did not stop. He pushed on the handle of the bat, shoving the fat end deep into the girl's throat.

No one on the bus moved. Everyone just watched.

Grace could not sit and watch. The girl was sick, and these boys seemed set on killing her. Jumping to her feet, she stepped over Tank-top, and strode down the center aisle. "Stop it! Stop this right now!"

"Lady, go sit back down," the third teen said. He stood in a fighter's stance, resembling an old school boxer. He looked ready to throw jabs and uppercuts. His feet kept moving. "This isn't what it looks like. There's something wrong with her."

"You boys are what's wrong with her," Grace said, as she reached the back of the bus.

She saw it, though. There was something wrong with the girl. It was more than just her having a bat shoved through her face. The kid couldn't be more than sixteen, she was thin. She wore a short shirt that showed off a diamond pierced navel. Her stomach boasted claw marks. These boys didn't just act like animals, they were animals. "Give me that bat."

"Lady, you have no idea what's going on! She attacked us! She came at us. We weren't doing nothing. She bit J-Dawg." The boxer pointed.

Grace looked behind her.

J-Dawg was growling at Anna.

Surreal was a word she'd read in novels. She understood the definition of the word, but had never truly experienced anything even remotely surreal until then, at that moment, when life switched gears. The way time unfolded changed. Everything went to slow motion and color drained from her vision. Grainy and gray was how she saw everything around her. The only color she could make out was the red jacket Anna wore. It was vibrant and seemed to radiate with the limited daylight that streamed in from heavily tinted bus windows.

The man who had the girl with the bat in her mouth escaped from under her. He dropped to his knees onto the black grated aisle and crawled forward a few inches before collapsing flat onto his belly.

He couldn't be dead.

He maybe passed out or was having a heart attack. He couldn't have been more than fifty years old.

Grace needed to get over him, past him, and to her daughter.

People by Anna refused to react.

"Grab my baby!" It was the only thing Grace could think to yell. She needed to motivate people to react and not sit by as idiotic bystanders. She stepped onto the fallen man's back.

"J-Dawg caught it, Richie. J-Dawg's sick!" Boxer dropped his fists to his side.

Anna's eyes were open. She watched everything. Her lips quivered. Even from this end of the bus, Grace saw the tears.

J-Dawg's going to wish he was a whole lot sicker when I get through with him, Grace thought as she crushed the man's fingers under the heel of her shoe. Bones crunched. That woke the guy up. He howled and raised his head.

He tripped Grace, catching her back foot as she brought it around. She went down fast, hands reaching for anything to grab onto.

Why on earth was the bus still moving?

"Stop the bus! Someone, get him to stop the bus!"

Grace pulled herself up onto her knees and screamed as J-Dawg bit her daughter on the arm.

Anna screamed.

Grace pushed her way forward; she brought a leg back and kicked J-Dawg in the jaw. His head snapped back. Blood, Anna's blood, flew from his mouth and sprayed a woman on the seat across from them. In a swoop of her arm, Grace lifted her daughter up.

Now the bus stopped.

"How could you!" Grace was not yelling at the man who bit her daughter, but at the people who sat by and watched the assault.

At the front of the bus, the driver was unbuckling his seat belt. "What's going on back there?"

"I don't feel good, Mommy," Anna said.

Grace pressed Anna's head to her chest, her arms wrapped tight around her child as she made her way off the bus. "You better keep this bus right here; I'm calling the police."

"Ma'am—"

She shouldered her way past the driver, noted his name on the displayed license and stepped off the bus. Setting Anna down on the curb, Grace searched for her phone. She was calling 911. Her phone was not in her pockets. She didn't have her purse. Anna had been playing with the phone. She must have dropped it. There was no way she was going back onto the bus for her things until police arrived.

Grace placed her palm on Anna's forehead. "It's going to be okay."

There was no telling what kind of disease the junkie had. Probably shared dirty needles shooting heroin. AIDS. She clapped a hand to her chest, knowing she needed to do something to stop her heart from beating so fast.

Someone must have called the police from the bus, she heard sirens.

Two police cars sped toward them. Grace stood, waved her arms to flag them down.

They blew past her.

Grace swore and raised a middle finger at them. She charged the bus and banged on the closed doors. "Call nine-one-one. Get the police here. My daughter needs an ambulance. Do you hear me?"

She took a step back.

She peered into the tinted windows.

She saw the fight was still taking place. Although muffled, she now heard screams. People on the bus were crying out for help.

Something was wrong. Terribly, terribly wrong.

Grace turned and saw Anna on the ground. She was losing a lot of blood. The bastard had torn a chunk of flesh off her daughter. She ran back and scooped her up. Anna was lethargic. Her eyes rolled around, showing off mostly the whites. "Hey, honey. Hey, baby," she said. She held her daughter draped over her arms; her legs and head dangled.

She needed to get away from the bus. If those crazy passengers got off, there was no telling what might happen. All she could think to do was run. With Anna bleeding in her arms, Grace ran. Every step on the concrete pounded inside her skull. It felt like her brain had jarred loose and was sloshing around inside her skull.

A block and a half away, she saw a group of people and ran toward them.

"Help me, please. Help me!" Grace said. The crying she held in caused her throat to hurt. "Call nine-one-one for me. My daughter needs an ambulance."

Her daughter was bleeding out. She knew she frightened people, the two of them covered in blood. That should make people want to help. It didn't, instead they took steps backward, scared.

"Please. Please, call nine-one-one for me. Why won't someone help us?" Grace said. She sat down. There was nowhere to run, they were downtown. She was without her purse. Without her phone.

A man had his cell out. He held up a hand. "I'm calling," he said.

Grace cradled her daughter close and held her tightly. "It's okay. It's okay."

"The operator has medical questions to give the ambulance information, okay?"

"Just tell them to send an ambulance!"

The man took a step back. "They said they are, but the questions help determine the response, okay? How old is she?" the man asked.

"Ten."

"Is she awake?"

"Does she look awake?" Grace knew it wasn't this man's fault. She didn't want questions.

"Is she breathing?"

Grace felt her eyes go wide. She didn't know. She placed Anna down on the sidewalk. "I don't know? I'm—I'm not sure."

"They want you to put your ear down next to her mouth and listen," he said.

She tried, but heard her own heartbeat thump around wildly inside her chest. She set her ear closer to Anna's mouth, listened—and waited. She couldn't hold back the tears. This couldn't be happening. It was a beautiful fall day, and they were just supposed to go buy some new clothes for school and maybe grab some lunch somewhere. That was it.

She shook her head, unable to say that, no, Anna was not breathing.

"They want you to lay her flat on her back," the man said.

Grace stared at the man. "She is!"

"Make sure there is nothing in her mouth. Place your hand on her forehead, and the other under her neck."

Grace opened Anna's mouth and stuck her finger in and under the tongue. "There's nothing in there. Nothing."

People on the street crowded around them. The spectacle taking place drew their attention when her simple pleas for someone to call 911 went initially unanswered. She hated people. Hated them.

"I don't know CPR," she said. "I don't know what to do!"

"They're going to talk us through this, okay? They want me to tell you you're doing good. I'm going to tell you how to give mouth-to-mouth. With her head carefully tilted back, pinch her nose closed and completely cover her mouth with your mouth, then blow two regular breaths into the lungs, about one second each, just enough to make the chest rise with each breath. Did you feel the air going in and out?"

Grace did as instructed. "Yes."

"Did you see her chest rise and fall with each breath?"

"Yes."

Grace closed her eyes. Her vision was blurred with tears.

"Put the heel of your hand on the center of her chest between her nipples. Then put your other hand on top of that one. You're going to push down on her chest. About two inches. Let the chest come all the way back up. We're going to do this thirty times, twice per second, and then another breath, and repeat, okay?"

Grace went through the instructions again in her head. "Where is the ambulance?"

"It'll be here. It's coming. They said it's on the way, and you're doing great—"

"I'm not doing great! I'm not," she said. Grace did not mean to yell at the only man willing to help her. This was not his fault.

He held up one hand, perhaps meant to calm her. In a way it did, but not as much as when he knelt down on the opposite side of Anna and put the phone to his chest and spoke just to Grace. "We're going to get through this okay? I want you to start the compressions, and I am going to count them off, okay? Thirty compressions, two per second, and then a breath." He put the phone back to his ear.

His talking helped. It kept her calm, focused. "Okay."

"One, two, three," he said.

It seemed like she was pushing too hard, going too fast. Something snapped inside Anna. "Oh, Jesus. Jesus," Grace said.

"She broke something," the man said into the phone. "We heard it. We heard something break."

Grace dropped over her daughter. She couldn't keep it together. She couldn't do this. "Anna, baby. Anna, breathe, honey. Breathe."

"Listen, listen," the man said, he had a hand on her shoulder. "It's okay. You can't stop. You have to keep doing this."

"I broke her ribs," she said.

"That happens," he said.

"Anna!"

The man pulled Grace off her daughter.

"What the fuck do you think you're doing?"

He dropped his cell phone, pushed up the sleeves on his jacket, and set his hands on Anna's chest. He didn't hesitate. He started compressions and counted them off out loud. His own breathing matched each thrust. Short, quick breaths.

Grace watched, but couldn't stand seeing her little girl's body cave inward with each compression. She looked lifeless, fake. He was going to kill her.

She didn't stop him. She didn't help him. She couldn't help him. Grace felt paralyzed.

Someone draped an arm around her shoulder. An elderly woman sat next to her. She looked frail, deflated. Her skin was marked with brown spots. The woman did not say a word, but continued to pat her on the back softly.

The first responders on scene was the city fire department. An engine pulled up, lights flashing, sirens off; five men climbed out of the red machine. They wore helmets with turnout gear boots and pants, but no jackets, while the suspenders were fit over firehouse tee-shirts. Two firefighters rushed up and took over CPR. One did compressions and the other placed a mask over Anna's mouth and gave breaths through it when it was time.

When the ambulance arrived a few moments later, they loaded Anna into the back of the ambulance. The paramedics did not interfere. The firemen had a routine going that could not be interrupted. The four of them rode in the ambulance with Anna.

A police officer gave Grace a ride, following lights and sirens behind the ambulance.

Chapter 7

"One of the worst things was that I never got to thank that man for helping me. He was the only one that helped me, and I never thanked him. I don't know his name and can't even remember what he looked like," Grace said. "I just wish I had a chance to thank him."

Char and Grace sat silently inside the rig. Char was not sure what to say, what she could say. "We should see if the guys need anything. I think we're going to camp down here for the night," is what she said, finally.

Grace nodded, lips pressed tightly together, her hands folded in her lap. "Looks like the day's just starting."

"Been a long night," Char said. "I'll come around and help you down."

"I'm okay." Grace did not look up. "Char?"

"Yes."

"I'm sorry I laid all of that on you. I had no right."

Char knew the images would stay inside her head forever. She could only imagine what happened to Anna after being bitten. "We're family, Grace. I'm here any time you need to talk. Any time."

"I know you are. I love you for it. We all have sad stories. We just know better than to live in that horrid past. We don't talk about it. That's our group's little unwritten rule, and I just violated it."

"That's Tony's thing. He's a guy. Guys suck at sharing feelings. We can talk. You and me. Okay?" Char was not sure she'd ever open up. The horrors that made up her past were her own. The weakness of sharing could cripple her strength. She did not want to risk that. People depended on her.

"You mean that?"

"I do."

Grace nodded again and sniffled. "Look at me all crying and slobbering like an infant."

"Stay there. I'll come around and get you, okay?"

Char climbed out of the rig.

"How she doing?" Sam said. He wrung his hands together. "She going to be all right?"

"She's going to be fine."

"What were you guys talking about in there?" Sam said.

"None of your business," Char said. She knew she sounded curt. Sam should know better than to ask. "Give me a hand getting her out of the rig. She might not be ready to walk. Her head needs to be bandaged up. She wasn't bleeding, but she has a gash across the temple."

"Tony was digging through the back of the truck for medical supplies. I think he found some peroxide and gauze."

"Good. We can clean it, keep it from getting infected. It's a start."

They walked around to the passenger side and opened the door.

Grace smiled. "I'm really high up here, aren't I?"

Sam held out his arms. "I'll get you down. Nice and slow."

"Nice and slow," Grace said.

"You got this?" Char said. "I want to check on Tony."

"We're good. I have her," Sam said. Char heard the love in his tone of voice. His time with Grace was about the only time she could tolerate him. He was more mature and responsible when around her. Their relationship was good for him.

Char planted her palm on the hilt of her sword and walked toward the back of the trailer. Her boots crushed on dirt and loose gravel. As she neared the end, she could hear Tony inside the trailer grunting and moving things around. She reached the back of the trailer and held onto the open door. "You need a hand or anything?"

Tony had two boxes in his arms. He tried looking over them to see his path as he walked toward the back of the trailer. "Take these. They have medical supplies in them."

"You think we put enough distance between us and them?" Char took the boxes, expecting them to be heavy, but they weren't. She set them down and pulled open the cardboard flaps. She dug through the contents, finding bottles of aspirin, gauze, scissors, medical tape, splints, peroxide, allergy pills, Percocet, and penicillin. "Penicillin. This is good for Grace, right?"

Tony jumped out of the back of the trailer. "We'll see how bad the cut on her head is, but yeah. We'll start her on that. Just in case. It will help fight any infection. You guys alright? You were in there a while."

Char wasn't sure why when Tony asked the same question Sam had, she wasn't as annoyed. "She was telling me about her daughter. What had happened to her."

Tony nodded, leaving it at that. He didn't like background stories, saying they didn't help people move forward. "She okay?"

"I really don't know. She seems broken."

Tony planted fists on his hips and sighed. "We have to hide this truck."

The conversation about Grace was over. Char left it alone. "We really only drove along the road. If Broadhurst is coming after us, he's not going to have to look very hard."

"No. No, he's not. There just weren't places to make turns onto any other roads. This is kind of it for now. Think we should keep going?"

"I think Grace needs some medical attention and a chance to catch her breath."

"I agree. Let's get situated back here; keep the rig running. We'll have something to eat. Hell, we have enough food in this thing to have a feast."

"I could head down the road a ways, keep an eye out for raiders."

He shook his head. "No. Not this time. We're staying close, *together*. We'll let Grace rest some, but by this evening, before the sun sets, I want to be back on the road. We're going to have to find some other roads, get some real distance between us. It's the only way."

"There's another way," she said.

"And that would be?"

"We load up supplies. Between the four of us, and with the horses, we can take quite a bit and we leave the truck."

She saw Tony's expression. The thought of leaving the truck didn't sit well with him.

"This thing is going to run out of fuel sooner or later. We don't have any diesel. What good will it be to us then? We would have to leave it anyway. Whether we do it now or later really makes no difference, the end result is the same. We pack supplies and leave the truck. The benefit is that once Broadhurst finds it, he might be happy enough to have his things back that he just forgets all about us."

"Wishful thinking."

"Naturally," she said.

"Let's go have a look at Grace," he said.

# # #

They set Grace up inside a sleeping bag, using a rolled up one as a pillow. It did feel good to rest for a while. Char had her own wounds to lick. The last several hours had been brutal. She rubbed her shoulders and tried to massage away some of the knotting and pain.

Char hated the sound of the rig's chugging engine. She worried it would eventually attract unwanted attention. They were parked in a small clearing just off the main road.

Tony knelt beside Grace. "I came across a needle and thread. I'd like to sew up that gash. It's pretty deep. The bleeding has stopped, but I'd feel better knowing we can keep it clean. The only thing is, I don't have any anesthesia for the pain, and it's bound to hurt. A lot."

"We've got this," Sam said. He sat on the back of the trailer, legs dangling. He held up a bottle of whiskey. "She takes a couple good swigs, she won't feel a thing."

Tony regarded Grace with a look.

"Give me the bottle," she said.

The first gulp, she gasped. Her mouth fell open and she drooled. After wiping her face with her forearm, she smiled. "Smooth."

They all laughed.

Tony was eventually successful in threading the eye, and then used a lighter to sterilize the needle.

"You ever done this kind of thing before?" Grace said.

"Only when I was operating in the O.R.," he said.

Char looked at Tony, confused. "You were a doctor?"

"It's sarcasm," he said. "I promise I'll do my best to keep you from looking like Frankenstein."

"Frankenstein's monster," Sam said.

"What?" Tony said.

"Frankenstein was the doctor. Not the creature. People do that all the time. Confuse the two, but what you meant to say was, 'I promise I'll do my best to keep you from looking like Frankenstein's monster," Sam said, placing heavy emphasis on the last word.

"You done?" Tony said.

"Yeah. Done."

"Then come down here and hold her hand," Tony said.

"I'm not going to fight you," Grace said to Tony.

"It's for support," Tony said. "I know you can handle it. There's just no reason to do this without someone holding your hand, not when we've got people here to hold it."

Char smiled at the thoughtful gesture. "Maybe while you guys do that I can scrounge around and see what we might want to have for dinner."

"Burgers and fries sound good," Sam said, sliding out of the trailer and taking a knee beside Grace.

"Yeah. I'll see what I can dig up. If I find any hamburger meat inside that hot trailer, you are welcome to it."

Chapter 8

After a hearty lunch of canned beans, canned spinach and canned fruit cocktail, the group slept in shifts. Grace, who should have been out cold the entire time, stayed awake all day.

Large white clouds moved fast across a blue sky. The sun peeked in and out. Looking over the ridge Char watched the shadows race over tree tops toward them, over them, and then away from them. She loved the mountains. There was a serenity to the inspirational views that sort of balanced the shit of a world they lived in. She wished her father and brother were alive to see what she saw, knowing they would appreciate the beauty, too.

"You good?" Tony stood next to her, his hands stuffed into his front pockets.

"I am," she said. She wasn't. He knew she wasn't. None of them were good. They existed, worked to stay alive. They kept moving. There was no chance to settle down and grow roots. It wasn't an option.

"We're going to start packing it in. Figure out what supplies we want to pack. Give us a hand?" he said. She wasn't sure if Tony actually wanted help, or knew that keeping her busy would preoccupy her mind. Either way she felt thankful for the distraction.

"Can't believe Grace didn't sleep."

"Might be a good thing. If she has a concussion, we want her awake. Not sure why, exactly. It's just what I've always heard.

Might have something to do with the brain swelling or something. Not sure how staying awake prevents that. I do know one thing, she's going to be tired as all get out later." He laughed. "Come on. Let's get packed."

Once back behind the rig, Sam and Grace sorted through boxes pulling items they fit into backpacks.

"Know what I found?" Grace said.

Char shrugged. "Hamburger meat?"

"Better." Grace held products up in the air. "Toothpaste, shampoo, soap, anti-perspirant, and body lotion. Yes, you heard me, body lotion!"

Char could not have hidden her smile if she tried. "I would love to wash my hair. I mean, really clean it good."

"You and me both. Know what else? With all the squirrel meat Davy Crocket has us eating, I found a dozen boxes of toothpicks. Nothing worse than trying to set free sinew stuck between your teeth with nothin' but your tongue!"

"I don't want to jinx anything," Sam said.

"Then don't," Grace said.

"But, how long's it been since we've seen an infected? Hours? I must say, I'm liking it up here in the mountains."

Sam was right. "It is kind of odd."

"Not really," Tony said. "Not when you think about it. Not much population up in the mountains before everything went to hell. What civilians were here probably ambled down the mountain toward the . . . food. It's kind of why I wanted to come this way. I mean, it was more of a hunch. Seems to have paid off though."

"I have a question," Grace said. "I see two horses. We doubling up on them?"

Char eyed Dispatch, but didn't say anything. It was a horse, but she didn't want to see him strain to carry two people and supplies. It didn't seem fair.

"I think I have an answer to that," Sam said. He set down two cans of food and stood up. Everyone watched him as he climbed into the back of the trailer and disappeared inside.

There was something of a ruckus from inside the trailer. Some curse words were said. The sound of boxes tumbling. More curse words. Char smiled at Sam's antic, they always surprised her. "What is he doing?"

Tony and Grace shrugged.

A moment later, Sam re-emerged from the back of the trailer. He held up a mountain bike. "This is one. There's two more in here."

Tony took the bike from Sam, and Sam went back into the trailer for a second bike.

"That could work," Grace said, as she waved a dismissive hand through the air, "because there was no way I was getting up onto a horse. I'm just saying."

Tony clapped his hands together. "Let's pack everything back into the trailer. We can't really lock it up, but we can secure it as best we can and try to camouflage it. Never know if we may stumble back this way sometime. It's wishful thinking, I know," he said.

With the saddlebags on the horses packed, and backpacks stuffed full, and the trailer as camouflaged as possible, the four of them bid a silent farewell to the trailer, each knowing that at some point they were going to wish they had kept the truck forever.

Sam and Grace pedaled side by side. They talked, laughing, enjoying the last bit of sunlight as they led the way along the main road.

"Are they too cute together, or is it just me?" Tony sat on his horse, the reins in his hands. The horse stepped back, to the side and then settled in with a shake of his head and a snort. Its breath plumed from large black nostrils.

Char laughed. "We better follow closely behind. No telling what more trouble those two can get into." She made a few clicking sounds with her tongue and guided Dispatch forward. Her scabbard clapped softly against the side of the horse, which she found a comforting sound.

It was far easier making lefts and rights, getting off and away from the main road. Broadhurst would need a bloodhound to track them now. The few times the horses made a mess they'd stop and clean the shit off the road. It would be pointless trying to get lost, if they left proverbial bread crumb along the way.

Up ahead Sam and Grace had stopped. They stood beside their bikes. They were at the top of a hill. What lay beyond could be anything. It had to be something for them to have stopped. Char and Tony caught up, and pulled on the reins to stop the horses.

"Took you guys long enough," Sam said.

"What's up?" Char said, and sat leaning forward, her arm draped over the saddle horn.

"I mean, I could be seeing things, but are those lights? Like, electric lights?" Sam pointed straight ahead.

The road went down the side of the mountain. It was a steep decline that lead to a wide stretching valley. In the distance, toward the center of the valley, was what looked like a town. The town was lit with lights.

"What the hell?" Tony said.

"I see smoke coming from chimneys," Grace said. "Smell that?"

Char took a whiff of the air. The aroma must have been there all along, but combined with seeing the billowing smoke below she now could smell burning wood. It reminded her of being at Grandma Patty and Papa Phil's house. They'd light the downstairs fireplace and keep it going most of the winter. She and Cash used to sit close to the bricks and roast marshmallows. He always pulled his out when the marshmallow was blackened and had caught fire. He'd watch the flame dance for a few moments before blowing it out and popping the marshmallow into his mouth. She liked hers toasty brown.

She wanted a marshmallow badly now, and wondered if any had been left behind in the trailer.

"Let's get off the road. See if we can get a closer look," Tony said.

"Aren't they worried about attracting infected, or raiders?" Grace said.

"Could be where Broadhurst is from. We could be walking right to them," Char said. "I don't like it. I think we should just get out of here."

Sam shook his head. "It's a town, Char. For some odd reason they have power. I mean, look at the lights. Look at all of those lights. I don't hear gunshots, or screaming. It looks like something out of a picture, or a … ah, what do you call those things you mail?"

There were not that many lights, but what few there were lit the darkness like a beacon.

"Letter?" Grace said.

"No. The stamp goes right on it."

"It's called a letter," Grace said.

"They were cheaper to mail than letters. It was two sided. A picture on one side and you write a short message on the other side. Stamp went on that same side with your message."

"What the hell are you talking about?" Tony said. "Forget it. I say we watch the place for a little while. See if we can tell what's going on. If it doesn't look safe, we're out of here, like Char suggested."

"I think we should just get out of here now. We don't know anything about what's down there."

"Which is why we watch it. Just over night. In the morning we'll decide what to do next," Tony said.

"Postcard," Sam said.

"What about a postcard?" Char said.

"That's the word I was trying to remember. The town down there, it reminds me of something you'd see on a postcard." Sam smiled, and nodded, as if pleased with himself. Grace patted him on the back. It was done mockingly. Sam couldn't tell the difference.

Char dismounted and led Dispatch to the nearest tree and tied him to a low hanging branch. "I'm going down there. We're not going to be able to observe anything from this far away. And if you have any plans of going into that town, then I want to know firsthand what's what. Because, like it or not, Tony, I know what you're thinking."

"What am I thinking?"

"You want to go into town and check things out."

He shook his head. "They have electricity. I won't lie. I'm intrigued."

"We do fine without it."

"You're not going down there alone. If you want to scout things out, take Sam with you," he said.

Sam held both hands and shook his head. "I didn't say *I* wanted a closer look."

The sun had set fast. It was autumn. Dusk came earlier and earlier each day. Walking through the dense forest at night would be dangerous, whether they'd seen a lot of infected recently or not. "Sam, follow me," she said, and then pointed at Tony. "You and Grace stay hidden. Don't wander far. I don't want to have to come looking for you guys when we get back."

"Don't be gone long, okay?" Tony said. "Take a look around, get a feel for the place and report back."

He worried about her. She knew that. "We'll be careful. But I'm not going to return until we have something worthwhile to report."

"I still don't have a weapon." Sam looked left and right, like something lethal would magically appear for him to use.

"Take one of the assault rifles," Tony said, referring to the rifles they'd taken off Broadhurst's men.

"Do we want something that loud?" Char said. She handed over the machete. "Here, use this."

# # #

They were already on more of a hiking trail than a road. It snaked down through the forest toward the town. It would be the most direct approach if they just stayed on it and the most obvious if there were posted guards or lookouts. They'd be spotted for sure. For the moment, Char decided to follow the trail until she felt it was no longer safe.

"What? You don't like the idea of finding a town? They have lights, Char. Lights," Sam said. They walked side by side. He kept bumping his shoulder into hers. It didn't seem like it was on purpose. He just appeared preoccupied with straining to see everything around him, and it, for some reason, affected his balance.

"No," she said, "I don't."

"And is there a reason?" Sam said.

"There's always a reason." Char and her family had fled Rochester, New York when the apocalypse started. There had been a military rescue. The Coast Guard boated a group of survivors across Lake Ontario up to the mouth of the St. Lawrence. There was an internment camp being utilized like a FEMA and medical research facility. When they docked, they quickly learned the camp had been overrun with infected. It was also where Cash was shot. Brothers with a cabin in the woods helped them, but turned out to be freaks. Things got crazy. She remembered the fire. She'd never forget the flames.

"And the reason?"

"Stop talking," she said. His chatter started the moment they left Tony and Grace. He did not stop talking. If he wasn't telling a story, he was asking question. She wasn't in the mood for answering. The sound of his voice distracted her. The key was to stay focused, alert.

"Think what you want. I don't see how finding a town could be a bad thing. Wouldn't it be nice to get back to normal?"

"Normal is over, Sam. The past is gone. If things ever change for the best, it's decades away. It's not going to be because we found some small town with power in the Blue Ridge Mountains."

"See, that's where you're wrong. It has to start somewhere, with a town someplace. Why can't it be a town here, like the one down there?"

Char didn't have an answer, and hated that Sam's argument actually made sense. "Can you, please, do me a favor and give it a rest? It's not asking—"

A tree branch snapped to the right.

Char stopped walking, and threw an arm in front of Sam to hold him still. It was a move not unlike what her father used to do when driving and had to stop the car fast. He'd throw an arm across her when she was in the passenger seat. She'd have a seat belt on, and his arm would not prevent a single injury, but he did it every time.

Sam bent a little lower, arms out in front of him, head swiveling slowly to the left, and around to the right. He looked ridiculous. If the situation weren't so dangerous, she might have laughed at him.

As quietly as possible, she removed her sword from the scabbard. She held it in both hands, a white-knuckle grip. She stepped off the trail into the trees on the left, and Sam followed. They wove their way deeper into the thicket, stepping carefully.

It was dark under the canopy of trees.

Blackness surrounded them. It would take a few minutes for their eyes to adjust. Char just hoped they had minutes.

They could not see the town lights, nor the moon or stars in the sky. They stood still, listening for movement.

It could be anything. It didn't have to be infected. It could turn out to be worse, a bear, or mountain lion. Either way, Char now felt as if they were being hunted. A point was coming when staying still would not cut it, would no longer be the safest thing to do. They would have to decide whether to stand their ground and fight the unknown enemy, or just risk it and run.

"I don't hear anything," Sam said.

"Shhh!" Char held a finger up to her lips. She rolled her eyes. Was he kidding?

Slowly, the darkness ebbed away. She could make out shapes and shadows. It was little more than trees that took form. Detecting movement seemed an impossible task. What worked to her advantage was the wind.

"Infected," she said. She repositioned her grip on the sword. She whispered, "Stay still. Stay quiet. Stand back to back."

Char could see between the trees, and the main trail. She was thankful her eyes kept adapting better and better to the night, and that the adjustment hasn't stopped. "How are your eyes doing?"

"I wish I ate more carrots as a kid," he said.

"Can you see?"

"I can see. I can see the trail."

"Me, too," she said, "let's keep moving."

Another branch snapped. Then another. Leaves rustled. The infected was not trying to mask its presence.

"I can't tell where it's coming from," Sam said. "The sound is bouncing. It's impossible to narrow down where it is."

Char shook her head. It wasn't impossible to narrow anything down. The sound wasn't bouncing. The sound was coming from more than one location. "We're surrounded, Sam. I think they're coming at us from every direction."

Chapter 9

"It's the lights," Sam said.

"What?"

"The town. Their lights. It's got to be attracting them like moths. What do we do?"

It was a good question. Char looked around. She still could not see a single infected. It was more than one. They were getting closer. The stench of rot was pungent and overbearing. "I don't want to run blind. We could wind up dead center and trapped."

"Just stand here?"

"I don't want to do that, either. I'm thinking we climb a tree. Get up high. The damn things won't look up if they can't smell us."

"But then we are trapped," Sam said.

"Not if you're right, if it is the light they're after. I say climb." Char replaced her sword into the scabbard. "Give me the machete."

Once the weapons were away they each selected a tree. Char grabbed onto a branch and pulled herself up. The limb was thick. She stood on it, staying close to the trunk, and maneuvered up another few feet. She twisted around, and set a foot onto the next branch, while reaching up for others. She heard Sam. He needed to quit the grunting, otherwise their plan to hide was for nothing.

Once she was twenty feet or so up, Char stopped. She knew she was high enough to be out of reach, and had a good enough head start that if any of the infected evolved enough to climb a tree, she'd still be alright. She stared down at the ground.

She heard Sam. He was a tree over. Not more than fifteen feet away. She couldn't hear what he said, but knew he was talking to her in a loud whisper.

Forced to reply, she said, "What?"

"I cut myself. Scraped my wrist on fucking bark."

Char closed her eyes. The infected reminded her of sharks, or vampires when it came to blood. They seemed drawn to the scent much in the same the way a normal person could smell a hot apple pie pulled from an oven a mile away.

Branches still snapped underfoot, but pinpointing where the sound came from was still impossible. The only thing that was obvious was that the noise was louder, and the sounded like it was much closer.

She wanted to know how bad he was bleeding. It didn't matter. An answer would not change a thing. If he was bleeding a lot, they'd be found for sure. If it was a little they might be able to keep hidden until the horde passed by them. It came down to time. It would tell.

"I don't know if I'm high enough," she heard him say. The tremor in his tone of voice was annoying.

Then climb higher. "Will you shut up?" She almost yelled. She almost screamed. She kept her calm. She kept her cool.

Sam would have been dead in hours if he'd spent any time in Mexico.

# # #

2 ½ Years Ago
Reynosa, Tamaulipas, Mexico

Char had not been a prisoner, but neither was she free to come and go as she pleased.

Antonio Velasquez occupied a piece of property down a dirt road off the Reynosa-Monterrey highway. It was the only parcel of land with green grass. The other homes along the street were built on rectangular plots of sun-cracked dirt. Halfway up the paved and winding driveway was a swimming pool. It wasn't kidney shaped but more oblong and resembled a huge pond. Erected in the center was a small concrete island complete with a hammock strung between a pair of palm trees. No one added chemicals or vacuumed the water, so it actually did look and smell exactly like a stagnant pond. Velasquez always said he'd like to sit in a kayak with a bottle of tequila and talk about grand plans of commandeering all of Mexico and making it his country, but there were far too many mosquitos, and he never trusted mosquitos not when it came to possible ways the zombie virus could be transferred.

Too many times Char had been tempted to remind Velasquez that zombies ruined any real planning, and that Mexico was too dry and hot to bother fighting over. She never did. She was well aware of the pride he felt for his country, regardless of when he once told her he made a steady bundle smuggling Mexicans into America. Then there was his temper that prevented her from saying much of anything, ever. She'd witnessed too many of his own people wind up flat on their backs when on the receiving end of a flare-up. Velasquez suffered from —undiagnosed— bipolar tendencies.

The main house was shy a bathroom or two of being called a castle. The three-tier structure contained fourteen bedrooms, two kitchens, a game room with four billiard tables, three stocked wet bars, and a spa complete with a sauna and hot tub. The full basement resembled a liquor store. There was an all mahogany, temperature and climate controlled wine cellar, too. When the electricity was up and running, the place had to have resembled a mini version of Heaven. The owners must have thrown wild, talked-about parties. In the backyard, once off the sprawling marble block patio and well past the double row of ten-foot high shrubs were two in-law homes set on the property corners. Each house was at least 3.000 square feet, dwarfed when compared to the main residence, but not small either, and each house also had a good sized in-ground pool of their own.

Velasquez might not have worked to earn a place like this, and might have only killed residential zombies to get where he has gotten, but the guns and ammunition were all his. His band of followers feared and then respected him. He was a leader. Char knew that much. She wasn't sure she had respect for the guy, but there was enough fear for her to feign respect.

It was while stumbling midday along the highway when he first found her. Dehydrated, sunbaked and weak from lack of nutrition, Char knew she could not survive. She'd been in Mexico less than a year, and stayed mainly because it was where her father thought she'd be safest. What she really wanted was to go home, back to New York. It didn't matter if she holed up in her father's old apartment with the door and windows boarded up, and had to fight zombies day in and day out. She'd be home, somewhere familiar. She'd die home, somewhere full of memories.

Mexico held nothing for her. She didn't want to die out here, alone and lost in an expanse of aluminum homemade huts and dust-covered everything.

She might have fainted, or was just delirious enough to want to lic down on the road. She was staring blankly up at the perpetually blue and cloudless sky when she heard revving engines approach. Every instinct inside her body sad to get up and run. Every muscle wanted to respond accordingly. Unfortunately, Char lacked the strength and ability even to roll on her side to see what was coming at her.

The man that stood over her was Antonio Velasquez. He was dressed in well-worn cowboy boots and blue jeans; the red and white checkered button-down shirt was unbuttoned and flapped in the slight breeze revealing a once white undershirt. The blue bandana wrapped over his head must have been used to sop up sweat, while the yellowed cowboy hat in his hands did its best to keep the heat from the sun at bay.

He introduced himself and stared with dark, dull eyes. The flat nose between pockmarked cheeks didn't help his appearance. Char tried shielding her eyes from the sun with a forearm across her forehead. Velasquez stepped to the side. His back blocked the sun, his body a black silhouetted form above her. "Can you stand?"

It was an immediate plus that he spoke English.

She hadn't realized just how dry her throat was until she tried to talk. "I'm not sure."

She also realized it may have been days since she talked last.

Velasquez held out a hand. She reached for it, and he pulled her up onto her feet.

After nearly a year of living in what she considered a commune—someone living in every available room, taking up every square foot of space among the three locations on the 3 acres of land—Char had had enough, but it came down to more than packed-in discomfort.

Although the band of Mexicans protected the property armed with assault rifles and handguns along the fenced perimeter day and night. Safety from zombies was not the issue.

The need to flee was essential to her survival.

Velasquez was a violent man, especially when drinking and he drank often. The way he treated her the last few weeks prior to deciding it was time to leave had changed, drastically. She noticed it first in the way he looked at her. He looked hungry. It was the only way she could describe it. At night, he visited her room when she was asleep, or when he thought she was asleep. He'd stand by the window, lean against the wall and finish off a bottle of tequila in silence. She knew better than to open her eyes. She heard his heavy breathing and could only assume how many more nights he'd allow her sleep to go uninterrupted before deciding to climb in next to her.

Getting away would not be easy. If anyone else at the commune fled, she did not think Velasquez would care. She had a feeling if she attempted to run he'd come after her. The best way to run would be not to leave the house.

In order for this to work Char knew she would have to hide somewhere and not make a sound. It might be a day or two before she thought it would be safe to move. She figured initially Velasquez would go looking for her, maybe bring a guy or two along and that they'd drive up and down the streets searching. When he couldn't find her, she hoped he'd round up more men and go back out expanding the scope of the canvas. At that point, when most of the commune was left unguarded, she would have the best chance to slip away undetected.

That was the plan, anyway, and it worked. However, it was nearly three days before a chance to run presented itself. She chose to hide in the attic. It felt like living in the belly of a furnace. She'd stored water and her weapons up in the attic ahead of time. On the day she "disappeared" she brought up food, too. She ate and drank sparingly. She held in urine, and refused to move her bowels until she was free on the outside. She spent hour after hour silent, and still. She worried about a floorboard creaking under shifted weight, and that sound alone would be enough to give up her location.

When the house was silent, she snuck down the stairs to the first floor. She opened windows and doors in the giant house, hoping zombies would filter in before leaving. She took the doors to the back patio and walked across the yard. It was flat land. There were no trees or structures to hide behind for miles in any direction. The best bet was to walk and just keep walking until she was no longer visible even if someone like Velasquez used binoculars. She stayed away from roads, cut through yards and hoped she'd make her way back to the border.

She just wanted to go home, back to America. It might be crawling with zombies, but facing the walking dead seemed like the lesser of two evils.

The entire time she walked she felt like Velasquez and his men were closing in on her. Many times she wanted to run. Running caused two problems, it used up her energy, and it looked suspicious. Conserving strength was important, that went without saying. She only had limited supplies left, and rationing them was going to be essential to her survival. Although a woman walking in what appeared like nothing more than the middle of nowhere was already suspicious. Running without being chased would raise a flag to anyone who noticed.

Chapter 10

"They're coming this way, Char," Sam said. He hadn't climbed any higher in the tree, and was still talking. The quiver was apparent in his voice, the tone an octave or two higher than normal. Char was almost certain she could hear him sweating.

She did not answer him. Eventually, he would have to catch on and realize just how golden silence truly was. She tried listening to the night. Sam *might* be right, the infected seemed to be headed toward them. It could be the scent of fresh blood that Sam dripped onto the tree trunk that aroused their senses.

This gave her second thoughts about climbing into the trees now. A pack of infected would just stay at the base of the trees and moan. She couldn't imagine being stuck in a tree with the tree surrounded by infected. The more noise they made, the more moaning they did, the more infected would show. They often reminded her of seagulls. When her dad, Cash, and her went to McDonalds, they oftentimes ate in the car in the parking lot. The seagulls knew the cars in the area were filled with people eating food. One seagull always approached. He'd caw, squawk and slowly make its way closer and closer. Cash was notorious for throwing at least one French fry out the window. Dad would yell, but not as if he was seriously upset. Just before that seagull snatched the fry up off the asphalt, it would give out one last high-pitched squawk. That was the tone, the alarm the other seagulls waited for. Once it sounded, they all came. It was almost as if Char could understand Seagull. If translated, the seagull would have said something along the lines of: "They're giving away foooooooood!"

They were in trouble. "We should get down. Now. Make a run for it," she said.

"Climb down?"

"Before they get here."

"They sound close, Char. Real close," he said.

Their conversation wasn't helping the situation. It wasn't like he had very far to climb down, either. Wasting time debating didn't help any. Char started down the tree. She took each step carefully, one branch step at a time.

"And then what? What are we going to do?"

"Get down from the fucking tree now, Samuel!" She jumped the last five feet and bent her knees to absorb the impact. It was distant, but distinct. The moaning was awful, a steady groan that was both guttural and phlegmy. Char wanted to plug her ears and block out the sound. There wasn't much point, though, once it was heard it could never be unheard. It was one of the only sounds she vividly recalled from nightmares that plagued her sleep when she actually did sleep.

Sam landed on his feet.

"Back to the trail. We're making a break for the town." Running along the road would be easiest. There would be less obstacles, no fallen branches, or wild weeds to trip them up. Char always hated movies when someone, usually a female character, tripped and injured an ankle. Half the time directors didn't even have the actor trip over anything. They just tripped. They'd sit up and coddle and ankle, without even having put any weight on it first. It was part of what made cheesy movies classics.

"Why not back to Tony and Grace?"

Char ran past Sam. If he was more interested in asking questions, then he could. She just wasn't planning to hang around an answer them.

"We might be running straight into them!"

Char heard heavy footfalls, and heavier breathing behind her. At least he was running, following her lead. If she could only get him to shut up she would be as close to happy as she could be in a situation as dire and dangerous as this. As she ducked under branches, and jumped over stumps, she almost smiled. More and more she was looking forward to thoroughly kicking his ass.

For all the moaning and all the groaning, Char was surprised they had not yet seen one infected. They had to be close. It had sounded as if they were closing in on them at one point. So where were they? Where were all the infected?

Char saw the trail. They had not been that far away from it in the first place. She slowed, and then stopped by the last row of trees. Sam came up behind her and wheezed.

She cringed waiting for him to talk. Just to be safe, she pressed a finger to her lips and he nodded, a hopeful indication that he might finally get it.

They stood still.

The woods had fallen silent.

She walked out from between trees and stood on the trail. She did a three-sixty searching for signs of anything in the brush around them. There was nothing. Not a single infected. She motioned for Sam to join her.

"This doesn't make much sense. I don't like it here. I have a bad feeling about this, that town, all of it. I think we should go tell Tony and just keep going south, or west, or wherever. Anywhere but staying here," she said. She knew that cheesy horror movies had the chicks with sprained ankles, and she realized, they also had the pessimist who was also given lines that foreshadowed upcoming events, and almost laughed. She couldn't help it. It was how she felt.

"You wanna go and tell Tony, what? That we thought we heard a bunch of infected, we ran and climbed trees to hide? Are you gonna tell him that nothing ever showed up, we got down, and whaddya know, everything is okay?"

Char sucked her lower lip into her mouth and bit down on it, just hard enough not to draw blood. Sam was right, and that was what pissed her off. "Keep your eyes open," she said.

Sam raised an eyebrow, a silent way of saying, *Duh*, without saying it.

The steel sword felt like it weighed close to a hundred pounds. It didn't, but perception ruled. She laid the blade over her shoulder like a ball player waiting for a turn at bat. The lights from the town below did look warm, and welcoming. They were like nothing she had seen in a long while. There was an overall Hansel and Gretel feel to the situation only it was the draw of lights instead of a gingerbread house decked out in candy. The power of a lure to poison was always dependent on the cravings.

Char stopped when she saw a sign posted on the side of the trail. They were less than a few hundred yards from where spotlights sat perched aiming toward the forest. She read it to herself, and then out loud, "Welcome to Arcadia. No Stealing. No Fighting. No Murder."

"Remember that bad feeling you had, about this being a bad idea and everything?" Sam said. "I don't know if I have a bad feeling, or if I find this sign the exact opposite of welcoming and more —I don't know— just creepy as shit."

"We are going to need the both of you to lower your weapons and then lace your fingers together behind your head." There was a distinct pump-action sound. First it came from the left, then the right, and then from directly behind them. "You heard me. Weapons down."

Char lifted the sword off her shoulder. She squatted as she set her sword onto dirt and loose gravel.

"Sir, your machete."

Sam looked at Char. She made a face at him. Did he not just see her set down the sword?

"Sir, I will ask one more time politely."

"Sam, put the fucking machete down," Char said. Damn him for looking so stupid, it made her look stupid too. How could they ever give off an impression of confidence with stupidity in such abundance inside Sam?

"And your knives, ma'am. All of 'em."

She thought they might have missed those. Perhaps it wasn't as dark out as she thought.

"We don't want any trouble. We saw those lights over there, and wanted to take a closer look," she said.

"Which is fine. I have no problem with that. Before I can bring you into town, we just have to make sure that there are no surprises. You and your boyfriend going in with weapons leaves the town open to surprises. See what I'm saying?"

"We're not a couple," Sam said.

Char winced, as if a razor had just sliced skin on her back. She removed her knives and set them alongside the sword. "But we'll get them back?"

"Eventually."

"These were from my father," she said. It was partially true. Together they ransacked a cabin's arsenal grabbing up as many weapons as they could carry. "They hold sentimental value."

"You're not going to need weapons on the other side of that wall."

"Wall?"

"We can talk about Arcadia here, or we can go to Arcadia and talk about the town over a cheeseburger and Coke. Your call."

Cheeseburger and Coke? Char's mouth watered. It was a ploy. The guy holding a gun to the back of their heads was teasing them. It would be no different from offering a bottle of Voss to a dehydrated man in the middle of a desert. "How about we pick up our weapons and just go back the way we came."

"Is that what you want to do?"

"Yes. It is."

"Then do it. We'll watch you go. Just understand, if you come back the same thing will be expected. Turn your weapons in at the door. It's not unfair or unreasonable, if you think about it. And if harming you was our purpose, then wouldn't we have already?"

Char could think of many reasons why guys like him might keep girls like her alive. "Just because you didn't shoot us on site, doesn't mean you don't mean us harm."

"Good point. It's your call. What do you want to do?"

Char knelt down. She picked up her knives. She strapped one in place on her thigh, the other on her belt. She lifted her sword. "Sam, pick up the machete."

"Nice and slow, you two. Nice, and slow."

The man speaking did not sound apprehensive at all. He sound calm and in control. Still, Sam moved at a snail's pace. She wanted to bend over, grab the machete, and kick him in the ass. "We're going to leave," she said.

"I figured that out when you picked up your stuff. Be safe out there."

She hated when someone was condescending. She slid the sword into the scabbard. She didn't want to give the men with rifles any reason to shoot. Turning around, she was surprised to see a boy about her age standing behind her. He held what looked to be a twelve gauge shotgun. The barrel was not pointed at her, but instead lay cradled over the crook of his arm. His jaw was accented by a dark haired goatee and the rest of his face by a bit more than a five o'clock shadow. She hadn't expected. . .him. "There were a lot of infected in the woods not long ago. And then. . . nothing."

"Infected?" he said.

"Zombies," Char said. "We could smell them. We heard them."

"Did you? You have a lot of questions. Maybe coming in to town and talking with us would be best?" he said. "I'm Benjamin. Ben."

Had he held out a hand, she might have shaken it. He didn't so she walked past him instead, and only hoped Sam was behind her. She didn't want to have to look back and see. Regardless, she kept walking up the trail.

She thought she heard someone say, mockingly, "I'm Benjamin, but you can call me Ben."

This made her smile.

"What do you think?" Sam said, walking beside her. "We were right, huh? The place is crazy. We go tell Tony and we hightail it as far away from this place as possible. Don't you agree?"

"Yes. No. I'm not sure."

"You're not sure about what? Giving them our guns, what supplies we have —because you know they're going to want that stuff too, all of it. You're not sure about just turning everything over because one stranger, oh, excuse me, one cute stranger demanded that we have to do so before being allowed entry into their precious Atlanta?"

"Arcadia."

Sam said, "Atlanta, Arcadia, what difference does it make?"

"For one, Arcadia stands for. . .*Utopia*."

Chapter 11

"We didn't get that close," Char said, addressing Tony and Grace. Sam couldn't be more wrong about everything. The idea of turning over their weapons and supplies just to enter a town was ludicrous, regardless of what Ben looked like.

"We did, however, meet some of the locals. At gunpoint," Sam said, adding his narrative to the rendition.

There was a bite in the air. Tony refused to start a fire. He didn't want to tip anyone off to their location at this point. Instead, they sat huddled together in a circle wrapped in their sleeping bags.

Grace used a camping spork to eat fruit cocktail from the can. "So they want our guns?"

"If we want to enter, yes," Char said. She wished she'd been able to gather more information, get a closer look. Ben made it sound like the town was fortified with walls. At least that was how she interpreted what he'd said. She hadn't seen a wall, though. Just the Arcadia sign.

Tony pulled his sleeping bag tight around his shoulders and rocked forward. "I say we walk."

"I second that," Sam said immediately after Tony spoke.

"Grace?" Tony said. "What do you think?"

She held the spork in one hand while tipping the can to her lips and drinking the syrup. She smacked her lips then drew a sleeved forearm across them. "I don't know. Part of me thinks it's worth checking out, still. We don't know enough about the place. I'm not comfortable with turning over our weapons though."

"No one is getting my bow." Tony cocked his head to the side. "They'd have to kill me to get it out of my hands."

"I feel the same way," Sam said.

"You don't even have your own weapon," Char said.

"You know what I mean. I had one. Before," he said. "I'm going to need a new weapon, Tony. We've got to find me something. I can't keep borrowing Char's machete. Unless you just want to give me that to keep, Char?"

"Ah, I don't think so," she said, almost snickering. "We'll find you something. Somewhere."

"Then it's settled?" Tony said.

Grace held up a hand. "I haven't said one way or the other, yet."

"Neither have I," Char said.

"Well?" Tony shrugged. "What are you thinking?"

Char sucked in a deep breath and slowly exhaled. "I really don't know. I have trust issues. The idea of turning over our weapons doesn't sit well with me. Not at all. I hate lending my machete to Sam. I keep waiting for him to lose it so I can kick his butt."

Sam said, "I really don't think—"

Char held up a hand. "The guy we talked to made it sound like there is a wall around the town. They have lights, which means they've somehow figured out how to run electricity. They were protecting their borders. It would have been easy for them to kill us and take our weapons if that was what they were after. Once it was clear that Sam and I meant no harm, they relaxed. We were allowed to leave with our weapons. Entering the town seems voluntary. I don't think in and of itself that's a bad thing. The Welcome sign said no stealing, no fighting, no murder."

"Not exactly the Ten Commandments," Sam said.

"But it kinda is," Char said. "It covers the general bases."

"General bases?" Sam said.

"Do you know the commandments, Sam? Can you recite them for us?"

Sam lowered his head.

"I think we shouldn't just walk away. Not without knowing. When daylight comes, I think we should go back. All of us."

"And give them our stuff?"

"And bury our stuff."

Tony pursed his lips. He shook his head slowly from side to side. "Bury our stuff?"

"We go in. We don't give them anything. We spend the day checking it out. Then we leave. Unless we love the place, unanimously love the place. This is my family. You guys. Even Sam."

"Gee, thanks."

"You're welcome," Char said.

"What if they don't let us just leave?"

"They going to lock us up in a prison?" Char said. "I don't think so. We can get out. If we decide to leave, we'll get out."

Grace just stared at Char. "I don't know if I like that plan or not."

Tony said, "Sam?"

"I don't know. I thought I did, but I'm just not sure."

They decided to sleep on it. In the morning, they'd revisit the proposals.

Char volunteered to take first watch.

# # #

Char sat with her back to a tree, shivering. The sleeping bag provided little protection against the cold. It was only going to get worse. They needed someplace real to stay. She didn't want to leave the mountains. It was beautiful and calming, if not inspirational. There were cabins and houses everywhere. The problem was finding the right one. The four of them were used to moving around since the whole thing started. Was it the idea that stopping just didn't seem plausible because they didn't know how to stop moving around?

That was possible.

Eventually, they would have to stop. Rebuild. Start over.

Eventually, but when?

Tony stirred around inside his sleeping bag, and sat up. She watched him rub his eyes and pass a hand through his hair. It was getting long. Soon he'd ask her to cut it for him, again. He crawled out of his bag, picked it up and sat down next to her.

"Mind if I join you?"

"It's not your watch yet," Char said. She had no way of knowing how long she'd been guarding them. Usually when she started to get tired and felt like she could no longer keep her eyes open it was the next guy's turn.

Tony leaned his head back against the tree bark. "Not very comfy."

"Could use your bag as a pillow."

He draped it over him. "Need it as a blanket, though. Brrrr. Maybe we should have started a small fire?"

"You think?"

The silence that followed was not awkward. Neither felt like they had to talk to fill the space between words. The night stretched on for several minutes until Tony cleared his throat.

"I, uh, before all of this, I was an attorney," he said.

Char was thankful for the darkness. She knew her jaw had dropped. Tony was violating his own rule. She did not stop him, but wanted him to talk.

"Corporate law. I handled employee issues."

"Like firing people?"

He shrugged. "Before a manager fired anyone in their department, I'd make sure all the T's were crossed and I's dotted. You know, I'd ensure that there was documentation filed, and actual written policies broken. Nine times out of ten that was good enough. Bob's been an hour late to work once a week for the last five weeks. First time he received a warning, then some documentation, a final warning, and then termination. That tenth time, the former employee would sue, file a complaint with the EEOC, and claim one of their rights was violated. We terminated them because they were black, or pregnant, or a transvestite, or in the military, because they worshiped Allah instead of God. You know what I mean?"

Char nodded.

"It was a good job. I enjoyed the work. Before everything happened we had this case. A group of former employees filed a class action suit. It's where they all alleged the same discrimination, had one lawyer representing them. It had been going on for years, but we were finally getting close to a trial. Discovery was a nightmare. We had to turn over a room full of documents. All those papers had to be scanned, and identified numerically. There was a room we turned into what we called a War Room. It had phone lines and fax machines, copiers, and filing cabinets. Staff worked in there from sunrise to well past sunset. Judge was giving us two weeks on the docket. There were a ton of witnesses and expert witness to meet with. I mean, depositions were completed long before, but just to touch base before they took an oath on the stand wouldn't hurt."

When he fell silent, Char waited. If Tony was opening up, she didn't want to rush him. Maybe that was all he wanted to say. If there was more, she'd wait.

"Nina. She was just eleven years old then, but my wife and I, we knew something was, I don't know, different by the time she learned to walk. She liked to push a toy vacuum. All kids kind of like to do that. Her room, spotless. Socks rolled. Everything on a hanger, hung in a particular way in the closet. She would cry if the end tables in the family room were dusty. Cry. A guy on TV threw a toothpick into the street, she got off the recliner to pick it up. It was on TV. There was no toothpick to pick up. By the time she was, I don't know, around seven, we told the pediatrician what was going on. She was diagnosed with Obsessive Compulsive Disorder. They put her on a prescription. After a while it worked. She still cleaned, but it wasn't as necessary, if that makes sense. The side effects, though, had her putting on weight. My wife and I, we didn't really notice it. It upset Nina, though, and she kept it to herself.

"She started wearing hats. Every time we went to the mall she'd buy a new hat. She had fedoras and those cabby hats, baseball caps," he said, and touched the brim of his cap. "This was hers. One of her favorites for some reason. I'd bought it for her at a game.

"It was after her eleventh birthday, October fifteenth, when I saw her in the bathroom. The door was opened just a crack. I wasn't spying on her. I was planning to use the bathroom, had almost walked right in. For whatever reason, I stopped, you know. Through the crack I could see her staring at her reflection in the mirror. I could honestly say it was the first time I'd seen her without one of her hats on. And I just stood there, and I just stared. I might have been crying. I don't know.

"She was missing clumps of hair. It looked like she'd pulled out almost all of her hair. If I didn't know she wasn't sick, I'd have sworn she'd been getting radiation treatment. Right when I was about to turn around and find her mother, she pulled open the door. The hat —she'd put it back on. She stopped when she saw me standing there. I know I tried to smile. It had to look so stupid, me standing there grinning. She knew. She could tell by the look on my face. She started crying. Her shoulders shook. And I said, 'Honey,' and I went to reach for her. It was the only thing I wanted to do. I just wanted to hold her, to hug her. She looked ashamed. Her cheeks got all red, but she pulled away, went back into the bathroom and slammed the door closed."

Char thought Tony might be crying. She didn't know how to handle it. She was not used to seeing him like this. There was no way to know how he'd react to a hand on his shoulder. She knew it scared her, all of it, him talking, the crying, and her not knowing how to respond.

"Doctors said she had something called *trichotillomania*. It's an actual condition where people pull out their hair. It was going to take a little more than a prescription to fix this. Someone even told me the pills she was taking could have triggered the hair pulling behavior. So we checked out a hospital in Arkansas, a children's hospital. They agreed to take her as an in-patient. There was no start-finish date. It was kind of a program and when she was ready to switch to out-patient, she could come home.

"My wife went with her. I couldn't leave work. We had so much going on with that class action suit, but I wanted to go. I wanted to be there.

"A few nights later, after they'd arrived, I was talking to Nina on the phone. Sirens started going off in the hospital. I could hear them. I told Nina to let me talk with her mother. Neither of them knew what was going on, and that they'd call back. So I figured a fire drill or something, right? It wasn't. My wife called back and was screaming that one of the doctors had just bitten Nina and that she was bleeding badly.

"While I was still on the line, I heard what sounded like a football team crash into their room. My wife was screaming, my daughter was. . .she was calling out for me, for her Dad, and then the line went dead.

"I kept calling and calling her number, and the hospital, and their nine-one-one center. I felt so helpless. I wanted to be there. I knew I needed to be there, but I didn't want to do anything until I knew what was going on."

The silence lasted several minutes this time. Char figured it was the end of what he'd want to tell her. "Did you ever find them?"

"I made it to Arkansas, to the hospital. It took me a while, nearly a week. By then, I knew what was what. I knew that if my Nina had been bitten then she was gone. It didn't stop me though. I kept on track and I made it to Ohio. It was a mess there. The city was the worst I'd seen. The halls of the hospital were either deserted or littered with infected who weren't coming back. I couldn't find my wife or Nina. I'm no fool. I don't hold onto optimistic bullshit. I accepted it, and then I started walking. Just, walking."

"Tony, why are you telling me this?" Char said. "I'm glad you did. I just, I'm confused about why."

He leaned closer to her. "Did you ever just feel like everything is about to go to shit?"

"You mean like Arcadia?"

He shook his head. "I mean beyond Arcadia. All of this. Everything."

"Why are you saying that? We're doing good, Tony. We're surviving."

"But we're not living, Char. This is no life for you."

"For me?"

"I say we go into town tomorrow. We bury the guns, the supplies, like you suggested, but we go in and we see what it's about."

"You're scaring me. You know that, don't you?"

"Don't be scared, honey. Just keep your eyes open. Be ready."

"Be ready for what?"

"For anything."

# # #

They stood side-by-side on the trail after burying their weapons and supplies in a small clearing by where they'd camped for the night. They placed a pile of fallen leaves and twigs over the freshly dug earth so it appeared less conspicuous. They each kept a knife as a meager means of protection for the walk from the burial plot to the town. Just because they were checking out a town didn't mean the infected weren't still sniffing around.

Thick morning fog rolled over the ground like clouds passing across in the sky on a windy day. Somewhere a fire burned. It might be coming from Arcadia. It smelled wonderful, the way a hearth fire in the middle of winter did. Char assumed it might even be coming from a fireplace, a controlled burn. It had been a while since fires raged out of control. That happened all of the time years ago, not so much anymore.

"I feel naked," Tony said. "I don't like not having my bow."

Char knew what he meant. She felt awkward without the weight of the sword on her hip. It had been strapped around her waist for years. It was the first thing she touched when she woke up from any kind of sleep.

She held onto Dispatch's reins. They'd talked about freeing the horses. Tony let his go. Char couldn't.

"It isn't right to bring him in. We have no idea what we're walking into. I'm not going to tell you what you should do."

"Can I take a minute with him?"

"Of course you can," he said.

Char walked her horse along the trail, away from Arcadia. She stayed close to his head to pet his nose. "You go and find Tony's horse. You two stay together."

She knew she shouldn't be crying. She wiped tears away with the back of her sleeve.

"We'll meet up again, I promise. This isn't goodbye."

She kissed the side of the horse's face, and it neighed as if it understood what was happening. She stepped toward the back of the horse and slapped its hindquarters. "Go on! Git!"

Dispatch sprinted away.

She stood silent, watching until he was no longer visible before joining the others.

Ahead, they saw the posted Welcome sign.

"Think they're watching us?" Char said. The joy she felt brushing her teeth after breakfast was short lived. Her conversation with Tony prior to dawn continued to replay inside her head. She didn't like knowing he was afraid or that he was losing hope. Her courage and confidence fed off his. She felt rocked now, off kilter, and she didn't like it. When on her own, she was strong and took care of herself. It just made things easier when the energy was shared between two or more people.

"You can bet on it," Tony said. "Wouldn't surprise me if they followed you last night, and watched us bury everything."

"You really think so?" Sam said.

"It's why I said it," Tony said.

"Then let's not keep them waiting." Char started walking and did not stop when they reached the Arcadia sign. She glanced at it out of the corner of her eye, but kept pushing forward.

"I just want it noted, for the record, I'm still not comfortable with this," Sam said. He shook his head.

"I don't think any of us are," Grace said. "Winter's coming. We haven't really found a safe place to settle down, to grow some moss. It could start snowing any day now. Winter in the mountains is a harsh thing. I had family in Colorado. They'd get drifts against the house that kept them from even getting outside to clear a path."

"They get a lot of snow up here?" Sam said.

"Perfect ski conditions," Tony said. "Yeah. It snows."

Char thought about the Mexican heat. She'd hated it, sweating all the time and thirsty. Winter wasn't much better. They were the extremes, she supposed. Spring and Autumn were her favorite times of year, even before the apocalypse. "We're going to have to learn how to skin animals and make coats and boots and stuff," she said. "You know how to do that, Tony?"

"I do not." He laughed.

Ahead of them was a ten-foot high wall that appeared to be made of cinder block.

"Will you take a look at that," Tony said.

They stopped.

Char looked right and left. "It just goes on forever."

"The place is fortified," Grace said. "I see it, but I don't believe it. Did you know something like this was here?"

"No," Tony said. "It sits down in the valley kind of hidden from everything. Makes me wonder if they built it recently, or if it's always been here?"

"It's got a Lord of the Rings feel to it. You don't think there are Orcs in there, do you?" Sam said.

"Nerd," Char said. She spun around. "Mountains are all around us. I mean, we are deep down in a valley. I can't help but feel a little claustrophobic about it. It's like they are closing in on us. Does anyone else feel that way?" Char remembered taking a ride with her father and brother to New York City. The Holland Tunnel went under the ocean and brought them out on the other side, where it looked like they'd landed on another world. Giant buildings and flashing lights. She would never forget how difficult it was to breath under the tunnel. Her dad teased her at first. When she started to cry, worried the walls might cave in and they would drown, he stopped, realizing perhaps that she was truly suffering from a panic attack. It wasn't as significant right now, but she felt it in her chest, a slight tightening as her breathing became a little more rapid.

"It's beautiful," Grace said.

It was beautiful. The blue sky and fluffy white clouds moved slowly over red, orange, yellow and green leaves. Add to that the aroma of several fireplaces burning wood, and it was nothing shy of picturesque, if not confining and overbearing. Char shook her head as if that might clear the steadily mounting fear that grew inside her mind.

"Anyone see a doorbell, or do we knock?" Tony said.

As if voice activated, they heard a latch release. The large double doors swung open.

"I do the talking," Tony said.

No one argued.

Char's breath caught in her lungs for just a moment. In that moment a wave passed over her. It was a sudden sense of dread and hopelessness. It was complete and enveloped all of her. She had never felt such a powerful push of emotion before. As quickly as it came, it passed. It left an empty and hollow sensation in her heart. "Is it too late to go back?"

Three men with assault rifles greeted them.

Tony reached for her hand. He squeezed it. "We've got this."

PART II
Arcadia

Chapter 12

Arcadia, North Carolina

Vincent Forti sat behind a large desk. A small stack of papers set in the In Box required his attention. The work days were long. The things that needed doing increased day by day. The people of Arcadia had elected him to the position of mayor nearly two years ago. It was an election year. Although no one was running against him, he still wanted to run a strong campaign to reassure the community that their choice in a leader was not a mistake.

The barter system worked well enough for now, but Vincent wanted to reinstitute money. Getting such a program off the ground proved more difficult than expected. Decades ago, paper money had value because it was backed by silver and gold. People could exchange their paper for the exotic minerals. President Nixon changed that system in the early 1970's to something known as Fiat Money. This was how money worked from the 70s until the zombie apocalypse, but made little sense. Paper money had no value except the *belief* it was worth something. Gold and silver no longer backed the paper. There was no reason why a twenty-dollar bill should be worth more than a single, except for the fact that the number twenty is nineteen numbers bigger than the number one is.

The people of Arcadia had their own money from before everything crumbled. It was more worthless now than ever before.

Perhaps it was because there was no belief that the money held any value. It would be archaic to declare that paper money was once again worth something. The playing field would not be level. The best bet was to create new money, and distribute to everyone an equal share. Before that could be done, the government would need to assign weight and value as a means to establish a code of cost for things like vegetables, poultry, housing, medical needs, electricity, repairs, clothing, and so on and so forth.

For the time being, government had their hand in everything from farming, livestock and education, to religion, engineering and law enforcement. He preferred the term Peace Officers to Police Officers. Crime has been minimal. There was the occasional fight at the Bent Elbow, and the domestics that required an officer to intervene. As far as burglaries and murder, it didn't happen.

The stiff penalties might be considered harsh, but they worked as an effective deterrent.

Vincent sat back and closed his eyes. His thumbs massaged the bridge of his nose. Tension grew behind his eyelids. There was a dull steady throb, and it was barely nine in the morning.

He welcomed the knock at the door.

"Come in."

Gary Priestly stuck his head into the office. "Sir, they've returned."

Gary was the Deputy Mayor. The two were exact opposites. Gary was in his late fifties, thin, had a full head of grey hair and a neck like a turkey. He wore round glasses that made him look every bit like an elected official or a C.E.O. Vincent was forty-two, and beefy. Dark thinning hair and a thick, flat nose made him look more like a mobster than a mayor. He'd often been told he should wear bowling shirts, because if he did, he'd be the spitting image of James Gandolfini from that old HBO show.

"They?"

"Four people. Two were spotted last night. Gathering Patrol came across them, offered a chance to come in, but they declined. It was in the report," Gary said.

Vincent didn't miss the dig. The Sheriff's department filed three reports a day. One per platoon. The end of shift reports detailed an hour-by-hour log of activity, even if there was nothing to report. The executive order brought to attention anything at out of the ordinary, or that required highlighting. "They in the Hall?"

"They are, sir."

"Weapons?"

"Couple of knives. They had swords and machetes last night. Must have ditched them between then and this morning. It was in the report, as well."

Vincent was surprised when Gary didn't announce intent to run against him this fall. Every indication was there, especially the seething animosity the deputy mayor often forgot to mask. "Your initial take?"

"Two men, two women. All seem generally fit. If they are welcomed, we'll have medical give them physicals. I haven't talked with them. Just saw them led to the Hall. We'll have them complete an assessment for work assignments *if* we get to that point."

Vincent leaned forward, set his elbows on the table, hands folded in front of him. "I'll be there momentarily. Make sure they're comfortable. See if they want anything to eat or drink while they are waiting," he said, treating Gary more like a butler or servant instead of the deputy mayor.

"Of course," Gary said, and closed the door.

It wasn't often that new people showed up to Arcadia. There was room for growth, but space was limited. While no labor laws existed, everyone put in more than eight hour shifts. There was much that needed to be done, especially in the fall. Winter's in the mountains could be crippling if enough food was not gathered and stored in preparation of four to six months before the spring thaw. "Gary?"

The door opened. "Yes?"

"Who's with them?"

"Sheriff."

"Okay. Give me two minutes, I'll be right over."

Gary closed the door.

Vincent put his face in his hands and tried to wash away the pain ebbing inside his skull. He took a bottle of aspirin from the center desk drawer and swallowed three maximum strength pills with a glass of water. It would be at least a half hour before the medicine kicked in. Unfortunately, he didn't have that long.

While bowling shirts might wear more comfortably, Vincent retrieved his suit coat from the rack behind his desk. He shrugged his arms through the sleeves, adjusted his shoulders and the knot on his tie, fitting it against the buttoned collar. He gave himself a once over in the full length mirror on the back of his office door before he headed downstairs to the Hall, as ready as he'd ever be to greet the strangers.

# # #

Arcadia's City Hall was a three-floor brick structure. The outside steps led to four Greek pillars in front of the entrance. Vincent and Gary had offices on the third floor. The D.A. and defense attorneys kept offices on the second, along with the municipal court judge and her clerk. The sheriff and his team used offices in the back on the first floor, where holding cells were located.

New people were escorted to the large conference room on the first floor. Vincent gave a respectful knock on the closed door before pushing it open. He surveyed the people briefly, taking in as much as possible without staring. First thing he noted was the lack of hygiene. The collective group required a bath, complete with serious scrubbing and delousing. He wished that could be done before he met with anyone. The flip side was if they were not allowed access, or chose to leave, the use of water and supplies proved a waste. He ran a palm down the front of his tie, as he stretched to shake hands and introduce himself to each of the four people standing across from him.

"Please, please, have a seat," Vincent said. He moved to the front of the table and sat in a high-back chair, Gary sat at the opposite end. "Sheriff."

"Mayor," Gus Huber said, nodding his head. He was beefy, roughly thirty-seven, and loved to boast about his 20-15 eyesight. Gray touched his temples and whiskers when he neglected to shave. The bright blue eyes turned cold as ice if he wanted them to, transitioning him from something of an older GQ model, to more of a dangerous looking man. Gus had been the town sheriff prior to the beginning of the end. He ran a tight, no-nonsense community. When Vincent became Arcadia's mayor, one of his first actions in the role was to appoint Gus back into the law enforcement position. He had not regretted that decision. It was a four year term, but Vincent did not foresee anyone, or any strong potential candidates running against his man. Still, nothing much surprised him anymore. It could happen.

"First," Vincent said, clasping his hands together, setting them down on the table folded in front of him. "I want to extend to you a warm welcome to Arcadia."

"We are not sure we are staying," Tony said.

He must be the one in charge. Vincent merely smiled. "I can understand that. I am sure you have questions—"

"How do you have electricity?" Tony said.

Vincent needed to remind himself that for three years, people have been living like scavengers, doing what needed to be done just to survive. The fact that these four had made it living beyond Arcadia walls amazed him. "We have something of a generator that runs twenty-four seven."

Char shook her head. "A generator? It powers the entire town? How can you possibly have fuel for something like that?"

Vincent knew he'd pursed his lips. He preferred to deal with one person. "It is not an actual generator. It does not run on fuel like you might be thinking. The resources we have are limited, and there are rules to using the electricity. People here are very conservative with the luxury. Usage is monitored closely, trust me. We can't have lights on in every house all day and all night. In fact, people in homes are encouraged to burn candles. Some of the businesses, like our medical center, diner, and City Hall, we use more electricity than most any other place. You'll forgive me if I am not comfortable answering more specifically at this point of our interview."

"Interview?" Tony said.

"It's what it is, isn't it? You are trying to decide if you want to stay in Arcadia, and to be frank, we're also here to decide if we want you." Vincent leaned back in his chair, crossed one leg over the other. "This has become a close knit community. Self-sufficient. We pride the progress we've made on maintaining order, expecting civility and compassion. Everyone has a job to do, and everyone works hard at the job assigned. We have doctors, and garbage collectors. We have farmers and factory workers. There are firefighters and school teachers. No task is unimportant. Without functions being performed, this —all of this— won't work, it can't work. If people slack on their responsibilities, Arcadia falls apart. I know this must sounds like some kind of political spiel, but I am giving it to you straight."

Vincent watched their reactions. The small group remained silent, perhaps letting sink in the information just shared. It was a bit overwhelming, he supposed. Seated before him was a different breed of survivors. He might not know their backstories, but just by the looks of them the last several years have taken a toll. He knew he was fortunate, having been part of Arcadia from the beginning. The land was purchased by preppers more than two decades ago. The wall that turned the town into a fortified city took years and countless dollars to erect. "Questions?"

"How are people compensated for the work they do?" the young woman said.

"And you are, Charlene?"

"Char."

"*Char*. That is an excellent question," Vincent said. He stood up and walked slowly toward one of the windows. The mini-blinds were closed. He parted them with a finger and peeked outside. People moved about, on the way to work, on the way home, headed to and from the marketplace. "Currently, it is something of a socialist economy. Everyone performs their job to the best of their ability and everyone shares in, well, everything. Most of the food is grown and harvested. We have canned food and bottled water, as well. We use that sparingly. Eventually, the goal is to reinstall a common currency and transfer from socialist to democratic, toward making things more like the way they were."

"So a doctor performing heart surgery is going to earn the same as a guy picking up trash?"

"Mr. Dibella, is it?"

"Tony."

"Tony, I'm not going to lie. Sometimes I wonder if the direction we want to head in is the right path. Pretty soon you will get a tour of the town. What I believe you will see is not just content, but happy people. To answer your question, yes. Someone who is in the O.R. all day is going to receive the same each week as someone who picks up garbage. There are no wages being paid. There are staples that everyone gets, regardless. Your break a shoelace, you receive a new shoelace. If a light bulb burns out, you are given a new light bulb. Unfortunately, other items are allotted. We call that allotment *chips*. For example, you want to serve chicken breasts and garden salad for dinner. That's fine. You are allotted x-amount of chips per month. If you elect to use chips for one meal because maybe your family is celebrating a birthday, then so be it. The Mercantile keeps detailed records of who earns and uses what. Same goes at the Bent Elbow."

"I'm Sam. Sam Gerringer. What is the Bent Elbow?"

"That is the one and only watering hole in Arcadia, Sam," Vincent said. He made his way back to the table and sat down.

"And how exactly does that work?"

Vincent pointed a finger at the black woman, and cringed. "Don't tell me," he said. "Grace?"

She nodded.

Smiling, Vincent said, "People work hard. Day in and day out. While we don't have an unlimited supply of alcohol, we do have alcohol. These mountains were also once very popular for moonshining operations. I won't confirm or deny that outside the walls there might or might not be a few distilleries distilling. And it works exactly the same as the food and water. Each person, of age, is allotted x-amount of chips for recreational purposes. People *are not* permitted to commingle allotments, though. This way a person can't spend food chips on moonshine. Does it happen? I'll bet it does. I'll guarantee it's not from poor book keeping, but nothing in our laws prohibits people from trading the two different types of chips. A guy who lives alone, eats very little, but is more thirsty than most, might end up working out a trade so he can spend more time at the Bent Elbow than the Mercantile, if you follow what I'm saying."

"Laws?" Char said.

Vincent cocked his head to one side. "You've met our sheriff, haven't you? What good is having Sheriff Huber, if we don't have rules and laws in place for him to enforce?"

"No stealing. No fighting. No murder," Char said.

"Those are the highlights, yes. Add to that the basics, no arson, rape, burglary, domestic violence, and so on and so forth, and we've covered the bases. No different than any town or any city in pre-apocalyptic times."

"How many people live in Arcadia?" Grace said.

"We have just over five hundred adults and seventy or so under the age of sixteen. Isn't that right, Gary?" Vincent said.

Gary nodded. "Working with round numbers, yes. That sounds accurate."

"With under six hundred people and in a place as serene as this, I imagine crime is low? Why would you need a sheriff?" Grace said.

"Our sheriff's office consists of Peace Officers." Vincent smoothed out his tie. "We still have crime. It's not a lot, but it does happen. People like Sheriff Huber are necessary. We also have a D.A., a defense lawyer, and a judge. All licensed by the bar prior to the events of three years ago. They rule based on case law, and facts, same as courts did years ago."

"And the sheriff and his deputies are the only ones with weapons in town?"

Vincent nodded. "That's correct."

"I'm curious how you power this place?" Char said.

"And I guess I'd like to know why you are letting people move in. I mean, why are you even considering us for, I don't know what you'd call it, citizenship? If the community is working smoothly, everyone has a job to do and everyone is doing their job, why even entertain people like us?" Tony said.

"The power is something we'll talk about later. Like I said earlier, it's not something we just disclose to people," Vincent said, addressing Char's question. "The thing is that there is still some room to grow. There are still jobs openings that need to be filled. Some are pulling double duty. Rotating with others. There still is a cause for concern that people working that hard will suffer burnout. People get sick. Die. Leave."

"Why would someone leave?" Char said.

"Why would people choose to trade food chips for moonshine?"

"You have that many job openings?" Char said.

"What's that saying, many hands make less work?" Vincent smiled.

"Light work. Many hands make light work," the deputy mayor said.

Vincent hoped no one noticed his smile crunch into a cringe. "You are right, Gary. Thank you."

Tony said, "You mentioned a tour of the place?"

"That's correct. I did," Vincent said. "Are you interested in seeing the town?"

The four people at the table looked at each other, back at Vincent, and then all four nodded.

# # #

Vincent's suit coat was back on the rack behind his desk. He'd loosened the knot on his tie and unbuttoned the top button. Standing by his window, a tumbler of whiskey on ice in his hand, he watched as Sheriff Huber led the four from City Hall toward the marketplace.

Chapter 13

Char wanted time alone with her friends. Sheriff Huber kept up a steady flow of monologue. He pointed out different businesses. She was most impressed that there were two tailors. Clothing didn't grow on trees. Maintaining what they had was important. It made sense.

There were no vehicles anywhere. The power the mayor talked about must have been limited to electricity, moonshine, and not refined petroleum. People walked everywhere. Char did not miss eyes giving them a once over any more than they missed an equal seizing up from her. Several people greeted the sheriff, and nodded a silent hello to Char and the others. The sheriff waved, and said hello in return.

Char stayed close to Grace. While the woman's questions over the last hour were helpful, she noticed Grace wince now and then. She was anxious to see if one of the Arcadia doctors could give her friend an exam and just ensure them that everything was all right.

"Is that a bakery?" Sam said.

"Finest bread and pastries for miles around." Huber laughed at his own dark humor.

"If we decided we wanted to stay, and all of you decided you wanted us, what is there, like a vote or something?" Sam said.

Huber shrugged. "Nothing as formal as that, really. Because of our size, the mayor, deputy mayor, Rebecca Bowmen, and myself, get together and discuss the pros and cons."

Char wanted to ask what defined a pro as opposed to a con, but didn't. She wasn't sure it was worth asking because she wasn't sold on the place just yet. Everything seemed too perfect, too smooth. She might be only seventeen, but she'd learned long ago to reserve trust until earned.

"Rebecca Bowmen. Who is she?" Grace said.

They stopped in front of a white building. The tall steeple was complete with a bell in the bell tower. Some of the paint peeled off the clapboard. The wood steps were bowed. The handrails, also wood, were weathered and worn. Char worried if he ran a palm up them she'd be picking out slivers the rest of the day.

"Ms. Bowmen is the Arcadia priestess."

"Priestess?" Sam said.

"She's … Well, let's just say she is a very spiritual person. I don't know that she is ordained by any church, but she is in touch with a high power, and that much I am certain." Huber shifted his weight from leg to leg, his hand resting comfortably on the butt of his revolver. "She's also a highly intelligent person; has always reminded me of one of those contestants on Jeopardy. Know a little about everything. There's not a conversation that goes on that she can't contribute to in some fashion. She even helps George Hermann, one of Arcadia's best engineers."

"If she has a say in whether we're allowed to stay, do we get to meet her?" Grace said.

Huber waved an arm toward the front door the white clapboard church. "She's right inside, and if I'm not mistaken, she's expecting us."

Char wasn't sure what to expect. They entered the church. It did not look different from small churches she'd seen around home. The main aisle led to an altar with rows of wood pews on either side. The center runner was red carpet. Stained glass windows let in some outside light. Mostly it was dark, shadows filled corners and crept out across the eggshell white ceiling. The only odd thing was the relics. She did not see a Crucifix or anything related to Jesus. On the wall behind the altar hung a dreamcatcher with an eagle in a web of beaded strings perched on the ring. Dangling from the ring were four large and long brown feathers. On another wall was a peace pipe and across from it a hatchet.

From somewhere inside incense burned; the odor strong and pungent.

"Priestess Bowmen?" Huber walked backwards down the aisle looking up toward what Char presumed was a balcony.

A woman emerged from through a beaded doorway. She had long, straight, raven black hair, and an olive skin complexion. Her nose was long and thin. She had dark eyes and white teeth. "Sheriff. I was hoping you would show, and these must be our newest candidates?"

Huber spun around. His hands went to his sides, his fingers played with his utility belt. "There you are," he said. "Priestess Bowmen, I'd like to introduce you to. . ."

"Tony Dibella." He held out his hand.

They each introduced themselves.

"Would you like me to stay while the five of you talk?" Huber looked fidgety. He didn't seem to know what to do with his hands. Char thought she saw beads of sweat on his forehead. For some reason, the priestess made him uncomfortable.

"That won't be necessary. I'm sure after we talk, they'll be ready for lunch. I can walk them over to The Diner for something to eat, if that will be alright?" Rebecca never looked away from Huber. Her eyes stayed locked on him.

"That will be fine. I'm sure that will be okay. I'll swing by and pick them up from there a little later," he said, and then he bowed as he backed away from the priestess and slowly made his way back down the aisle toward the doorway they'd entered. "I'll see you all soon."

It wasn't until the sheriff was gone and the door closed all the way behind him that Rebecca Bowmen smiled. She motioned toward the row of pews on the left side of the aisle. "Why don't we sit down and talk; make this a little less formal?"

Tony, Char, Grace and Sam filed into a pew, and the priestess opted a pew two rows ahead. She knelt on the bench, and rested her forearms on the back, facing the others. "I think I'd like to start by asking if you have any questions for me?"

Sam raised his hand.

"You don't need to do that, Sam," Rebecca said.

"I guess I have a question. I hope this doesn't sound rude, but are you like, are you. . .a shaman?"

Char looked from Sam to Rebecca, curious about how she'd answer.

"Shaman is Native American. I am not. I do consider myself like something similar to a shaman because I use magic to heal and prevent illness, physical, physiological and mental," she said.

"Magic?" Sam said. Char thought he had rolled his eyes. She knew he was all about technology, computers and science. This wasn't Oklahoma University. Infected roamed the earth. If monsters actually existed, why couldn't magic.

"I know what you're thinking. I don't have some black cauldron that sits on an open fire where I stir in leg of frog, and eye of newt," Rebecca laughed. "What I try to do is use things from nature as ingredients for natural healing."

"Wouldn't leg of frog and eye of newt be natural?" Sam said.

"I was thinking more about roots and herbs, but I suppose it will all depend on what ails you, won't it?" she said.

"Point made," Sam said.

"I might just have been imagining it, but the sheriff seemed awfully —I'll say— apprehensive around you," Tony said.

"Very perceptive," Rebecca said.

"I noticed it, too," Char said, and immediately regretted the words. It sounded like she wanted credit for being perceptive, as well. "Why was that?"

"I'll tell you a story. It was maybe a year ago. The sheriff suffered from insomnia. He said every time he tried to sleep the only thing he saw were those decaying creatures. If he slept at all, he explained that he felt more tired and worn out when he woke up. He came to see me. The mayor suggested it to him. The sheriff was born and raised Baptist. I suspect he considered Indians, shaman and a priestess, like myself, to be more like New Orleans witches, casting spells and practicing voodoo. He didn't think I could help him. He told me as much. He said he didn't believe in the hocus pocus I practiced. I explained to him that he didn't need to believe in anything for the medicine to work. He wasn't having it.

"I mashed together a collection of herbs and other ingredients and told him to make a hot tea out of the prescription, and drink a cup, only one cup every night before bed, and that before long, he'd be sleeping like a baby," she said.

"It didn't work?" Sam said.

"Oh, no, it worked," Rebecca said. "It worked so well that he even stopped having nightmares. Hasn't had a one since, best I can tell."

"And that's why he's uncomfortable around you?" Char said.

"Because it worked. Yes. That is why he is uncomfortable around me. Once a month though, like clockwork, he stops by to refill his prescription."

"So you are a doctor?" Char said.

"I am a spiritual person. I can see, hear and heal. I do not possess any more power than you do. The difference is that I am in tune with my surroundings. I try to be one with nature. I listen to the wind. I feel the leaves change color and fall from branches. I see through the eyes of eagles and hawks that soar above the mountain tops. I use these senses to heal pain that is physical and physiological, pain in the limbs and joints, and pains that deteriorate the mind and soul."

Rebecca had spoken slowly. Char felt almost entranced listening to the words. In a way she felt in awe of Rebecca if only because of the inner peace that radiated from her.

"Like you, Grace. You have been recently injured," Rebecca said.

It wasn't anything supernatural. The injuries they'd earned were worn for all to see. Cuts and bruises were visible on all four of them. They'd come from tough times and were ready for worse.

Bowmen stood up. She moved out of the pew she was in, to the pew between them. She stopped in front of Grace. "Lean forward, dear."

Grace was hesitant, but responded. She reached for Char's hand, gripped it tight as their fingers laced together.

The priestess held out a hand and let fingertips trace along Grace's brow, down the side of her face and under her chin.

Char shivered. She thought she felt electricity pass between their palms and almost pulled away.

"You are a strong woman, Grace. Your body and mind are strong. You are healing yourself right now, even as we speak," she said.

When Char was finally able to look away from Rebecca, she saw the steady stream of tears roll down Grace's cheeks.

There was heat between their hands. It nearly burned flesh.

Chapter 14

Rebecca led Char and her friends through town.

Downtown consisted of connected red brick, non-descript buildings. Hooked street lamps and cobblestone sidewalks on either side of the paved road made the place resemble Anywhere Small Town, USA. Char hated to admit it, but she'd fallen in love. If she had to choose to live anywhere, this was it. She envisioned an apartment above one of the businesses. Walking the sidewalks, window shopping, bundled up for winter, with mittens wrapped around a mug of hot apple cider. Dreams like that were painful. Usually she kept them from her mind. This one snuck in, and she regretted having allowed it.

Char watched the priestess walk. The steps flowed. Underneath a heavy biker's black leather jacket with a U.S.A. and Bald eagle patch sewn on the back, the woman wore a long blue and yellow dress. There was no other way to describe it. Her every movement flowed. Char could not remember the last time she wore a dress. It was at least three years ago. Maybe it was for her birthday, or there was that time when she just wanted to look nice at school. Her father always liked her in dresses. He called her his "princess." She liked that, missed it. She missed him.

Rebecca stopped in front of a door. The building sat in the center of the row. "This is the diner."

A wood sign hung over the door: The Diner. Char looked up and down the street. People still watched them in a curious kind of way. Strangers were excellent at drawing out curiosity. It was no different from when a new kid showed up at school. The first day hardly anyone said boo to the transfer. In time, that new kid had friends, same as any. Some worthy, some backstabbers. Char figured it wouldn't be all that different in a town like Arcadia.

Rebecca opened the door. A bell jingled. It was far too cutesy, as if Arcadia was on another planet, or lost in a unaired episode of Rod Serling's *Twilight Zone*. The hair on Char's arms stood up. While there was no reason to suspect anything other than genuine hospitality, it was all she could focus on. She wished she had her weapons. It was hard not to feel naked without them.

The priestess talked with a woman behind the counter. It was conversation just louder than a whisper, but still not easy to listen in on. Char took this opportunity to lock eyes with Tony. He bit down on his upper lip and cocked his head slightly to the side. It seemed like his senses were on high alert, as well.

Char reached for Grace's hand. The woman took it, and gave her hand a squeeze.

"Not gonna lie," Sam said, "I could eat."

"Friends, Mona is going to show you to your seats. Anything on the menu, I recommend. Mona's husband is culinary genius with rations, and that is not sarcasm. I hope you enjoy your tour and consider staying on. Should you decide to stay, please, please stop by and visit. I love the company. Now, unless you have any more questions for me, I'll be going."

They each thanked Rebecca for her time, shook her hand, and then stood silent watching the priestess as she exited the diner. When they turned around, Mona stood before them smiling.

"Hungry?" she said and sat them in a corner booth, by the front window. She was in her fifties with red hair and wrinkles around her eyes. Blue eyeliner and red lipstick only accented her age, not making her look younger. Her apron was tied around a pudgy and soft stomach. "This is probably the most coveted seat in the place. Everyone likes to people watch. I'm not sure it's because they're nosy, as much as they just like to keep a pulse on what's happening around them." Mona laughed. "Oh, who am I kidding? People are nosy!"

After they ordered, and while they waited for their food, the bell over the front door jingled.

Benjamin walked in. Char watched him look around the diner.

The place was empty, except for them.

His eyes stopped on her.

Although she couldn't help it, she smiled.

The man walked into the diner, smiling, too.

"Hello," he said. His wave was small, timid. He wore a tan shirt with a silver badge and blue jeans with cowboy boots. He approached the table nodding. "How is everyone?"

"We're good," Tony said.

Char noticed Grace was not looking at Benjamin, but at her. Her lip curled into a smile all her own.

"You were the guy we ran into last night," Sam said. He pushed out the chair next to him. "Going to join us?"

Benjamin held up a hand. "No, thank you. I just wanted to see how you guys were doing. See if there was anything you needed. And yes, I met you and..."

"Charlene," she said. Everyone stared at her. "Char."

"Char," Benjamin said, "I met you and Char last night. I'm glad you decided to come back. Arcadia has its faults, but all and all, it's a pretty cool little town."

"What are some of the faults?" Tony said.

Benjamin shrugged. "I can't actually think of any. Just figured it would sound more believable if I didn't just brag about how perfect it is here. Hard for people to accept that sometimes. Perfection is tough to come by," he said.

Tony seemed to bite his tongue. Char might have added a thought or two of her own to the conversation, but refrained. She hadn't noticed any faults. The place might just be cosmetic. Might not be until after you'd lived in Arcadia a while that you began to see through any facade. "How long have you been here?"

"Me? Since the whole thing started, really. My father and I. Where are you from?"

"New York," she said.

"I always wanted to go to New York," he said.

"Not the city. Rochester. It's between Buffalo and Syracuse." Char dropped her hands into her lap once she realized her fingers couldn't leave the silverware alone. "But I've been to New York City once."

She'd gone on a day trip with her father and Cash. They went to the bus station at 2 AM. It was a seven hour ride. There were so many stops along the way. She sat with her brother, and he wanted the window seat. She used her father's phone and listened to music most of the way. As the sun came up they had the city skyline in view. They'd passed the stadium where the Giants and Jets played, and then went through the Holland Tunnel. They emerged inside New York City, and her life changed. Leaving the bus station and stepping out onto the city streets, she knew when she was older that she wanted to move to Manhattan. She didn't care what she did for a living as long as the city became her home.

Char didn't share the memory. It was hers, and although Tony opened up to her a few nights ago, she did not have any intention of doing the same.

"How about the rest of you?" Benjamin said.

The bell over the door jingled again.

"Ben?"

"Hey, Olek," he said.

"We gotta roll. New shipment coming in."

"Yeah, okay, Olek. Well, it was nice meeting all of you. If you decide to stay, the sheriff's office is at City Hall, where you all met with the mayor earlier today," he said, and backed away from the table.

Before he stepped out of the diner, he gave a final wave.

Char stared at her hands in her lap for a moment, and then looked up.

They stared at her.

She ignored them and picked up her fork. She set the fork down and took a sip of water. Setting the glass down, she widened her eyes. "What?"

"Nothing, nothing," they all said.

"And here we are," Mona said, showing up with plates of food on a tray that she carried balanced on the palm of her hand and shoulder. "Good and hot for my hungry guests!"

# # #

Char and her friends were given two adjoining rooms at a Holiday Inn Express. It was a four story hotel with an indoor swimming pool and exercise room. The stay was compliments of the mayor. They were to meet with him in the morning. This gave him time to talk with the deputy mayor, sheriff and priestess. It also gave them time to talk. This was the first chance they had to talk since they'd entered Arcadia that morning.

Tony and Char sat on the double bed across from Grace and Sam. Sam was lying down on his side, his elbow on a pillow, hand propping up his head. "I don't know about you guys, but I'm loving it here. Loving it. It's like the first time I've gone an entire day without thinking about the infected. I mean, man, not once have those decaying flesh walkers entered my mind. Not once." He was right. Char couldn't recall the last time she'd spent an entire day not worrying about the infected. She hadn't looked over her shoulder once. She knew she wouldn't be surprised if Rod Serling *did* appear and narrate this particular TV episode, except for the fact that he'd died decades ago. However, she also knew that being dead didn't mean a thing.

"I will admit, this place is cozy. Problem is, it's too cozy, if that makes any kind of crazy sense," Grace said. "The people seem friendly enough. I have never met a mayor before, nor have I ever been escorted all over town. We're getting red carpet treatment, all right. My question is, why?"

Tony folded his arms. "It's the one thing I keep thinking about, too, Grace. *Why?* I know the mayor indicated that because the town is relatively small he can dedicate time to meeting personally with anyone that wants to enter.

"This has to be one of the largest and best run towns we've *ever* come across, or may ever come across. The mayor said they had job openings that needed filling, but he never said what those openings were, and never once asked us what we're good at, what we did for a living. For all he knows, the four of us have spent our lives on unemployment and won't be able to contribute to this society at all."

"I've never had a job," Char said. "I've been killing zombies since I was fourteen. It's the only thing I know."

"I worked at a pizza place making chicken wings, and at Wal-Mart stocking shelves. That's it," Sam said.

Tony and Grace laughed. Eventually, Sam and Char joined in.

"What do we want to do?" Tony said. "I'd really like to make this something we either all decide to do or not do. Together. But if some want to stay and others want to go that will be okay, too. We each have our reasons for wanting what we want. No hard feelings, agreed?"

Char said, "Agreed."

"What do you want, Tone?" Sam said.

Char knew Tony hated when Sam called him that. She waited for the backlash, but it never came.

"I'm not sure. It's tough to make a decision like this so quickly."

"How much time do you think we have to think it over?" Grace said.

"I don't know," Tony said.

"How long do you think they take to decide whether they want us or not?" Grace said.

Tony uncrossed his arms and held them up in surrender. "No idea."

A knock at the door stopped their conversation.

Tony pressed a finger to his lips. Char and the others stood up, and moved toward the edge of the beds ready for anything.

At the door, Tony looked out the peephole, and sighed. He removed the security chain and unlocked the door. "Deputy," he said.

Char strained to see over Tony's shoulder.

"I was wondering, actually, the mayor wanted to me to ask if you guys wanted to come down to the Bent Elbow for dinner and a drink?" Benjamin said. "Hi, Charlene. Guys, how are you?"

"What time is dinner?" Tony said. "You know we don't have, what is it? Chips?"

"An hour or so. I can stop back. Walk you guys over, if you'd like. And you don't need to worry about paying. Like with lunch, it's on the mayor."

"Well, then, thank, you. We would love to, and appreciate the invitation," Tony said. Char cringed, hoping the deputy didn't pick up on the sarcasm that she'd become so accustomed to. He shut the door and turned around. "Looks like we all have a date with the deputy."

Sam laughed.

Char threw a playful punch at his chest. Over-exaggerating the situation, Sam fell back onto the bed writhing in mock-pain.

"This is a good thing, really," Tony said.

"A double and a half date," Sam said, throwing a pillow at Char.

Tony caught the pillow, threw it onto the other bed. "Come on, dammit. Nothing's changed. We don't know these people. We know nothing about this town except what they've allowed us to see, and we've only talked with people they want us talking to. We can't let our guard down just because there aren't infected sneaking up on us."

"So how is going to a bar a *good* thing?" Char said.

Tony repositioned himself in the chair, setting his elbows on the table. "People drink, they talk. If we're given even half a chance to mingle, then maybe we'll get a more accurate perspective of Arcadia. I don't mind everything smelling like roses, but there's got to be shit somewhere."

Chapter 15

The bar was Downtown and sat on the west corner, not far from The Diner where Char and her friends had recently enjoyed the closest thing to a home cooked meal that they'd had in years, prepared by Mona and her husband. Over the bar entrance hung a green shingle. Under the words, "Bent Elbow," a poised and bodiless arm tipped back a frothy mug of beer. Below the sign Benjamin stood with his back to the wall, hands stuffed in pockets; illuminated beneath the vapor of a street light, his breaths plumed from his mouth in puffs like grey smoke.

Tony whispered. "The kid's cute and everything, but keep it slow. We don't know anything about these people. I am far from comfortable with everything. I'd rather we concentrate on being safe right now."

Overprotective, like her father. She loved him for it. "You have nothing to worry about," she said.

Tony let out a gasp of sarcastic snicker. "I'll be keeping an eye on things, young lady. You understand me?"

She wrapped an arm around his. "Deal."

The streets were far less crowded. Some couples milled about, and Char figured chips were used sparingly. Perhaps the best thing about the apocalypse was the appreciation of limited resources and the death of gluttony. Not for everyone, she was sure, but for most.

"Hello." Benjamin pushed off the wall with his shoulders, and waved. "It's really getting cold at night. Winters up here are kind of rough. Not a ton of snow, but the cold is relentless."

Tony and Benjamin shook hands. "Again, extend our thanks and appreciation to the mayor. Any chance he'll be joining us?"

"Not likely," Benjamin said. "He wants you to get a feel for the place. If he showed up people tend to get phony. Brown nosing, and overly friendly."

Tony nodded. "Understood."

Benjamin pulled open the door. "I've reserved us a table. Right this way."

"So you'll be joining us?" Grace said, giving a Char a casual bump with her arm.

"If that's all right? I don't have to."

"It's fine," Grace said.

Char was the last to enter, just in front of Benjamin. "How was your day?" he said.

"Pretty interesting, overall. You?"

The Bent Elbow was dark with wood floors and wood paneling. A buck with an impressive rack hung over the center of a polished gold-trim outlined L-shaped bar. The bar was fully stocked with an array of bottles of booze sitting on two-tier shelves in front of the mirror behind the bar. A barmaid with big breasts squished into a too-tight t-shirt used a white rag to wipe away wet glass rings off her countertop. Char assumed tipping was encouraged. Chips were chips. The more things change, the more they stay the same, she thought.

"Busy. Had an issue with a supplier of ours. Claimed half his shipment was stolen by bandits. He assured us he'd be able to retrieve the cargo. Had people out looking, feeling pretty confident the truck's been ditched somewhere close by," Benjamin said.

Char felt her breath catch in her lungs. "Really? Hmmm."

"Just a day in the boring life of a deputy, I guess." He laughed.

When Char finally exhaled, she felt light headed. She had questions she knew better than to ask. Even a young cop like Benjamin would see everything she said as a red flag. Somehow she needed to talk with Tony. A sense of dread filled her as she saw the dream of sanctuary slip away. As she followed the others to a table in the center of the barroom floor, she wondered how to get Tony's attention.

Wood chairs scraped on the wood floors as people sat around the table.

"Very. . .rustic," Sam said. "I like it. You guys add a mechanical bull, and I'm telling you the place will be packed. Have to set up those velvet line thingies. Have people outside wrapped around the building waiting to get in. I don't know. I could be like the guy with sunglasses and clipboard at the door checking who's who on a list before letting anyone in. They got a job for a guy like that in Arcadia?"

Benjamin laughed, shaking his head. "No, sir. They do not. I'll run it by the mayor, though, see what the demand is for creating a position like that."

"Appreciate it. Job like that would be awesome," Sam said, placing his fingertips on the edge of the table and leaning back to look around. "I do like it here. It's homey."

Char tried to imagine what the Bent Elbow had been like pre-infected days. Mining town like this, it was probably packed full on pay days, rowdy as hell. She envisioned fights between friends and the odor of stale warm beer as part of the polish on the wood floors. The thing that caught her eye was the jukebox in the corner. Tube lights ran up the sides in soft blues and reds. The bubble glass displayed columns of songs. Every few minutes the pages automatically turned. It had been a while since Char last heard music. When she was in school, music was most important to her, especially after her parents divorced. Songs seemed to get her better than ever.

"It works," Benjamin said.

Char looked at him. "What?"

"The jukebox. It's free, too. No chips needed," he said. He wore a sly grin. "Go check out the playlist. It's rather impressive."

Char felt her face grow warm. She knew she blushed at the idea of listening to music. "I wouldn't know what to play."

"I'll go over and look through the selection with you. Come on," he said, and held out his hand.

Char pushed back her chair and stood up. She eyed the hand suspiciously, but did not take it. She was more than capable of getting out of a chair on her own.

"When you get back," Grace said, "you and I are going to have to spend a little time talking."

"About what?" Char said.

"Birds and bees, honey. You were probably too young before all of this to understand what you missed just now," Grace said. She smiled and batted her eyes.

Sam laughed.

"Am I missing something?"

"When you get back. That's when we'll talk. Now go play something with a beat. I am not going to lie, the idea of dancing has got some appeal," Grace said. She snapped her fingers and moved her shoulders some. "It has been a long, long time."

"With those moves," Sam said, "maybe it's better that way."

He groaned and rubbed his shoulder when Grace punched him in the arm.

Char made eyes with Tony, and shook her head as if indicating Sam and Grace had lost it. She followed Benjamin to the jukebox, and stared through the bubbled glass at the list of songs and artists. "My dad used to take my brother and me to this diner on Park Avenue. The place looked like a chrome trailer in the back of a parking lot. The counter was lined with stools that spun, and booths lined the front windows. Everything about the place just screamed 1960's. The food was so-so, you know? It was good, but nothing fancy, tuna melts and meatloaf, that kind of thing. My brother always got the mac and cheese and French fries."

"What did you get?"

"I always got the same as my dad, The Western Burger. It was a half-pound burger with lettuce, tomato, pickles, and a giant onion ring, with a little mayo on the bottom bun and a ton of homemade barbeque sauce on top. It was a mess to eat."

"Sounds delicious."

"It was. We went through a ton of napkins, but the best part, or at least what I remember most, was the jukebox. Dad always had money for us to each pick like four or five songs. Anything we wanted. I don't know why, but that was exciting, and we never left, even if we'd finished eating, until all the songs we'd selected were played." Char tried to smile as she looked up to see if Benjamin was about to laugh at her.

"Pretty great memories."

"You don't think it's silly?"

"What part would I think was silly? It all sounds amazing."

Char turned her attention back to the jukebox. As much as she wanted to hear music, she couldn't concentrate on reading. The words on each artist tab blurred.

"Hey! Mayor's kid," someone said.

Char looked up.

Benjamin turned away. "Mr. Broadhurst. How are you, sir?"

Mayor's son?

Broadhurst?

Char lowered her head, slipped away from Benjamin and the jukebox, and made her way back to the table.

"I don't hear any music?" Grace said.

"It broken?" Sam said.

"Tony. We need to get out of here," Char said.

"Why?"

Benjamin walked up next to Charlene. "Hey, everyone, I want to introduce you to one of Arcadia's suppliers, Frank Broadhurst."

Chapter 16

Char felt her breath catch in her lungs. A whirlwind of thoughts spun wildly around inside her mind. Would Broadhurst recognize any of them? It was dark inside the bar. If he did, would he make a scene? If Broadhurst didn't recognize them, how would Grace and Sam react? There were far too many variables.

She caught Tony's eyes. He was staring at Benjamin. She was certain the thoughts that flashed through her head were passing through the minds of her friends, as well.

"I'm Frank, just Frank. Nice to meet you," he said, nodding a hello to everyone.

"Nice to meet you," Tony said, as if he hoped to keep the introductions short.

"This is Tony," Benjamin said.

Broadhurst held out his hand. Tony shook it. It resembled a reluctant action, forced. Apprehensive.

"And this is Sam," Benjamin said.

Broadhurst made a move to reach across the table to shake Sam's hand. His eyes picked up Grace. He stopped, stood up straight, and dropped his hands to a holstered weapon.

Grace looked like she might scream.

Why did he have a gun?

Broadhurst pointed at Sam. "These are the people who stole the town's supplies!"

The gun was out and pointed at Sam's head.

Tony jumped up and slammed his arm across Broadhurst's. The gun discharged once, twice. Broadhurst aimed and fired off a third round.

Char bent low, wrapped her arms around Broadhurst's waist, and drove him sideways, dropping him hard onto the floor.

Chairs skidded across wood as people moved out of the way.

Broadhurst wasn't going to let it go. He rolled Char off, and delivered a blow with his elbow into her ribs. She grunted and tried to pull away.

Sam dove onto Broadhurst.

Char saw things moving too fast to be real. She heard cries, screams, and the echoes of cries and screams as Grace helped her up.

A glass mug smashed over Grace's skull. The woman's legs wobbled and she crumpled to the floor. Blood and shards of glass mixed seeping into the wood.

Spinning around, Char caught a fist across her jaw. Benjamin grabbed for the man who struck her. This man wore a gun around his waist, too.

Someone yelled for someone else to get the sheriff.

A woman got past Benjamin and the man he struggled to restrain, and kicked Sam in the side of the head. Sam fell off Broadhurst.

Face bloodied, Broadhurst didn't relent. He pummeled Sam. His fists crashed into Sam's face. The flesh was turning to pulp.

Char needed to help Sam. She couldn't find Tony.

She knelt next to Grace, who was unconscious, but breathing.

Sam was limp under Broadhurst. He didn't struggle. Broadhurst never stopped. The punches smacked like a baseball bat repeatedly into Sam's face while the woman kicked Sam wherever she could, growling with each slam of her heel into his groin, and thighs.

They were going to kill him.

Benjamin had the one man in a half nelson, and the man continued to struggle and resist. Char grabbed the gun from the man's belt and checked the clip before she fired a shot into the air.

Patrons of the bar had mostly cleared out, only those in the back half who couldn't safely get around the brawl to an exit stayed huddled close in the back corner.

Tables tipped as the man knocked Benjamin backwards.

"This is over!" Char said.

The woman who had been kicking Sam turned around. She withdrew throwing knives from a harness worn slung over her shoulders. Char didn't hesitate. She fired the gun. Bullets tore into her chest. Blood soaked through the shirt as she stumbled to the side, lost her balance and dropped onto a table. The table barely moved. She slid forward and off the table hitting the floor face first. She didn't move again.

This caught Broadhurst's attention. He skidded around Sam's lifeless body, snagged an arm under Sam's head and pulled him up onto his lap. "Drop the gun, girl. I'll snap his fuckin' neck."

Sam looked dead already.

If blood didn't bubble from his nostrils, Char would have thought he was dead.

Char raised the weapon.

"Char, don't," Benjamin said. "Frank, let him go."

The guy he'd been holding dropped an elbow into Benjamin's belly. It was enough of a distraction that he could wiggle free of Ben's hold. He tackled Char. The gun flew from her free from her grip.

Char saw one of the knives the woman dropped.

The man punched her, his first slammed into her temple. She saw black stars clearly, while everything else in front of her fell out of focus. Her ears rang.

She locked her fingers around the knife and stabbed the man in the neck.

His blood sprayed. It was warm, sticky, and covered her face.

Broadhurst still held Sam by the head.

"Let him go, Frank," Benjamin said. His voice quivered more with each of the four words. He stood with his legs spread, bent forward, and one arm out. It was awkward, but he was able to pull the man off Char. "You all right? Let me handle this."

"He's mine," she said.

"Char, let me handle this. I'm a deputy. Please, just let me take care of this."

She rolled onto her stomach, pushed up onto her knees, and then lunged forward, over Sam. She dove onto Broadhurst and Broadhurst screamed.

"Char!" Benjamin said.

She didn't stop, couldn't stop. She stabbed Broadhurst in the chest. She pulled the knife out and plunged it in again. Broadhurst was dead. His eyes were open wide. She stabbed the throwing knife into his heart one more time and then twisted the blade. Once she felt the edge scrape across bone she pulled the knife out and wiped the blood off on his blood soaked shirt.

Someone grabbed her from behind.

She spun around, slashing out with the blade.

Benjamin winced, and backed away. "Charlene!"

She saw Tony. He was on the floor, under the table where they had been sitting. She crawled toward him. The wood floors seemed to drink the blood that spilled from his body.

"Tony?"

He didn't answer, didn't move.

She knelt next to him.

His eyes were closed, his mouth open. The hole in his forehead had been accidental, but fatally placed. She looked back at Broadhurst. He'd done this. She wanted to stab him again. The man had died too fast, too easily.

"Olek. I'll get her," Char heard Benjamin saying.

"Ma'am, drop the knife."

She stared at Tony. This wasn't right. It shouldn't have happened. They'd fought side by side taking on hordes of infected together. It didn't end this way. It couldn't. Her friends had been cheated.

"The knife, Char, put it down," Benjamin said.

She couldn't go through this again, being alone. The loss was too much. Her heart ached. She lowered herself onto Tony, hugging him. She cried.

# # #

Sheriff Huber locked the barred cell and stood there with the ring of keys in his hand.

Char sat on a thin mattress. She wanted to wash the blood off. It was dry and crusting on her skin. "I want to know how Grace is," she said. She didn't look up, or at the officer. Instead she stared down at the gunmetal gray floor.

"Right now, I think it will be best if you worry about yourself."

Char didn't respond. She pushed back on the cot, pressing her back to the cinderblock. She drew in her knees and wrapped her arms around her legs.

"I'll be back in a little while. You and I are going to have a talk. I want your side of the story," the sheriff said. "I'm not sure what you'll be able to tell me to make this any better. You do have the right to an attorney. Deputy Olek told you that when he arrested you, correct?"

Char could not believe that Tony was dead. She also wanted to know how Sam was. This place had doctors. She wanted to assume they were being cared for.

"Charlene, did Deputy Olek read you your rights when he arrested you?"

"Is Sam okay?"

"Your friends are being taken care of. I need to know if you understand what I'm saying to you."

It was her idea to come to Arcadia. It was her fault they'd stopped running. The smart thing would have been to keep pushing on, putting more distance between them and Broadhurst. She wanted her weapons back. She wanted to collect her friends and leave this horrible town.

Maybe they wouldn't want to go with her. She couldn't blame them if they decided just to cut her loose.

"I'll be back, ma'am. We'll talk more then, okay?"

Broadhurst deserved a much slower death.

"I just want a moment with her," a woman said. "Please, sheriff."

"Talk through the bars," Sheriff Huber said. "I'll give you five minutes. Not a second more. Do me a favor. See if she wants a lawyer. I can't get her to answer me."

There was a moment of silence. Char hoped they had both gone.

"Char?" The woman had stayed. It was Rebecca Bowman. "What happened tonight?"

What happened tonight?

Char lowered her forehead to her knees. She tried to hold back tears. The crying started, regardless. The sobbing made her shoulders shake. She didn't deserve to cry. She didn't deserve to feel this way. Self-pity was reserved for innocent people who were wronged. "This was my fault," she said. "Tony's dead and it's my fault."

"Tell me what happened?" Rebecca said. "Please. I want to help you. You're going to need help now. Let the sheriff get you an attorney."

"You don't get it. They started this. They kidnapped my friends. They had Sam and Grace bagged, tied and loaded in the back of a rig. Tony and I, we didn't steal from Broadhurst. We just got our friends back. We did what needed doing."

"You didn't steal the supplies?"

"We stole the supplies. After. After we got back our friends back."

"Charlene, if this wasn't your fault—"

Char punched fisted hands into the mattress. "This was my fault. All of it!"

"You can't say things like that, Char. Please. You don't understan—"

"Go. I don't want to talk. I don't want to talk to you. Leave!" Char got off the bed and walked into the furthest corner, she faced the cinderblock and tried to pull herself into the shadows. She just wanted to disappear.

Chapter 17

Sheriff Huber and Benjamin Forti sat across the desk from the mayor.

"Let's run through this again," Vincent said. He leaned back in his chair, his fingertips pressed so tightly together they were white. When he'd learned of the events taking place at the Bent Elbow he had been home, getting ready for bed. He'd put back on the clothing he'd just taken off. The wrinkles and tie loosely around his neck annoyed him. Most of the time he enjoyed the position as mayor of Arcadia. In the last three years they'd had some crime, there would always be crime, regardless of laws, regardless of the punishment. That baffled him.

"When I got there—"

Vincent held up a hand. "Start with you, Ben."

"I don't know, dad," Ben said. "I mean, it was going well. Then Broadhurst and his crew walked into the bar and I brought them over. Figured I'd introduce the prospects to the suppliers. Let them see how friendly the place is, and Frank freaked. He accused them of stealing the supplies."

"He reported that earlier today. Showed up without the rig," Huber said. "Claimed raiders hit him. Lost some men during the attack."

"Next thing I know, Frank's got his gun out."

"Why do we allow the suppliers to keep their weapons when they're in town? I don't see why they can't drop them at the gate and pick them up when they leave," Vincent said. He picked up a pad and pen and jotted notes onto the paper. "We're going to readdress this issue. I'm sorry, Ben. Go on."

"The guy, Tony, tried to get the gun out of his hand. The gun went off and he was actually shot and killed. Charlene attacked Frank. Knocked him down. From there, it was just out of control. I'm not sure I can even recall how everything happened," Ben said, and shook his head as if he were trying to wipe the memories out of his mind.

"But Char shot and killed a woman?" Vincent said. "Ben?"

"Yes."

"And she then killed two men. Stabbed them to death?" Vincent said. "Ben?"

"Yes, but—"

Vincent held up a hand, silencing his son. He then closed his eyes and rubbed the bridge of his nose. "Look, I know you like this girl, Ben, but you know how the courts work here."

"I don't think it was her fault."

"Who's was it? Frank's?"

"He pulled a gun, dad."

"And he's dead. How is he going to stand trial? This girl — woman— killed three people. That is excessive violence. Three people! These weren't zombies."

"She was protecting her friends," Ben said.

"We have three rules here, Ben. They're simple. No stealing, no fighting and no murder. It's kind of the Ten Commandments in three simple rules. She violated all three."

A knock on the door interrupted his train of thought. He sighed. It was the middle of the night. The building was busy with people. Four people were dead. Everyone in town seemed to have learned the news already. City Hall was busier now than it was during the day.

"Come in," Vincent said.

The office door opened and Deputy Sheriff Olek leaned in. "The boy, Samuel Gerringer? He didn't make it. I just received word. Brain was swollen. Doc tried to relieve pressure. Drilled holes into the skull. He hemorrhaged. Was nothing more that could be done."

Vincent silently nodded. "And the black woman?"

"No change. She's still non-responsive. Doc said she's in a coma."

"She going to make it?"

"He said too soon to tell," Deputy Sheriff Olek said. "And mayor?"

"Yes?"

"Rebecca Bowman is here to see you."

Of course she is, he thought. "Send her in," he said. He didn't look at the deputy or his son. "Five people are dead. Five."

"Mayor?"

"Come in, Rebecca. Please, come on in," Vincent said as he stood up.

Benjamin and Huber stood up, as well. "Priestess," they said.

"Close the door, would you?" Vincent said.

Rebecca closed the door.

Vincent went to a small closet and removed a folding chair.

"I'll sit there," Ben said to Rebecca. "You can have my chair."

"That's not necessary, but thank you," she said. "Vincent, I just talked to the young girl."

"And your thoughts?"

"She is angry and confused."

"Remorseful?" Vincent said, sounding hopeful.

Rebecca shook her head. "It's not that black and white. She blames herself for her friend's death."

Vincent thought about telling the priestess the newest death count, but refrained.

"She claims that Frank Broadhurst and his men kidnapped some of her friends and that they fought his men to get them back," she said.

"And stole the supply truck?" Deputy Sheriff Huber said.

"They did."

"Point is, whatever happened outside of Arcadia, I don't have much control over that. I don't want control over that. I have my hands full with everything that takes place inside these walls," Vincent said, pounding his finger onto his desk blotter. "Inside this town, my town, *our town*, they let shit come to a head. They all but destroyed the Bent Elbow. They turned that place into a bloody mess. How many people were there tonight?"

"A few families," Benjamin said. "I'm not sure. Twenty people?"

"Twenty people witnessed a killing spree," Vincent said. He pointed at Huber. "You get statements from everyone?"

Huber nodded. "We did."

"We have never seen anything like this. Last thing even remotely close was...I can't think of a single thing even remotely close to the shit mess this girl caused in less than a day inside our borders," Vincent said.

"It wasn't her fault," Benjamin said.

"I'm not saying it was all her fault, but your story, Rebecca's, they aren't much different. The bottom line is, the two groups had bad blood. They went at it. People are dead. If Broadhurst was alive, I'd be charging him as well. But he's not. He's dead. His crew is dead. Those deaths are far more important to me than those of prospects are. Frank and his team were our best suppliers. I don't know where they dug shit up, but whatever we needed, they got. How do you replace a crew like that during times like these, Ben? Huh? How?

"When the town finds out that we don't have the supplies we ordered..."

"Dad—"

"We put the laws into place for a reason, Ben. We can't let this woman get away with stealing, fighting, and murder. There is just no plausible way around this. It isn't the first time someone's been sentenced, it won't be the last. It wasn't easy then seeing someone sent to the Cog, it won't ever be easy."

"The Morales Gang," Ben said.

Vincent shrugged. "There is always an exception. The thing is, we have to follow the laws we've put in place. It is the only way to prevent chaos and anarchy. It's why Arcadia works. We have structure. We have order, Ben. We have order."

# # #

Char was the only person in the holding cell. The windowless room was dark, despite cased fluorescent lighting. Everything was a deep hunter green or dark grey. There was no way she'd sleep, despite how heavy her eyes felt. She closed them and hoped she'd drift off, but it didn't happen. Instead she paced, or stood gripping the bars; her head placed against them and stared at the floor.

She counted off steps. Twenty-four from one end to the other, and twenty-four from side to side. She wanted to keep busy. If she wasn't going to be able to sleep, she needed something else to occupy her mind.

No nightmare lasted this long.

Three years, and counting.

There had to be an end it. There had to be a way to stop the pain, the suffering.

Truth was, she'd tried. She'd done her best. After her brother and father died, she didn't think she'd be able to push on. She hadn't wanted to keep at it. There seemed no point. She remembered sitting on the side of the road under a hot Mexican sun, wondering why she'd continued the fight. Why had she decided life was worth living?

She wished she could recall the reason.

Something had convinced her not to give up.

Then.

Right now, she didn't bother searching for that conviction. She saw the hopelessness. Arcadia was a facade. It couldn't last. The lights, the electricity, all that was cosmetic. Appearance.

It was little else.

Char unmade her bed, tossing the blanket onto the floor. She balled up the sheet and stood on the mattress. Her father would never approve. He always wanted the best for her, and for Cash. He sacrificed for them.

He never told them as much, but she knew it. She'd always known it.

"I can't do this anymore," she said. Her lips quivered. She wanted him to be here. If anyone could fix this mess, he could. He had a way of making her feel safe, confident, and special. "Don't be mad at me, daddy. Don't hate me for this."

She looped the sheet over the bars that ran along the top of the cage, and knotted it in place.

She had no idea about heaven and hell, despite having been raised to believe in God and to fear the devil. Certain things were a sin, according to the Bible. She wondered how God could hold anything against her at this point in the game. She's worked so hard at staying alive. If anything, He should be delighted that she's finally coming home.

She wanted to see her father and brother again.

She wanted to join them.

If there was a Heaven, that was where they'd be. Together.

Soon the three of them could be reunited.

A tear slid down her cheek and she smiled as she brushed it away with the back of her hand.

Unsure how to construct and actual noose, Char tied the opposite end of the sheet and knew once she placed her head into the hole and jumped off the bed, the knot would slide tight around her throat.

She didn't care if it didn't kill her right away. She would die, suffocating eventually, and that was reassuring enough. Holding the sides of the hoop wide she stuck her head in and stepped off the mattress.

The knot tightened.

Char gasped. Her legs kicked, at first.

Survival instinct, she assumed. She forced them to go limp, and closed her eyes and waited. She thought, *Who could tell me I'm wrong? Who could say I haven't tried my hardest? I still failed. Despite it all, in spite of everything I've overcome, I still failed. You can't blame me now for finally deciding just to give up.*

This had been easier than she thought. There was no fear of dying. She felt nothing except empty and alone and tired. She welcomed death. She only hoped she didn't have to wait much longer.

Spots floated past on the insides of her eyelids.

Her lungs began to ache. She wasn't sure if she was holding her breath, or if her weight dangling off the knot prevented her from breathing. What she did know was that it was working.

As the oxygen to the brain was severed, her legs began involuntarily to kick. Her body twitched, and spasmed.

She was dying, and in only a few moments more she knew she would be dead.

Chapter 18

Through mostly closed eyes, Char saw blurred light. A shadow loomed above her. It grew larger and smaller and larger again. She heard something hiss and gasp, hiss and gasp. It was slow, steady and rhythmic. Someone was talking to her. The sound was muffled, and difficult to understand. She closed her eyes. The odor of rubbing alcohol or of something strong and sterile assaulted her nostrils.

Convinced there was no such thing as an afterlife, Char was surprised by the sights, sounds and smells.

"Charlene?"

She knew the voice. While it sounded familiar to her, she knew immediately that it was not her father, or her brother. She thought for sure the first people she met in Heaven would be them. Maybe she assumed they would have been told she was on her way, and would have been first in line to welcome her.

"Charlene?"

This wasn't right. Any of it. It wasn't making sense. She felt discombobulated. Aside from the voice calling her name, the hiss and gasp she heard sounded like something she'd heard before. It was a sound from a long time ago. She remembered her great-grandfather. He'd been in the hospital. He had been in his late eighties and suffered a stroke. He was dying, and they'd gathered around his hospital bed waiting. They'd waited for nearly a week and a half before death took him. The entire time they spent in his room there was that same hiss and gasp. It came from a machine that her father explained helped great-granddad breathe.

Something wasn't right; the strong aroma of sterilization, the hiss-gasp, the voice calling her name that wasn't her father or brother's.

She wasn't in Heaven.

Char tried opening her eyes again. They fluttered. The light wasn't as bright this time and what she saw was not as blurry.

The shadow leaning over her slowly came into focus.

She wasn't in Heaven, or Hell.

She was in Arcadia.

Her eyes closed and she fell thankfully into a dreamless sleep.

# # #

When Char opened her eyes she found herself sitting in an upright position in bed. She no longer heard the machines inside her room. There was a single light on. The glow was soft, relaxing. What bothered her was the cuff on her wrist attached to the bedframe. The steel clanked on the rail as she gave a useless tug of her arm.

He was asleep in a chair by the bed. It had been his voice she'd heard calling her name earlier.

She looked around and knew she was in a hospital room. The curtains were drawn closed across the window. She had no idea what time it was; if the sun or moon was out. "Hey, Benjamin!"

He sprang out of his chair, eyes open wide scanning the room. His mouth was open, and his breathing heavy. When he looked at Char, he settled down some, as if catching his breath. "You call me?"

"You were sleeping."

"Everything okay? You're awake. I should get the doctor," he said.

She held up her un-cuffed hand. "Wait. Not yet."

He moved closer to the bed. "Are you okay?"

"I'm thirsty."

"I can get you some water. I think."

"What's going on?"

"You don't remember?"

"I thought I'd killed myself," she said.

"You nearly had. I came in and found you hanging in your cell. We got the door open and cut you down. Why would you do that?"

"Why wouldn't I?"

Benjamin looked away. He didn't have an answer. She didn't suspect he would.

"I have nothing, Ben, and I'm being charged with a murder in a town I don't belong in. They can't do this to me," she said, and raised her cuffed arm as high as it would go. "I know we have no government, but this isn't justice. You were there. Broadhurst started it. He attacked us. Did you tell them that?"

"I told them exactly what happened."

"So why am I cuffed to a hospital bed? Why would you bother to save me? Just so I can serve some made up prison sentence for murders that were committed in self-defense? Does that even make sense to you?"

"You haven't been found guilty, Charlene."

"It's Char."

"There will be a trial. Jurors. You'll get a chan—"

"A what? A chance to tell my side of the story? I'm not from Arcadia, Ben. I know someone has to take the fall for this, for what happened. I don't think it should be me. I wasn't going to let it be me."

"Our patient is awake, I see." A woman in a white lab jacket entered the room. She held a clipboard. "How are you feeling?"

"Fine."

"She's thirsty," Benjamin said.

"Will you get her a glass of water, please?" The nametag on her coat read: Dr. Sophia Debes.

"I said, I'm fine."

"You don't want water?" Ben said.

"Please, Ben. Get her water. If she isn't thirsty now, she will be."

Ben left the room.

"How are you feeling, aside from fine?"

"Bruised."

"Your neck is black and blue. You're lucky to be alive. If the mayor's son hadn't found you when he did, you and I would never have met." She was young, with light brown hair worn up and a warming smile. She looked tired, as if she had worked multiple double shifts without much downtime in between.

Char wanted to tell the doctor that she wanted to be dead. She saw no point in sharing that much. She wasn't in the mood to be psychoanalyzed. "Am I all set? I mean, can I have my things, and a key," she shook her wrist, "and leave. I've had my fill of Arcadia. I think I like my chances on the road outside of your walls a lot better."

"I'm afraid that's not for me to decide, but I would like to check your vitals, if you don't mind." The doctor pulled the stethoscope off from around her neck.

Char thought about protesting. Instead, she let the doctor listen to her heart and lungs, flash a light into her eyes and take her pulse.

"Everything seems okay," she said.

Char didn't feel relieved. "What happens next?"

"I'll notify the sheriff that you're awake. I'm sure he'll be by in the morning. The two of you can discuss the next steps together," the doctor said. "Is there anything I can get for you? Are you hungry?"

Char might have been hungry, but wasn't sure. Regardless she wasn't sure she could eat. There wasn't much point in taking her anger out on the doctor. "I'm okay for now."

"I put some ice in the water," Benjamin said, coming back into the room.

"I'll be down the hall if you need anything else," Dr. Debes said.

Char nodded.

The doctor left the room.

"Want me to set the water down over here?" Ben pointed to the nightstand next to the bed.

Char held out her hand. "I'll take it."

"I have a straw."

Char removed the paper and sipped up ice cold water. It tasted wonderful. "So did your daddy assign you to keep an eye on me?"

Benjamin stood beside the bed, both hands on the rail. "I'm not on the clock. I told him I wanted to stay with you."

"What?" she said. "The way you're looking at me."

"It's nothing."

"It? If you are referring to an 'it,' then it is something. Tell me."

Ben could not look her in the eyes.

"I'm not fooling around here. What's going on?"

"Your friend, Sam? He, ah, he didn't make it."

Char felt deflated. She didn't want to be here, to be alive. Sam's death was proof that she didn't want any of this. She knew she was crying. She couldn't feel the tears. Her skin was numb, her muscles, her heart.

"I'm sorry," he said.

She stared at the thin white sheet over her legs. She was in a hospital gown. She hadn't even noticed earlier. Where were her clothes?

Why do I care about my clothing? she thought.

Tony was dead. Sam was dead.

"Where's Grace?"

"She is alive."

"I want to see her. She must be here."

Ben looked at the door.

"Is she down the hall? Please. Take me to her."

"She's not awake."

"I'll be quiet," Char said.

"She's in a coma."

Char struggled against the cuff. She yanked on the rail, gripped it with both hands and pulled. She heard someone screaming.

She was the one screaming.

"Char! Charlene!"

"I want to see her, Ben," she said.

"I can't. There's nothing I can do," he said, motioning to the handcuff.

"You don't have a key?" she said. "You do. You have a key!"

Ben fumbled a hand into his pocket. "I can get in trouble for this. Big trouble."

Char wanted to remind him that he was the mayor's son. She wasn't trying to escape. "I want to see my friend, Ben. Please."

He unfastened the lock on her wrist. "Are you okay to walk?"

"I'll manage," she said. He helped her out of bed. Her bare feet on cold linoleum sent a shiver up her spine.

They stepped out of the room.

Dr. Debes looked up from the nurse's station at the corner. "What are you doing?"

"We're going to visit Grace. Down the hall. We're not leaving the building," Ben said.

The doctor did not look happy.

Char turned away and let Ben lead her toward the room. It was three doors down. The door was open. Grace looked small and frail under the bed sheet. A machine beside her bed beeped. The woman was not cuffed to the rail. She wouldn't have been. She'd done nothing wrong except help Charlene.

Char approached the bed, stood next to her friend, and cried. Her shoulders shook as she tried to hold in sobs. "This wasn't our fault, Ben. It wasn't hers. She shouldn't be lying here like this."

She remembered the story Grace had shared with her about her daughter, Anna.

"I have to get out of here, Ben."

"This is a pretty good little hospital," he said.

"I don't mean out of this place, well, I guess I do, but I mean out of here, this town. Can you get me past the wall?"

Benjamin turned away from the bed and walked around to the foot. "I can't do that."

"What's going to happen to me? If they find me guilty of these killings, what is the punishment?" All she could think about is that sign out in front of Arcadia. No stealing. No fighting. No murder. It didn't get clearer than that.

When Benjamin refused to answer, Char felt despair settle in.

"Are they planning to have a funeral for Tony, for Sam?"

"I don't know."

Chapter 19

Carl Trieste introduced himself as he set a briefcase down on the table. He reached across and shook Char's hand.

"How are you doing?"

"I told them I wasn't interested in being represented by an attorney," Char said.

Trieste had military-style cropped white hair; buzzed on the sides and a little longer on top. He couldn't be over five-eight, one hundred and forty-five pounds. He wore glasses that magnified bright blue eyes, and suspenders that clearly kept his trouser up around his thin waist.

He unsnapped the locks on the briefcase. "They told me this. It's why I asked permission to talk to you. I know because of where the world is right now that something like a trial must seem trivial, but Arcadia is serious about upholding laws. This town is trying very hard to make things as normal as possible. The only way to get things back on track is by having and abiding by laws."

"Are you on my side?"

"I am interested in defending you against the charges that have been filed," he said.

"Were you a lawyer before the infected?"

He seemed to think about the question. "The infected?"

"Before the zombies."

"Yes. I was. A pretty good one, too."

"I acted in self-defense. I am not a citizen of this town. I just want to leave."

"That's not how it works."

"They can't keep me here," she said. It sounded hollow, empty, because she was sitting in a locked room, and after her meeting with Trieste, she'd be escorted back to a cell. Despite her protests, they were keeping her.

"If there hadn't of been an apocalypse, okay, and you were in, let's say, another country, and you were accused of committing crimes, you would stand trial in that country, even if you thought it was unfair and wanted to leave."

"I'm not in another country. I'm in my country. This is still America. I still have rights."

"Following that line of logic, then so did the people in the Bent Elbow," he said.

Char folded her arms.

"Do you want me to leave?"

Char stared at the attorney. She thought for a few moments about what she wanted to say, before answering him. "I want you to help get me out of here."

Trieste smiled. "I would like that. We have a lot to do in a short period of time. Your trial has been set for two days from now."

"Two days!"

"Docket's not exactly full. In fact, between now and your trial, there is nothing else on the docket."

"What about picking a jury? Doesn't that take time?"

"We're handling jury selection tomorrow morning. I want to be able to spend the rest of today, and after jury selection tomorrow interviewing witnesses." Trieste removed a legal pad and two pens from the briefcase and began scribbling down notes.

"This is crazy." Char pushed her fingers into her hair and along her scalp. "What are my chances of getting out of this? You think I've got a chance of being let go?"

Trieste set down his pen and leaned back in his chair. "This is a quiet town. Real quiet. People are not used to seeing or hearing about the kind of thing that happened at the bar. Most of these people were here right after, and some even before the zombies took over. This is shocking."

"So I don't have much sympathy from the townspeople?"

Trieste shook his head. "And to compound matters, the people you allegedly killed were suppliers."

"You mean raiders."

He shrugged. "They brought the town supplies. Where and how they got the items isn't what's going to be on trial."

"I am." Char ground her teeth. "Well. I killed them. If the situation came up again, I'd do it again. They got what they deserved."

"It's obvious to me that you and Frank Broadhurst knew each other. So, let's go back, okay? Let's start at the beginning. I want you to walk me through everything. Start with how the two of you met."

"What do you want to know?"

"One thing that was brought to my attention. The story going around is that you may have robbed Broadhurst, stole a truck with supplies meant for Arcadia."

"Is that a question?"

"Did you?"

Anyone who knew the truth was dead, or not in Arcadia, she thought. "I don't know anything about a truck with supplies."

"Because if we could send a team to recover the truck, it could buy some of that sympathy you were wondering about."

It was important not to think about the now, but to concentrate on the future. She did not want to wind up in prison. She did not feel hopeful that a sentence could be avoided. The truck was tucked away. If she gave that up, when the time came, she'd have nothing. "I don't know anything about a supply truck."

Trieste looked at her for a moment. She didn't think he believed her.

"You're sure?"

"Positive. Next question."

# # #

Char stood next to Carl Trieste just outside the courtroom. The nameplate slid into place on the large wood doors read: Hon. Rachel Walton.

Char hated how normal these people pretended everything was. It made everything surreal. Inside the Arcadia dome it was as if the world had never changed. That should be a good thing. She struggled to appreciate their progress, or lack of regression.

There were plenty of people milling about in the halls. She guessed they were waiting for the doors to open. Everyone probably wanted a good seat. Why wouldn't they. This had to be some of the best entertainment they've had in years.

Trieste rested a hand on her shoulder. "How are you doing?"

"I'm sick to my stomach," she said.

"Are you okay?"

"I will be." They'd talked more last night. According to Trieste, he was happy with the jurors selected. It was a mix of men and women of varied ages. She didn't think it would matter. He'd also had a chance to talk with witnesses from the Bent Elbow. They'd gone over her statement numerous times. As normal as they wanted their legal system to be, no depositions had been taken, and there had not been any discovery. Trieste was not aware of what the district attorney planned to ask, what evidence they possessed, or what witnesses they'd call.

"What happens? I mean, if we lose this. What should I expect?" Char knew how murder worked in the U.S. pre-apocalypse. Even at fourteen she was aware of high profile trials that took place. Media made sure people were aware. It just never seemed like prison terms were consistent. Some went to prison for twenty-five years for possession of weed, while manslaughter cases landed a defendant seven to ten years behind bars. It all seemed to depend on which state and city you were tried in.

"We have time to talk about that," he said.

"I'd like to be prepared."

"I don't plan on losing, but if we do, if you are sentenced to a prison term it could be anywhere from ten to life, depending on the counts against you. There are two counts of Second Degree Murder, and two counts of Voluntary Manslaughter. Worse case, we will spend the time during the trial to plant the seed of a self-defense manslaughter case. If the jury agrees, you could get one to six years and expect to be out in as little as three."

Three years. "That can't happen."

"Don't get nervous. We have our one ace in the hole," he said.

Benjamin. He was not just there; he'd been a part of the fight.

"Have you got experience with murder cases since Arcadia became its own country?" She chewed on a fingernail.

"Not murder, no. There haven't been any killings in the last three years."

"Great."

"But I tried a pretty big case at the end of spring. A gang had entered Arcadia, one and two at a time. They were real sneaky about it. Our sheriff noticed what was going on. They tried to rob some of our storage units, but the police were ready for them."

"You defended them?"

"They were innocent until proven guilty," he said.

"And you won?"

"I lost. The Morales Gang is in prison now."

"How long did they get?"

"Most of them received a ten year term. The leader, Gonzales Morales, he's doing fifteen with no time off for good behavior."

The door to the courtroom opened. An officer waved them in.

They were led toward the front, through a swinging gate and sat at a table on the left. Trieste set down his briefcase and made a show of unlocking it and removing items from inside.

Char turned to watch spectators file into the room and fill the seats. It became quickly apparent it was going to be standing room only for the show.

She pushed fingertips to her temples. It didn't stop the spinning she felt. She closed her eyes, hoping she wouldn't get dizzy and spill out of the chair.

"Char? Are you alright?"

She nodded, but stopped, afraid the movement would jar her brain loose. "I'm getting a headache."

"I can see if anyone has aspirin."

"I'll manage," she said.

The District Attorney entered the courtroom from a back door near where the judge would sit. He wore a dark grey suit that almost matched dark hair with a splash of gray along the sides and top. He approached them and held out his hand.

"Carl."

"Ed."

They shook hands.

"And you're Charlene McKinney? I'm Ed Connors. The D.A."

"Charmed," she said, refusing to shake the offered hand.

He took a seat across from them, his files and folders already arranged on the prosecution table.

Although the trial had not even begun, Char was anxious for it just to be over.

"All rise for the Honorable Judge Rachel Walton," the officer who had opened the courtroom doors said. He stood by the judge's bench with his hands folded together in front of him.

Everyone stood.

The door Ed Connors emerged from moments ago, opened again. This time a black woman in a black judge's robe entered. The red collar of a blouse worn underneath was visible. She took her seat behind the bench. "Please, be seated," she said.

"Court is in session," the officer said, as everyone sat and adjusted getting comfortable.

"I don't see Ben," Char said, whispering to her attorney.

"I'm sure he'll be here," Trieste said.

"What if he's not?"

"We'll have him subpoenaed."

"You have those?"

"I don't know. We've never needed them. One way or another, Ben will sit on that witness stand."

Chapter 20

Opening arguments were brief. Ed Connors spoke for less than fifteen minutes. Char's attorney talked for twenty. The twelve jurors appeared to listen intently to both attorneys. Char couldn't gauge their reactions to anything stated.

"Prosecution, are you ready to proceed?" Judge Walton said.

"We are, your honor," Connor said.

"You may call your first witness."

Ed Connors stood by his table and shuffled through some documents. He took a moment to bang them lightly on the table and evened them up sliding his palm over the top before setting them back down. "Prosecution calls to the witness stand, Benjamin Forti."

Char sucked in a breath and held it. She turned around to see if he'd entered the courtroom. The door to the hallway opened. Benjamin was led in by an officer. He was walked down the center aisle, head down as if unwilling to look Char in the eye.

Carl Trieste set a hand on her thigh. There was nothing sexual about the gesture. She knew he was merely trying silently to ask that she control her reaction. The jury would be watching. They'd see everything she did, every expression she made.

"He's testifying for them," she said. She thought she might be whispering. She worried that everyone heard her question.

He patted her thigh, a lame attempt at reining her in.

Benjamin took a seat in the witness box. He was dressed in his police uniform.

Ed Connors went through preliminary questioning, establishing that he knew both the victims and the suspect in question, that he was with them at the Bent Elbow on the night of the murders, and that he had witnessed the events from start to finish.

Benjamin's answers were simple *yes* responses. They required little else.

Char willed him to look up at her. His eyes rarely looked away from his own lap. He didn't make eye contact with the prosecutor or the jurors seated in the box to his left. His answers were weak and barely audible. She wrapped an arm across her stomach, she didn't like the way he testified. Something was about to happen.

"And, Mr. Forti, can you tell us about what happened that night in the Bent Elbow, starting with when Olivia Ragone, Jason Iamuzzi, and Frank Broadhurst entered the bar? In your own words, Mr. Forti. Please." Connors stood with his back to the defense. He stared directly at the jurors while addressing Benjamin.

Char hadn't known the names of the other people with Broadhurst. It didn't change anything for her. If put in the same, or even a similar situation, she'd still have killed them.

Benjamin recounted events truthfully. Char listened to every word said as if someone narrated while the events replayed in her mind. It was almost like sitting in a movie theater. She didn't cringe, or close her eyes. She felt no remorse.

"Olivia Ragone died from a gunshot wound. Did you see who shot Ms. Ragone?"

Benjamin nodded his head.

"You have to respond verbally," Connors said. "Did you see who shot Ms. Ragone?"

"Yes."

"And was it the defendant, Ms. McKinney."

Carl Trieste stood up. "Objection. Leading."

Judge Walton nodded. "Sustained."

"Can you identify the person who shot Ms. Ragone?" Connors said.

"Yes."

Connors waited a moment, but when Benjamin did not continue, he said, "And is that person in this room today?"

"Yes."

"Can you point to that person for the jury?"

Benjamin pointed in Char's direction.

"Are you identifying Ms. McKinney?" Connors said.

"Yes, but Ms. Ragone had pulled out a knife."

"Had Ms. Ragone attacked the defendant with the knife?"

"No, but—"

Ed Connors did not let Benjamin finish. "Mr. Forti, after the defendant shot and killed Ms. Ragone, did there come a point when you informed Ms. McKinney to stop?"

Benjamin pressed his chin to his chest.

Char adjusted the way she sat in the chair, leaning forward, her ribs to the table.

"I didn't hear you answer, Mr. Forti."

"Repeat the question, please."

"Isn't it true that, not only did you tell Ms. McKinney to stop, but that you told the defendant multiple times to let you handle the situation?"

It was one of the few times that she caught him looking up. He didn't look at her. He looked at the jury. She wished she could see his eyes.

"Mr. Forti?"

"I did tell her to stop," Benjamin said. He looked at his attorney. Their eyes locked. "The situation was still volatile, but—"

"And did she stop?"

"No, but Broadhurst still had—"

"And how many times did you tell Ms. McKinney that you would handle this, that you wanted her to stop so you could handle the situation?"

"You are not letting me answ—"

"Answer the question asked, Mr. Forti."

Trieste stood up. "I object, your honor. Prosecution is badgering his own witness."

"It's my witness," Connors said.

"Overruled, Mr. Trieste. Mr. Connors, if you ask your witness a question, I would like to hear his entire answer, if you don't mind," Judge Walton said. "Proceed."

"Read back the last question, please?" Connors said to the person taking notes. There was no stenographer.

"And how many times did you tell Ms. McKinney that you would handle this, that you wanted her to stop so you could handle the situation?"

"Thank you," Connors said, then turned to his client and repeated the question.

"A couple."

"How many times is a couple?" Connors said.

"I'm not sure."

Connors turned to look at the jurors. "More than once?"

"Yes."

"Five times?"

"I don't think so."

"Between two and four times?"

"I don't think I said stop, or let me handle this four times."

"Between two and three times?"

Benjamin nodded.

"You actually need to answer," Connors said. "Did you tell Ms. McKinney to stop and let you handle the situation between two and three times that evening?"

"That sounds about right," he said.

"Did she know you were a deputy? That you are a public figure with some authority in Arcadia?"

Char hated seeing Ben testify. She could tell he did not want to be up there, that he might be forced to testify. She figured the mayor was behind it, or possibly the sheriff. She couldn't say anything though. Everything asked and answered so far had been nothing but the truth.

"She knew."

"How do you know she knew?"

"She'd seen me in my uniform, I imagine. I'd mentioned it to her, as well, I guess."

"Objection. Calls for speculation," Trieste said.

"Sustained," Judge Walton said.

"Did the defendant ever see you in your uniform?"

"Yes."

"Do you wear a badge on your uniform?"

"Yes."

"So she knew you were a deputy. She heard you tell her to stop and let you handle the fight. And yet, she didn't listen to your commands."

"Objection," Trieste said. "Counsel is merely summarizing."

"Do you have a question for your witness, Mr. Connors?" Judge Walton said.

"Just a few more."

Connors enjoyed the drama. It was evident. He was into the theatrics. Char wanted to punch him the face. Even in the midst of an apocalypse people strived for personal success. She figured this guy wanted to win cases to vie for the mayor's seat during the next election. It was the only motivation she could fathom for why he acted like such an asshole.

"Did you then witness Ms. McKinney stab Frank Broadhurst?"

"I did."

"Where did she stab him?"

"The chest. But he was holding Charlene's —Ms. McKinney's friend hostage."

"Hostage?"

"Broadhurst had Sam by the head, was threatening to snap his neck." Benjamin sounded angry, and spoke for the first time with animation. He sat forward with his hands up, arms out, and trying to convey what happened with his actions.

"And this was when you commanded Ms. McKinney to stop and let you handle the situation."

"I didn't command her," Benjamin said.

"Did you, or did you not to tell Ms. McKinney to stop, and let you handle the situation?"

Trieste stood up. "Objection. Asked and answered."

"Sustained. Move on, Counselor."

Connors pursed his lips. Being chastised didn't bode well for him. "Did Ms. McKinney listen to you when you told her to stop and let you handle the situation?"

"No."

"Isn't it true that right after you told her to stop, and stand down, that she attacked Broadhurst and stabbed him in the chest?"

"Yes."

"Did he die when she stabbed him in the chest?"

"Objection," Trieste said. "We've not be given any supporting evidence to show Benjamin Forti's medical background."

"Sustained."

Connors smiled. "Do you believe Frank Broadhurst was dead when Ms. McKinney stabbed him in the chest?"

"He could have been."

"Did Ms. McKinney believe Frank Broadhurst was dead after she stabbed him in the chest?"

"Objection, calls for speculation."

"Sustained," Judge Walton said.

"How many times did Ms. McKinney stab Frank Broadhurst in the chest?"

"I don't know."

"Was it more than once?"

"Yes."

"More than five times?"

"I don't know."

"Less than five times?"

"I'm not sure. I can't be positive."

"If I told you that Frank Broadhurst was stabbed at least seven times, would that sound reasonable?"

"I don't know."

"He was. He was stabbed seven times."

Trieste banged a fist on the table as he jumped to his feet. "Objection. Counsel is testifying."

"Sustained."

Chapter 21

The two day murder trial was over, the jury deliberating.

Char sat Indian style on a bed without sheets or a blanket in her cell. She stared at the grey cinder walls. Outside thunder boomed. She could hear the wind whine as it whipped through the town. A storm seemed fitting; matched her mood. She did not think she'd have long to stew. The jury would be quick to render a decision.

Carl Trieste informed her that Sam and Tony had been cremated. They didn't bury people inside the walls of Arcadia. He promised she'd receive the urns with the ashes as soon as they were available. She wished she'd had one more chance to see them. Saying goodbye to a box filled with their remains just didn't seem like it would be the same.

Her attorney indicated that there was no change in Grace's condition. She was still alive, breathing on her own, but remained in a coma. Char figured the bangs on the head from the ride inside the trailer didn't help. She'd been certain her friend already suffered from a concussion. Getting cracked in the head at the Bent Elbow probably only exacerbated the original injury.

She hated the loneliness she felt. Entering the town, the mayor, the sheriff, and even the priestess had fawned over them. She wasn't surprised no one came to see her, but that didn't make it hurt less.

Where was Ben?

She thought, maybe hoped, that he would see if she was all right, or if she needed anything. The last time she'd seen him was when he testified against her in the court. It felt like weeks ago. It felt like she'd been sitting and staring at nothing for weeks. It may have been for days. She had some idea of time by the food trays brought, and taken away untouched. There was dinner, breakfast, lunch, and just moments ago her dinner tray was removed.

She wasn't hungry.

The deputies didn't seem to care if she ate or not.

A clap of thunder sounded like it had erupted directly over the City Hall. Without windows she could only imagine the flashes of lightning that must be like white fire finger-stepping across the sky.

Dispatch didn't like thunder. Char hoped that he was okay, that he'd met up with Tony's horse and the two were far from the storm.

Although she couldn't see them, outside her cell she could hear two deputies talking.

"You are missing the point," one said. "In zombie movies, the epidemic starts slow. Like one or two people are infected, and then they bite one or two people, and those four bite more, ya know? And so the virus spreads slowly. The military, they got time to get a handle on things before it's outta control. But in the real world, everybody and their grandmother got one of them flu shots. Think about that. Everyone turned into a freakin' zombie at about the same time. You know how crazy it was."

"You think it's going to settle down even more?" the other deputy said.

"I figure, it's gotta. The zombies seem to starve to death. Well —the ones outside Arcadia, anyway. Unless they're freshly turned, they're slow as shit."

"We hole up here a few more years, and maybe everything will get restored back to normal," the second deputy said.

"Be nice, but I like it here. Everyone is pretty cool. We take care of each other. . ." the first deputy said.

"Except for a murder now and then," the second deputy said.

"I don't even mind that. As long as it ain't too often. We're a lot like the U.S. as a country, ya know? We gotta patrol our borders better. We can't be letting aliens in left and right. Eventually they'll destroy what we've built. We got a prisoner that's proof of that."

Char fell back onto the mattress. She still had a pillow. She put it over her head and pressed the sides tight against her ears.

She didn't want to listen to them talk anymore. She didn't care what they had to say.

Closing her eyes seemed like the best escape. She didn't know if she could fall asleep, but wanted to try.

As she welcomed the darkness, the steady sound of her heart beating, and the solitude, she thought she missed something.

Sleep was coming.

She knew she was drifting.

Someone had said something important, though.

She just didn't know what, or when it was said.

# # #

Char was on her knees. Large raindrops fell from a black sky. Soaked, and shivering from the cold, she clawed at the ground scooping mud away in search of something she'd buried in the woods. Her fingers were bent and cramped like claws.

From every direction infected closed in on her.

They stumbled forward, moaning that hollow moan that filled her with fear.

She hated their moaning.

She hated the infected.

If she stood up, there'd be nowhere to run. She was surrounded.

She concentrated on digging. What she looked for was here. It had to be. She just couldn't remember what it was she hoped to find.

Thunder echoed in her ears. She thought her ear drums might pop.

The infected were so close. Despite the wind that whipped about around her, and despite the rain, she could smell them.

The infected were rank, raw with decay.

Inside the hole she'd dug, her fingertips scraped across something that was not muddy earth.

She'd found it, whatever it was.

She almost screamed with joy!

She did scream.

Not because she'd found what had been buried, but because they had her. . .the infected were falling onto her.

She lost her balance, overpowered by the infected attacking, and fell into the hole she'd dug. The hole was several feet deep. She crashed on the bottom, surprised that the hole had been so long, and wide, and deep.

The infected did not fall in after her. They gathered around the edges of the rectangular shaped hole and reached down for her, their fingers curling and uncurling in a desperate attempt to grasp any part of her body.

At least she was safe.

They weren't coming in after her.

The rain fell faster, harder.

The bottom of the hole began filling with water. It rose to over her feet. It didn't stop when it passed her knees.

She paced around on the bottom of the hole. The reprieve of feeling safe was short lived as the water rose to her waist.

The infected faces oozed loose flesh. It splashed into the deepening pool of rainwater that she stood in. She looked into glazed over eyes. There was nothing human left in them.

Tony had been wrong.

They were not infected. They were zombies.

The rain fell relentlessly from above, and the water levels continued to rise. Char couldn't touch bottom. She had to tread water.

Zombies didn't like the rain.

Why were they here? Why had they come for her? Why hadn't they run off to hide?

She was swimming now. The water, like an elevator, lifted her closer to the outstretched arms and reaching hands of monsters that desired only to tear her apart, limb by limb.

Plugging her nose, she went under water. She kicked and swam for the bottom. There had to be an exit, another way out. It was down here at the bottom of the hole. She knew it.

Her lungs burned.

She wouldn't be able to hold her breath for much longer.

Feeling along the bottom of the hole she knew she'd find, if anything, a drain plug. Once pulled, the water would recede. She'd be safe.

There was no way she could stay under. Not even for a second more. She kicked off the bottom and swam toward the surface. The moon was bright above the shimmy of the water, but she could see little else.

Her head popped up out of the water, and while she planned to suck in a breath of air and dive back down, it wasn't what happened.

Fingers twisted in her hair and yanked her up and out of the grave size pool.

She screamed.

They had her.

She was on her back, struggling. She kicked and punched at the zombies as they closed in on her. They said her name, over and over. At first it came in a moan, "Charrrrrr. Chhhhhaaaarrrr."

It changed, becoming more high pitched, and less gravelly sounding. "Chhaarr! Charrr!"

They had mouths open, teeth exposed and were ready to bite. .

.

"Char! Char!"

She screamed for help, for someone, anyone to help!

She sat up. Eyes wide open. She was alone in her prison cell. There were no infected around her.

No one calling her name.

Shivering, she hugged herself.

Outside, the thunder continued to disrupt the night.

She was hungry. Cold, alone, scared, and suddenly very hungry.

Chapter 22

"All rise." The deputy stood in front of the judge's bench.

The back door opened and Judge Rachel Walton entered the courtroom. Char found it difficult to regulate her breathing. She took small, quick breaths. She didn't want to hyperventilate.

Carl Trieste stood statue-still beside her. Across from him was the prosecutor, Ed Connor. Across from him twelve jurors filled the box. Char wanted to look at them to see if she could guess the verdict before it was announced. Their faces would have to betray a truth. She just couldn't bring herself to look. If they maintained eye contact she'd know they'd found her guilty. Even though she was minutes away from hearing her fate she wasn't ready to see it in the jurors' eyes.

"Would Counsel and the Defendant remain standing? Everyone else, please, be seated," Judge Walton said.

Char felt defeated, regardless of the outcome. She'd made it so far to wind up a defendant in a murder trial. She'd thought it before, but surreal seemed to have no boundaries. She forced herself to look up, to make direct eye contact with the judge.

"Would the foreman of the jury please stand?" Judge Walton said.

A woman rose. She was seated in the first seat, first row. She held a piece of paper in her hand.

"Have the jurors reached a verdict in Charlene McKinney vs the People of Arcadia?" Judge Walton said.

"We have, your honor," she said.

Char almost held her breath. The moment of truth was before her. She did not want to hear the verdict.

"For the count of second degree murder in the death of Olivia Ragone, what does the jury find?"

"Not guilty, your honor."

"For the count of second degree murder in the death of Frank Broadhurst, what does the jury find?"

Char felt hope well up inside her chest. She knew her eyes were open wide.

"Not guilty, your honor."

Char let out a long sigh. She lowered her head. She began to cry. Carl Trieste placed a hand on her shoulder. "It's not over, dear. Stay strong."

Not over? The jury had just found her not guilty for killing both Olivia Ragone and Frank Broadhurst.

Judge Walton was staring at Char. When Char regained composure, the judge returned her attention to the jury's foreman. "For the count of voluntary manslaughter in the death of Olivia Ragone, what does the jury find?"

Char had forgotten about the manslaughter charges. The nightmare seemed to have no end.

"Not guilty, your honor."

Char wanted to scream. She couldn't take much more. She'd rolled her hands into tight fists. Her fingernails bit into her palms.

"For the count of voluntary manslaughter in the death of Frank Broadhurst, what does the jury find?"

"Guilty, your honor."

# # #

"Charlene?"

She was curled up on her bed facing the cinderblock wall. She hated that a deputy sat in a folding chair outside her cell watching her. It wasn't the deputy calling her name though. She knew that voice.

She wasn't turning around. She didn't want to talk to Ben, much less see him.

"Char? Are you awake?"

She squeezed her eyes shut tight. He couldn't see her face, but it didn't matter. She tried to will him to leave.

"Char?"

It wasn't working. "I don't want to talk to you."

"I know you're mad at me."

She spun around, and sat up. Ben jumped back from the bars. "You're damn right I'm mad at you. What was that in there the other day? I'm going to prison, Ben. They're sending me to prison."

"They told me I had to testify. I was a witness. You heard the testimony of the witnesses after me. We all told the same story. All I did was tell the truth." Ben wrapped both hands around bars and pressed his face between them.

"You made me sound like a psychopath, Ben."

"The jury didn't see it that way. You were only charged with one count."

"It was self-defense. You were there. We were attacked. Broadhurst pulled a gun on us. You can leave. I don't want to talk to you."

Ben didn't move.

"Leave, Ben. Go be a cop somewhere. I got Barney Fife over there to keep me company."

The deputy stirred in his folding chair.

"I wanted to say I'm sorry it played out this way."

"Played out this way? Like it's a game? Like my life is part of some game? You know what you can do, Ben? You can go fuck yourself. You. Your father. The sheriff." No prison was going to hold her. She was going to find a way to escape and take it. She'd get outside the walls that fortified Arcadia and keep going. No one would come after her. There wouldn't be a posse on her tail. The assholes living here wouldn't know how to survive beyond the confines of their community.

Ben looked away as he stepped back from the bars. His hands still held onto them. "I talked with your attorney. He's not giving up on this case. He's going to file appeals."

"It's not a real court, Ben. This isn't even the real world here. You guys are living in a fantasy land."

Ben let go of the bars and took another step back.

"You don't have the power, the authority to lock me up for even a day. This is bullshit!"

He turned around and slowly walked toward the door.

"It's bullshit, Ben!"

He was gone.

She stared at the bars where he had stood. Part of her did not want to chase him away. There was no way she'd ever forgive him for testifying against her. Right was right. What he'd done was wrong. If he couldn't understand that, then she had no room in her life for him, no room for forgiveness.

Too wound up to lie back down, Char paced around the corners of her cell. Her arms were stiff at her sides, hands balled into fists. She ground her teeth.

There was no way the prison could hold her. She knew she'd find a way to escape. Climb a wall, scale a fence, sneak out in a delivery truck. She'd seen enough prison escape movies with her father. Her favorite was Stephen King's *Shawshank Redemption*. Hell, if she had to tunnel through a sewer drain filled with shit and piss to come out on the opposite side of Arcadia, she would. Whatever it took to get free. If she was lucky, the opportunity would present itself sooner and she could move on and be done with this ass-backwards town forever.

# # #

Char wanted to refuse breakfast on principle. She didn't. Her stomach churned. Going without eating only punished her. The deputies didn't care if she ate or not. They knew she'd never starve to death before being transported from the holding cell to prison. As long as she didn't hang herself, they could give two shits.

The scrambled eggs weren't bad. A little more salt would have been nice, but she didn't ask for any.

Rebecca Bowman walked into the area pulling along a small case with wheels by the handle and stopped when she reached the doorway. "Is it okay if I talk with you?"

Char shrugged. "If you don't mind me eating while you talk?"

Rebecca smiled. "Of course not."

A silence fell between them. Char figured if the priestess had something to say, she'd begin the conversation. As far as she was concerned, there wasn't much to say about anything.

"I talked with the sheriff," Rebecca said.

"About?" Char knew better than to get her hopes up. The judge sentenced her to three years. The sheriff couldn't get that overturned.

"They are transporting you late this afternoon."

"They sent you to tell me?"

"I received permission to give you a tattoo before you go. If a tattoo is what you wanted," Rebecca said.

"A tattoo? I don't know what you're talking about."

Rebecca came closer to the bars, wheeling her case along with her. "I want to give you a dreamcatcher tattoo. I will bless the ink before I start. Prison can be a horrible experience. I believe the tattoo can help you, protect you from things you fear, give you something to draw strength from."

Char looked down at her meal. It was half gone. She could not eat anymore. "I've never had a tattoo."

"It hurts a bit. Won't lie about that, but rarely is it as bad as people think." Rebecca smiled. It calmed and soothed Char. Maybe it was the priestess' face that chased away her anxiety. Char stared into Rebecca's eyes watched the irises expand and dance around the pupil like solar flares off the sun.

Char wasn't really sure how she felt about it. "And the tattoo machine, it's in that case?"

"It is."

She took a sip of apple juice and set her plastic cup down on the tray. "Why do you want me to have a tattoo?"

"I just—"

"I mean, why do you care?"

Rebecca stood in front of the bars and squatted down, so that they were eye level. "I've been to where you are going. I was not an inmate, if that's what you're thinking. I went to visit someone. I helped with some of the...mechanics of the operation. There's no point in sugar coating it. The Cog is an evil and vile place. I was at the trial. I heard all of the testimony given and I think the jury got this one wrong. They don't understand what it's like outside of Arcadia."

"They heard how Broadhurst and his people kidnapped my friends! They heard that he drew a gun on us at the bar! I shouldn't be in here." Char did not want to rehash this every time someone talked to her about the case. If felt pointless. It didn't matter if Rebecca disagreed with the jury. Nothing would change.

"I won't be coming to visit you."

"I wasn't expecting you to," Char said.

"Let me give you this tattoo. For courage, and strength, and to remember that you are not alone."

"But I am alone. I'll be serving my time alone, and like you just told me, you won't be coming to visit. I don't want your tattoo. Thanks, but no thanks." Char slapped her food tray off the edge of her bed. It rattled and clanked on the cement floor.

"You're going to clean that up!" The deputy was on his feet, pointing a finger at her.

Rebecca stood up and turned around. She folded her hand on the case's handle and started to walk away.

Char needed to control her temper. Her anger was justified, but shouldn't have been directed at the priestess. "Wait."

Rebecca stopped.

"Where were you thinking of putting it?"

# # #

Char straddled a chair, facing backwards. She'd pulled her hair down to the side, exposing the back of her neck. Rebecca stood beside her.

Char watched in silence as the priestess blessed the ink. The prayer of protection was poetic and impacting. Rebecca dipped the needle into black ink and told her to sit still.

The tattoo gun vibrated and hummed. The needle was drawn across her skin. The pain was sharp and continuous. It hurt most when passing over the bone of her spine.

"How are you doing?"

"It's not terrible," Char said.

Char stared at her toes and the cement floor and thought about as little as possible while Rebecca infused blessed ink forever onto her body.

"You're doing great. Just keep holding still like this and we'll be done in no time, but if you need a break, let me know."

Char winced now and then. The outlining hurt more than the coloring and shading. That just felt like being scratched. Every so often Rebecca rubbed ointment over the skin, and wiped away blood with a paper towel.

The pain came when they were nearly three hours into the inking, and Rebecca was still stretching sore skin to go over area that now felt bruised and raw. "We're just about done."

When Rebecca finished she gave Char a hand mirror, and then held another up behind Char.

Char angled her mirror so that she could see into the mirror in Rebecca's hand.

The dreamcatcher was big. Round. The web inside the ring was intricate and symmetrical. Coming off the bottom were three different feathers. They were grey and white and looked real.

"The feathers?"

"They are of an eagle. They symbolize freedom. The eagle is a predator. It is a bird known for being strong, courageous and cunning. There were many injured eagles held in captivity because they could not fly, or were unable to survive on their own after an injury. An eagle that can fly, that is capable of surviving on its own would never allow itself to be held captive for long. First chance it was given, it would soar away."

The words were not lost on Char. "I kind of wish we didn't do it on the back of my neck."

"Why is that?"

"Because I won't be able to see it."

"You don't need to see it for the powers it possesses to work. You know it's there. That is enough," she said.

"Powers?"

"You may find that times when you feel most alone, when you need to concentrate on happy things, the magic inside the ink will help you. It may lead you."

"Lead me?"

"It takes time to get used to," Rebecca said, "and the energy isn't apparent to everyone. With you, I think the energy will be not just apparent, but obvious."

Char had no idea what the priestess was talking about. She kind of understood why Sheriff Huber gave the woman room. She was a bit more than slightly odd. "Thank you for the tattoo. It's beautiful."

"I am going to bandage it for now. I am leaving you with some ointment. You apply it a few times a day. Do your best to keep it clean. This is blessed ink, so I know you will not need to worry about it getting infected."

"Maybe we'll see each other again someday," Char said, purposefully not saying when she got out of prison. Because it wouldn't be in three years, and once she was out, there was no way she was coming back, not even to visit with the priestess.

Chapter 23

Sheriff Gus Huber and Deputy Chris Olek stood inside the holding cell with Char.

"Turn around and place your hands behind your back, please," Olek said.

The cuffs rolled over her wrists and snapped into place, locking.

"You do what's asked of you, stay out of other people's business and listen to the warden and his guards, and your time down there will fly by," Huber said.

Down there? "Where is the prison? I didn't see one when we walked around town that one day I spent as a free person here."

"Be there soon enough," Huber said.

"This it? The two of you taking me?" She said, as they led her out of the cell and toward a door to the back of the City Hall building.

"Deputy Olek could have handled it on his own. I hope you don't mind that I am here," Huber said.

Char had secretly wished Ben had come, too. She hated that she felt that way. She was stronger than that, and he didn't deserve her attention. "If I make a break for it?"

"We'll be forced to shoot you."

She shrugged. "Might be the better alternative."

"Three years is the sentence. You be good, you could be out in a year and a half," Huber said.

"Be good?" She repeated what the sheriff said just to see if it still sounded as absurd. It did. "Yes, sir. I'll behave."

"An attitude is not going to help you," Huber said.

"No? That's too bad. An attitude is about the only thing Arcadia hasn't stolen from me," she said.

"When you get to The Cog, you might change your mind," Olek said.

He walked behind Char. She couldn't see his face, but she imagined a smile playing at the corners of his mouth. She stopped walking, and threw her head back.

The crunch made a distinct sound.

"Son of a bitch. She broke my nose, sheriff," Olek said.

Huber grabbed Char's arm with one hand, and backhanded her across the face with the other. She fell to the floor.

Olek stepped forward and kicked Char in the ribs.

"Enough, Olek," Huber said.

"But my nose," he said.

Char saw blood spill from between fingers as his hand cupped his face.

"Why do you have to make this difficult, McKinney?" Huber said. "Olek, go see Dr. Debes. I'll take the prisoner myself and check up on you when I get back. Charlene, get up. Come on, now. Get on your feet."

"Yeah, alright," Olek said, stepped forward again, and kicked Char in the side. She grunted and rolled over. "I'll see ya back at the office, I guess."

Huber bent down and helped Char to her feet. "I thought he might do that. I told you to get up," he said.

"Very thoughtful," she said.

"Don't turn this on me. You broke his nose. You can hate me, hate Arcadia, but it's not a bad place. When you were in the wild, you had to do what needed to be done to survive. I get that. This is a civilized town, McKinney. I warned the mayor about letting people from outside in. Everyone else here is living a pretty good, if not simplistic life. No one is bothering them. But they aren't killing people, either."

"Broadhurst pulled a gun on us."

"I'm not going to re-argue your case."

As they started to walk down the street, Char said, "You have a car or are we walking there?"

"You see any cars?" Huber had her by the arm, staying a safe distance to her left.

She did not like the idea of being paraded around.

"Remember how you and your friends asked the mayor about the power in Arcadia?" Huber said. When Char kept quiet, he continued. "The prison is called The Cog. It's where we get the power. It's down in the bowels of a mineshaft. There are multiple generators. They operate on a combination of converted garbage, the heat from the earth, which is called geothermal power, and manpower. I don't know all the scientific shit, but it comes down to kilowatts if I'm not mistaken. We've got a gifted engineer who designed, built, and runs this thing twenty-four seven. As his reward, he's also the prison warden."

"So it's slave labor," Char said.

"It is prison labor."

"In a mine shaft," she said.

"One way in and out," he said, as if he'd read her thoughts of escape and wanted to thwart them on the spot.

"Sounds claustrophobic," she said.

"It sure as hell is," he said.

# # #

On the edge of town was a hole in a mountain. The wall surrounding Arcadia was built around it. Two prison guards with rifles stood by the entrance.

"You're shitting me," Char said.

"You think I was kidding?"

"Kind of, yeah," she said.

"This is my last attempt at helping you. Do as you're told. Keep your nose down, and fly under the radar. What's below is like no prison you've ever seen before," the sheriff said. He greeted the guards with a nod.

"How big is this prison?" she said.

"Huge."

Char sighed. "I meant how many prisoners?"

"Prisoners? With you, fifteen."

"Fifteen? You have fifteen people running enough power to generators to supply this town with electricity?"

"Yes, but not exactly."

"Not exactly, what?"

"Those questions I will leave for the warden to answer." Huber didn't laugh, and he didn't smile. He just led her forward by the arm.

They entered the cave. It is what it was. A cave entrance. The sunlight did not penetrate even ten feet into the cave. The darkness would have been complete if not for a string of lights not much brighter than Christmas tree decorations strung along the ceiling.

They stopped at a gated cube.

"What's this?" Char said.

"Your ride down to The Cog," he said.

Char looked back over her shoulder. She could not see the cave entrance. She could barely make out the lights that were not immediately in front of her. If the sheriff was telling the truth about only one way in or out, and that one way being this elevator, she began to doubt her plan of escaping.

She didn't want to give up on the idea already, but as they stepped into the car and it slowly descended into sparse areas of complete darkness and passing areas of light, she felt hope slip away.

PART III
The Cog

Chapter 24

The elevator was a wooden plank platform with a mesh cage. It rattled as it descended. The view was of silt, clay, and grey rock with embedded crystals on all four sides.

"Just breathe easy," Sheriff Huber said. He stood stiffly, with one hand on the butt of his revolver and the other on the end of his long handled D-battery flashlight.

"What's that smell?"

"The shiny rock is called Rhyolite. What you are smelling is sulfur."

"Are we safe down here? I mean, breathing that in?"

"You will be given P.P.E.s once you get situated," Huber said.

"Yeah, I have no idea what that is."

"Personal Protective Equipment. A mask, gloves, and a prison uniform that will keep you safe from exposure to the elements."

"Mask?"

"A full face piece respirator." The sheriff mimicked putting on a mask. "They have acid gas cartridges that keep you from breathing in toxins. You'll be safe."

"Has anyone sentenced ever been released from this prison, yet?" she said.

Huber shook his head. "Not yet. No."

She couldn't think about that. Not now. To survive she shew she'd need to prepare mentally. Positive thoughts. "How far down are we going?"

"About two hundred feet."

Char sucked in a deep breath.

"Are you okay?"

She waved a hand in front of her face. "I might be hyperventilating."

"Breathe slowly, in and out. Nice and easy." The sheriff put hands on her shoulders.

The elevator rattled and shook.

"We're at the bottom," the sheriff said.

She sensed a change in his personality. He didn't seem like the bad guy she'd thought. "I'll be okay."

The elevator stopped. A guard stood in front of them. He held a rifle across his chest. His face was hidden behind the reflection in the face piece of his mask. The mask had a respirator cartridge on either side of his covered mouth and she could hear him breathing. He sounded a lot like Darth Vader.

"That's what I'll be wearing?" she said.

"That's what you will be wearing. Are you ready?"

The elevator gate rose and they stepped off the elevator. Lights lit the tunnel ahead.

"I guess I'm as ready as I ever will be." She wasn't ready at all.

"Take her to the warden, Officer."

"Wait," Char said. "You're not coming with me?"

"This is where we part. I do wish you the best of luck. Try to remember everything I told you, and you'll be okay."

She didn't want him to go. "Thank you, I will."

"I'll see you soon, okay?"

She didn't trust herself to speak. She just nodded.

# # #

"My name is George Hermann. This is my facility, my institution. It is a prison, yes. We have prisoners and armed guards. There is one way in, and the only way out is when you've completed your sentence, but the Cog is more than a prison. If you take any pride in yourself, you will understand that what we do down here is even more important than reformation. We supply more than just a service to the community of Arcadia. The Cog is the heart of Arcadia and possibly its brain."

Char sat at desk across from Hermann; the guard with the gun stood behind her. The framed degrees from M.I.T. and Stanford were hung on the wall behind Hermann's head and didn't impress her. She didn't think it was possible, but she missed Sheriff Huber. Hermann was not what she'd expected. When she thought of a warden she pictured a crotchety old man in a dark suit, with grey hair. Hermann couldn't yet be thirty. He had a head of messy black hair. He wore glasses with black frames and lenses so thick his eyes looked twice as large as normal behind the prescription glass.

"While you are here you won't just spend time wasting away in a cell. Your work will be meaningful. You will be contributing, working to ensure that power and electricity is supplied to the town," Hermann said.

"How does that work?"

Hermann stared at Char for a long minute. "I do not remember you asking for permission to talk, nor do I recall asking you a question. You are new. I will let it slide this once. The Cog is successful because we run on policy and procedures. Rules. You've just learned one of them. And, mind you, it is an important one. We don't tolerate much of anything other than a hard work ethic down here. Want your time with us to be painless, then follow the rules."

Char wanted to ask where to get a copy of the rules, but didn't. It would have been a sarcastic question that she was confident the warden would not appreciate.

"You are fed two meals. Breakfast and dinner. You begin work after breakfast, and finish around nine at night. When we are done here you will be fitted with the equipment needed to live down in this environment. You get one set. So take care of it. You will then be shown to your own personal cell. Today is your one and only day off, enjoy it. Tomorrow morning at six you will meet your foreman, be given your job assignment, and begin the labor portion of your sentence. And, Ms. McKinney, you want to hope that you and I never have to meet again."

There was no mistaking the threat in his tone of voice. She didn't even nod in understanding. For an engineer assigned to warden a prison, he was well suited for the position. The little creep was intimidating. He shouldn't be. That was why it bothered her so much.

# # #

Char thought about stirring up some banter with the masked guard escorting her from the warden's office, but decided against it. It made more sense to keep her mouth shut. She'd now been given the same advice by two people basically to fly under the radar. It was odd, but part of her felt relieved. She wasn't going to have to deal with the infected. The idea of living in a locked cell was somewhat attractive. She'd be able to sleep at night without keeping one eye open. She really couldn't remember the last time that had happened. Working every day might be just as Hermann indicated, rewarding; it might also keep her so occupied that she didn't have time to think about Tony, and Sam, and Grace. She would be kept so busy and exhausted that her mind might vacation from thoughts about her father, and brother. No one would be forgotten, but a break was needed. The last three years had been nothing short of hell.

Once they exited the main office area, Char was able to take in more of the mine. In a way, it was as she expected. The carved out caverns were chiseled rock. There were several guards with guns. They all resembled one another. There was no way to tell them apart. They were clad in black and masks and looked like Storm Troopers.

There were slotted metal walkways with guardrails. Char looked down and saw that the pit seemed bottomless. Powerful lights were strung up along the jagged ceiling. The odor of sulfur became stronger with each step taken. It assaulted her nostrils. Her nose kept twitching.

"I don't see the prison cells," she said.

"We're still in the administrative area of the prison," the guard said. His breathing heavy in and out while taking breaths.

Char had not expected him to reply. He did not remind her of a person in his uniform. Part of her had even considered him more of a robot.

Along the walls were mesh-metal cages. They stopped at the first one.

"We are going to fit you with a mask first," he said. He reached out and opened the metal door. They entered the room. Inside were totes. The guard looked at her face and the sides of her head. "Have a seat."

He opened a tote labeled small and removed two masks. From another tote he produced two round, cylindrical canisters.

"What are those?" she said.

"These connect to the mask." He pointed to the ones on his. "They filter the air from lethal toxins. We will give you fresh canisters each morning."

"They last that long?"

He didn't answer, but instead screwed them in place on one of the masks. "Lean forward."

He fit the mask over her face and fastened the straps tight on the back of her head.

"That kind of hurts," she said.

"It is important that the mask seals to your face. Otherwise, there is no reason to wear one. You will get used to wearing this, trust me," the guard said. "Breath normally for me."

She breathed in and out. Now she sounded like the daughter of Vader. She wondered when she'd get a lightsaber.

The guard put the second mask back in the tote. He wrote something on a clipboard. "Okay. We'll get you gloves and a prison uniform."

She wondered what color the jumpsuits would be. Blue or orange. It could be worse, she could be forced to pick trash up along the side of the highway.

In the next cage was where gloves were kept. The guard manipulated a tote and handed her a pair. They were suede, thick, and a little big on her hands. Her father had always claimed she'd play piano. "With long slender fingers like that, I can't imagine you *not* playing piano," he always said.

"They're kinda big," she said.

"Smallest we have." That ended that part of the conversation.

They stopped at the third, fourth, and fifth cages. The prison clothing was not what she'd expected. She was given three white tank tops, three pairs of black jeans and a heavy, black, Carhartt jacket. "This is what the prisoners wear?"

"They are for your protection," the guard said.

Char cocked an eyebrow. She again wondered about the work. What exactly would she be doing, and just how dangerous was it?

"Change into the clothing," the guard said.

"What, now?" Char said. She looked around. They were in the fifth cage. There were other guards on the metal sidewalks, but not near them. Anyone could see into the cages. They were more like chain link fence, the mesh was that open.

"You can't go into the prison in your street clothing. We'll place them in plastic and into a tote in the next cage. They'll be safe there and returned to you when you are released in three years."

"What about some privacy?"

"You gave up your right to privacy when you broke the law. Strip out of the street clothes and put on the assigned prison garb. I will not ask again," he said.

Char stood still. She heard just the two of them breathing inside their masks. She held the clothing she'd been given tight to her body. She felt dirty. Embarrassed. Violated.

He wasn't going to ask again.

There was no other choice.

She set the items down on a chair.

The guard just stared at her. His breath slightly fogged up the lower portion of the plastic faceplate and then disappeared. Then fogged up and cleared.

She undid her pants and slid them off. It was slow and humiliating. Goosebumps covered her thighs. Standing stooped over, she reached for the black jeans and quickly stuck her legs in. She pulled the pants up, zipped and buttoned them. She took off her shirt and kept one arm across her chest. The moment it took to slide the tank top over her head was the worst. She felt vulnerable, and could not stop her body from shaking. She knew he was staring at her breasts and hated that her nipples were erect.

It was over.

It felt like it lasted longer than a minute or two.

She grabbed the jacket, drove her arms into the sleeves, and immediately zipped it up. She put the gloves on last. Under all her new gear, she still felt naked.

"Grab your things. We'll secure them in a tote," the guard said. His tone of voice hadn't changed.

Char's face felt hot. She knew tears brimmed along her lower eyelids.

Fuck sleep. She no longer felt safe. She no longer thought being down here could be a good idea. She wanted to get out of here. If she had to stay a full day, it would be a full day too long.

Chapter 25

Char had been told there were a total of fifteen prisoners. She wondered how such a giant operation could be run by so few.

The prison was two levels. The cells lined three walls on both levels, in a U shape. The cells were barred, each with a locked door. The floor was cement. There were four picnic tables in the center. The guard station was at the open end of the U. It was a large office with a barred picture window. Behind it papers were posted on a corkboard, she saw a computer, and a few filing cabinets.

The guard led her up a set of metal stairs. He used a key and unlocked a door toward the center of the U. Her cell faced the office. Seemed like a prime location. She'd be able to see everything going on.

"This is your home. Make yourself comfortable for the night. Your foreman will be by in the morning to give you more of an orientation."

"And I keep this mask on all the time?"

"Hard to sleep with it on. It isn't as toxic in here. There is a ventilation system. Nothing fancy. I'd suggest wearing it when you work at the very least."

"So I can take it off?"

"Choice is yours, McKinney. It's your health. Not mine."

"You wear yours all the time?"

"I'm here twelve hours a day. I have no problem wearing it my entire shift."

She wanted to rip it off his face and punch his nose. "Where is everyone else?"

"Working."

He closed and locked the door. Without a word he walked away. She listened to his boot footfalls on the plank.

She stood with her hands wrapped around bars and stared at her new surroundings. She knew she was going to cry. It was the last thing she wanted to do. While she was alone, it was also the best time to get it out of the way.

The cell was maybe 8 x 8. There was a bed, and a toilet. The shelf over the john held a roll of toilet paper and nothing else. She removed her mask and gloves and set them on the shelf over the toilet. She breathed in deeply, exhaled loudly and plopped onto the bed. The mattress was a bit firmer than the one in the holding cell at City Hall. A pillow was at the head, and a blanket was folded at the foot. Bars made up the front and back of the cell. The left and right walls were solid. She mostly had privacy from the other prisoners, except for those cells across from her. Those prisoners could stare right into her cell. She looked at the toilet again, and shuddered.

She crossed her legs and sat with her back to the bars. Just behind her was the carved rock wall. Water trickled down the face. She reached an arm through the bars and her fingertip just touched the wall. The water was cold. She brought her finger to her nose and smelled it.

Sulfur.

She breathed in and out and was already tired of the sound the mask made with each breath. It echoed inside her head. She lowered her head onto the pillow. Using a foot, she shuffled the blanket up her legs, grabbed onto an end, and covered herself. The prison was lit, but held many, many shadows. The idea of sleeping seemed like the best escape for the moment, if falling asleep was even possible.

# # #

Antonio Velasquez raided other houses in the area. He did this daily. Supplies were always running out. His posse consumed everything. It reminded Char of when her Dad went shopping. She and Cash would dig through the groceries and pull out and devour the junk food. He wouldn't buy anymore until the next time he went shopping. When it was gone, it was gone. They'd never learned to ration the chips and soda pop.

Char stayed in the mix of raiders, armed with her sword, machete and knives. She knew if she had to, she could take on any one of Velasquez' crew easily. One on one that was. They were big men. Dangerous people. They were usually intoxicated. That added to the intimidation, but also incapacitated their reflexes, making them just slightly more threatening than fresh, fast zombies.

The house they surrounded looked vacant. They always did.

Guys barreled through the back door at the same time she and Velasquez rammed through the front.

Everyone yelled. "Get down! Drop it! On the floor!"

They weren't zombies. Overpowered, a Mexican man, woman, and three kids fell to the floor.

Velasquez spoke Spanish. He pointed his men to head off in different directions of the house.

She stood with her sword in both hands, daring the Mexicans to move.

The woman and her two daughters were crying. They were face down on the floor, arms over their heads.

Char knew this wasn't right.

They weren't looting from an empty house. These people needed their own supplies to continue to survive.

"Antonio," she said.

He shushed her. His eyes were dark, under thick eyebrows.

Some of the men returned. "There ain't shit here, 'Ntonio," Juan said.

"Si," Velasquez said. He jabbed the barrel of his rifle into the man's back. He spoke more Spanish at the resident.

The man didn't look up, but instead lifted his hands off the back of his head and raised them as high as he could. He was crying, and talking, and despite speaking a foreign language, Char could imagine what he said.

"We should get out of here if they don't have anything," Char said.

Velasquez jabbed his elbow into her arm. It was a powerful blow that sent her reeling. She lost her balance and landed on a sofa. A plume of dust rose and lingered in the air, sunrays spiked through it. The cloud danced in the light.

When Velasquez banged the butt of his rifle into the man's head, blood sprayed across dirty hardwood floors.

The women screamed.

The wife spoke fast. Her R's rolled constantly.

Char knew the mother begged for her daughters to be spared.

"That's enough, Antonio!" Char jumped to her feet.

The men were in a frenzy. Char knew they were making comments about the teenaged girl on floor. She was in a long white nightgown. She didn't like the hungry look on their faces. Velasquez was getting riled up, too.

He'd protected her from the men in his company. They never laid a hand on her. She knew if Antonio wasn't around, she'd of been in trouble. They'd have ravaged her relentlessly. Nightmares of an assault that never happened filled her dreams. She often woke in cold sweats and screaming from the torrid scenes that played on the screen behind closed eyelids.

Juan and Perez placed the rifle straps on their shoulders and bent down to scoop the teenager up. They had her under her arms. She struggled, kicking out.

The mother got up onto her knees. Tears fell from her eyes as her hands shot in the air and she screamed over and over, "Deténgase! Deténgase!"

Char felt bile rise in her throat. "Velasquez, this has to stop!"

When she stepped forward, Antonio grabbed her arm. She shrugged free. She raised her sword.

Something slammed into the back of her head. Juan, Perez, and the teen went cloudy in front of her. The floor raced up at her.

Laughter filled her ears, pounded around loose inside her skull as her eyelids fluttered. She knew she couldn't black out.

Three gunshots erupted from somewhere.

The bangs were close to her head. She waited for the pain from searing hot bullets passing through her flesh.

She never felt the pain.

Her eyes closed.

Part of her was thankful.

She fought to stay conscious. She forced her eyes open. It felt like weights hung from her lashes, opposing every ounce of strength left inside her and making the attempt futile.

She placed palms on the hardwoods and pushed up onto her knees.

She closed her eyes against a spinning room. When she opened them again, the sun was gone. No. Not gone. Just in a different place in the room. Not as bright.

The woman was dead, her skull shattered by a bullet.

The two young kids beside her were dead, too.

Bullets through the skull.

"They were not zombies," Char said, and she cried as she crawled toward them.

She heard them.

The noises came from upstairs.

It took effort to stand. She got up slowly, using a coffee table and the arm of a recliner to get to her feet.

She stood at the threshold leading from the family room to the foyer and looked at the bodies sprawled on the floor.

The people were dead.

Kids.

Holding her sword, she heard the rhythmic horror and shuddered as she climbed the stairs. Antonio and his men were animals.

She knew she had to stop them. Doing so would cost her life. It was an easy sacrifice, considering.

They howled. Beasts.

# # #

They howled like beasts, like animals . . .

Char sat up. The blanket fell off her.

The howling did not stop. The nightmare was not over. The prison was filling. The laborers were back from work and entering their cells.

Barred doors rang out as they were slammed shut.

She was thankful for the walls on either side of her cell. She could only imagine the monsters living beside her.

She grabbed the blanket and hugged it close to her body.

She wanted to go home, wanted her family back, wanted the infected gone, and life back to normal. Burying her face into her drawn up knees, she tried to muffle her crying. Tried.

Chapter 26

Char never fell back to sleep. It seemed like hours before everyone else was out cold. They'd worked all day. She didn't think they'd stay up long. She wanted to find some kind of inner peace, but every time she tried to concentrate her tattoo itched. Her skin felt a bit raw where the work had been done. All she wanted to do was scratch at it. The itch stopped, but started all over again the minute she focused on focusing. It was odd and annoying.

Once the lights went out, she sat curled on her bed, hugging the blanket tight, and squeezing her eyes closed.

They had taunted and cried out in the darkness. They knew she was here. Word must have spread.

When the lights came on, she waited. Prison life was about to begin. She wasn't ready for it. Her stomach muscles ached. She had to pee, but didn't want to be watched while urinating. She'd hold it as long as she could.

She heard footfalls on the walk and climbed off the mattress. Her mask sat on the shelf over the toilet, staring at her. It was her identity now.

"Rise and shine." The guard stood outside her cage. "I'm Kyle. Kyle Newstead. The second floor is mine from six until six. I get the luxury of escorting you to breakfast, to work, and to dinner. Lucky me. Grab that mask, those gloves and let's go," he said.

Char's hand trembled. She closed her fingers on her things, but thought she might drop them. She brought them to her chest, and pressed them tight against her body. Her throat felt dry, and it was difficult to swallow. She wondered about bathing. Her last shower was in the hotel up top, and aside from stepping into the frigid river to clean up, she couldn't recall how long it had been since she'd had that shower.

Char waited while Kyle used a key to unlock her door. "I open this door, you step out, and you stand here until I have all of the other doors unlocked. I give the word, you turn and follow the person in front of you. You guys head down the stairs and fill in the tables below. Sit where there is a food tray—that is if you want to eat. Understood?"

He pulled open the cell door. He tapped a long black rod onto his thigh. The handle displayed a yellow lightning bolt. She guessed the baton was electrified. He wanted her to see it, maybe to stop her from getting any funny ideas. Char wanted to tell him she hadn't had a funny idea in over three years.

She nodded, and then stepped out of the cage. A man stood to her left. He had his hands in front of him, holding onto his mask and gloves. Eyes forward. He couldn't be more than five-nine, with unkempt mixed dark and gray hair. She followed his lead and step forward toward the single safety rail and stared ahead with her gear held in front of her.

Peripherally she watched Kyle size her up for a moment, his eyes roamed over her from foot to head. He nodded, but still tapped the baton on his thigh. Perhaps finally satisfied that she wasn't going to run or get any other *funny ideas*, he turned and walked away.

She'd been holding her breath, but hadn't realized it until she exhaled. It was a slow, calming exhale. Then as soon as her lungs emptied, she sucked in another deep breath. The death grip on her gloves and mask was to keep her hands from shaking. It wasn't working. She needed to get it together. Char did not want these guys, the other prisoners, sensing her fear. Fear was weakness.

Eight prisoners occupied a cell on the second level. They all stood by the rail and stared straight ahead. Seven men were now being let out of their cage on the first.

Kyle stood by one of two staircases and waved his baton.

The group on the second level turned. Char turned with them. They walked toward Kyle, proceeded down the stairs, and went toward the picnic tables in the center of the prison.

Char walked up to a table.

The man from the cell next to her shook his head. "Not there. First three tables are for the guys on the first floor. We're over here."

She walked behind him.

"Sit here," he said.

As she sat, she turned to look at the first three tables. A man with a curved and jagged scar running from his chin to the top of his cheekbone watched her. The corner of his upper lip twitched. The seat where he sat was the one she'd been eyeing.

"Ignore him," the man next to her said. "If you can, ignore everyone at those tables. Don't look at them. Don't talk to them. Do your best to stay clear. Got me?"

Char nodded.

The man set his mask and gloves on the table ahead of his food tray, and then offered his hand. "I'm Ross MacNeil," he said.

"Char," she said, shaking his hand.

"This guy over here is Frank Ryan. And next to him is Chris Paleo."

Everyone said hello.

"What are you in for?" Ross said.

Char shrugged. "Self-defense. I defended myself against a group of people who attacked me and my friends."

"Fighting," Frank said, "same here. Had a bit too much at the Bent Elbow. Broke some chairs, some tables, and some noses. Told the judge it wasn't me, it was the alcohol. She didn't go for it."

Frank was big, burly. If he had a long curly beard, she'd of sworn he was Rubeus Hagrid from the Harry Potter films.

"It's not what I heard," Chris said.

Ross shot him a look. "What have you heard?" Char said.

Chris looked at Ross, as if for approval.

Ross said, "Rumor is, you're down here for murder."

"Self-defense," she said.

Ross held up his hands. "Just what's going around. That kind of puts a target on your back. You know the old saying, take out the biggest and the badest to establish a name, build a reputation? You aren't so big, but you might be the worst down here. No offense."

"Yeah. None taken." Char looked at the brown bag on the food tray. "What is this?"

Ross used teeth to tear open the plastic bag container. "M.R.E.'s."

"Meals ready to eat," Chris said. "Chicken fajitas."

Char opened her bag, dumped the pre-wrapped, pre-cooked food onto the table. There was a bag of corn chips, the fajita, an oatmeal cookie, dried apple slices, packets of pepper and salt. "This is okay to eat?"

Frank was biting into the fajita. "It's not bad."

"Cold? We eat it cold?" Char didn't feel hungry. She did not get dinner last night, and should feel like she is starving. Food was food, but something about shrink wrapped meals stored in potato chip-like bags didn't excite her.

"Eat up. Dinner is a long way off. You'll need your energy. Trust me," Ross said.

She opened the corn chips. "What do we do, exactly?"

Ross looked up from his meal, looked over at Frank and Chris. "It's not pleasant," he said.

She'd gathered as much on her own.

"We basically walk on a treadmill, or ride a stationary bike. It's how they power the generators that supply the town with its electricity."

"Treadmills?" Char said. It couldn't be like what she now pictured.

"You have to keep at a steady five miles per hour. Over five is fine. Under, and Kyle over there will remind you to pick up the pace with his lightning stick," Chris said.

"Same for the bike, you have to pedal between six and eight miles an hour. It doesn't sound fast, but after a while it isn't as easy as it seems," Frank said. "I run what's called the wheel. I crank it around and around by hand."

The chips crunched between her teeth. The taste of food hit her. She realized now how hungry she actually was. She opened the chicken fajita and took a bite. It tasted roughly like dry chicken with peppers and onions. Nothing Mexican about the flavor, other than it was wrapped in a tortilla. "But how is the power working if all of us are here eating breakfast? We generate that much power that we can stop at night and start again in the morning?"

This time Frank looked around the table. "We're not the only ones running the plant," he said.

"People choose to work down here? With prisoners?" Char couldn't believe that. It was a claustrophobic's worst nightmare. The sulfur in the air alone should keep people away.

"Not exactly," Ross said. "You get to meet any of the Gathering Patrol? They're a special unit with the sheriff's department."

Char pictured Benjamin Forti in his uniform. He'd mentioned more than once something about gathering, but couldn't recall anything specific. "Yes," she said.

"Let's say they help staff the generator plant who work twenty-four-seven down here."

"The Gathering Patrol works down here?"

"No, they find bodies to fill the positions," Ross said.

"I'm not getting it. You just told me that people don't work down here with us."

"They don't," Ross said. "Zombies do."

Chapter 27

It was hard to believe that the generator area was yet deeper into the bowels of the mine. They took an elevator similar to the one she'd ridden on with the sheriff. They descended four at a time, plus a guard.

"Stay close," Ross said. "If Lou's any kind of a guy, he'll keep you segregated from the gang and let you work near us. Near me."

Char could not believe the transformation. She felt like she'd stepped into a power plant. The place was loud. She was surprised they hadn't been given ear protection. There was a row of boxes about five feet tall with flashing lights and an array of toggle switches. The area was well lit. Lamps lined the ceiling. The walks were cement, and in certain areas, bright yellow handrails sectioned off hazardous areas.

Beyond were the guts of the operation. Her eyes saw but her brain failed to register what was in front of her. The central hub was a cylindrical shaped pillar. It rose at least fifty feet high. At the top, the head was bulbous, and translucent where strands of white lightning sizzled and danced against a glass encasement. Around the pillar it resembled a fitness gym. There were treadmills and stationary bikes. At the center, beside the pillar, she saw the giant wheel where Frank worked. Wires connected from and to everything.

"They built this in three years?" Char said.

"No. Arcadia has been planning for the end of times since the town's inception," Ross said.

If infected weren't already running the place, she'd have thought this was part of a futuristic lab from a Mary Shelley novel put in place to resurrect the dead.

The infected *were* running the place.

"Hello. I understand you are Charlene McKinney and will be with us for some time. Me, I'm Lou Kilmer. I'm the foreman down here. I'm your boss. I tell you to do something, you just do it. It's really that simple. I'm going to have Ross give you a quick tour—quick, being the key word," Lou said. "Then, Ross, you set her up on a mill next to you for the day. Good?"

"Yeah, boss," Ross said.

Lou Kilmer was tall and thin. He'd removed his mask to introduce himself. He had dark eyes under bushy eyebrows and a cleft in his chin. His Carhartt was rustic orange. Traditional. It helped him stand out from what the prisoners and guards wore.

"He pretty cool?" Char said.

"Far as bosses go, he don't bother you as long as you work."

She followed Ross.

"This is why you wear the Carhartts," Ross said, pulling at the lapel on his jacket. "The zombies are tethered with chains to the mills. It's what we call the treadmills. Mills. They can't go anywhere." He pointed at an infected walking on one of the mills. The shackles on his ankles gave just enough slack for it to amble forward. Cuffs bound its wrists to the handlebars on the side. "They don't ride the bikes, for obvious reasons. Usually those are for Gonzales and his guys, anyway. Guess it makes them feel like their cruising on Harley's or something. I don't know. I don't ask."

The infected plotted along. It couldn't be going five miles an hour. "How many are there?"

"Zombies? Around two hundred, two-fifty, give or take."

Char saw close to thirty under the lights. She squinted and noticed that beyond the light, extending deep into the darkness of the mine was row after row of infected on makeshift treadmills. She could not believe her eyes, or her ears.

They moaned. It was a constant sound, rolling sound.

It was not the usual moaning she'd come to expect from infected. She hated to think it, but they sounded sad. Made her think about the times she went to the zoo with her brother and father. When they got there early, the animals were up and active. By ten, they could care less about the visitors. They always stood at the Bengal exhibi and the majestic beast simply paced from one end of its cage to the other. Back and forth. It was perfect for the people watching the animal; it was clearly pathetic if you were the animal. It might not want out, but it surely did not want to be where it was. She remembered telling her father one day that she didn't want to go to the zoo anymore. Cash didn't understand. He loved the elephants and lions, the penguins and seals. Her father understood, though. She couldn't remember ever going again.

This was far from the same thing, only it wasn't. Tony refused to call them zombies. They were people once. That was his rationale. He was right, too. They were people who were once free, healthy, and alive. Seeing them enslaved didn't upset her, but neither did it sit well inside her.

"I like the mills," Ross said. "It is almost relaxing. The trick is to close your eyes while you walk. Imagine you are on a wooded trail somewhere. Picture birds, or falling leaves, or something peaceful, and just believe you are there. Not here. It's not always easy to do. The noise, the smells, but once you can escape to that happy place, it makes all the difference."

"How much time you get?" she said.

Ross stopped walking. "I'm out in another month or so."

"What did you do?"

He shook his head. "We need to start working. Boss gave us some leeway. I've showed you around. Now we've got to walk."

The first row of mills behind the rows of bikes was open. Ross pointed to the one on the end. Chris was on a mill, walking fast, swinging his arms back and forth. He reminded her of any guy on a treadmill at any gym. If he'd had earplugs, and was listening to music, she'd of sworn she was at a gym.

"You walk there, I'll take the one next to you," he said.

She could see Frank as she stepped onto the belt. He didn't wear his Carhartt. His muscles bulged as he turned the crank. The big wheel spun moved fast. It was dizzying to watch, almost hypnotic.

Chris nodded to them. Char waved.

"Are these powered?" Char said.

"Be self-defeating, don't you think? Manual."

"But the infected?"

"The who?"

"Zombies."

"Look closely in front of each of them," Ross said.

Char turned around. Fishing wire dangled a small piece of something in front of them. "Is that...meat?"

Ross nodded.

She didn't like the infected walking behind her. It made her feel like she was being pursued. Her skin crawled, the hairs under the jacket stood on end. "What kind of meat?"

"I don't know. I don't ask."

She didn't like the answer. It made her feel apprehensive. "I don't see how us doing this supplies the city with enough power."

"Start walking," Ross said. "It isn't just us. That thing in the middle there, it goes down further into the earth. It somehow converts the heat from the core into electricity. Then there is the underground river. Its power is harnessed as well, and turned into current Arcadia can use. The combined methods give the town just enough juice to be effective, and up top, they're not wasteful. It is used conservatively. It's not a bad operation when you think about it."

"But what if there were no prisoners to help?"

"People are always going to break laws, dear. It's human nature to fuck up. Excuse me," he said.

She smiled. He wouldn't see. Not through her mask. "I've heard worse," she said.

"Pick up the pace," Ross said. "We don't want to get talked to. You get one warning if you fall under the five mile an hour."

"What happens after a warning?"

"No dinner."

"A third? No breakfast?"

"Bingo." Ross shook his head. "The M.R.E.s might taste like shit —sorry, but they have the nutrition needed to stay healthy.

And down here, you want to get as many vitamins as possible. You might not have noticed, but we don't get too much sunlight here. Bam, there goes any Vitamin D you might need. Sometimes surprised we don't all have jaundice."

"Jaundice?"

"Babies get it. It's a Vitamin D thing. You need your Vitamin D. With those M.R.E.s you get what you need."

Ross was positive and upbeat and seemed to be a stickler for the rules. He was what you'd call a short-timer. She wasn't sure how much time he'd spent down here, his response being a little evasive, but with a month to go she felt confident he'd want no part in an escape plan. Still, he seemed to know the ins and outs. Picking his brain for information without alerting him to her plan might prove a challenge. "That river, it's underground?"

"The Chowan. It's mostly out in the open, but there's a part of it passes right under the mountain range."

"This far down?"

"No. It's more parallel with where our cells are," Ross said. His breathing was deep. He gripped the side rails and walked heavy. Each step fell hard on the conveying belt.

She looked ahead, concentrating on her walking. Each question he answered sparked more questions. If she fired them off, he'd get suspicious. The older guy might have taken her under his wing, but she didn't know him. Because she didn't know him, she couldn't trust him. The last thing she wanted to do was tip her hand. He might report it. Turning over information on a suspected escape plan could get him out early. She didn't know who Ross MacNeil was up top.

"You finding that happy place?" he said.

"Trying," she said.

"Give it some time. Close your eyes."

She closed her eyes. She heard her breathing. She heard and felt her heart beating.

Opening her eyes, she turned around. The infected lumbered on their mills. Some had milky white cataract-like covered eyes on the meat that dangled, but others, she thought, focused on *her*. The ones she thought were drooling with thoughts of her as their meal seemed to walk a little faster. The piece of meat was nothing compared to an entire person. It had to be why the front row of mills was reserved for the living prisoners. Motivation.

The white lights went red, and spun. She thought of the light bar on top of a police car.

A siren revved up from a squeal to a scream.

Char stopped walking and pressed her hands to her ears.

"Don't stop walking," Ross said.

"What?"

He rolled his hand around in a circle. "Keep walking."

She'd heard him. She began walking again. "What is it?"

Ross motioned with his head. Two guys were off their bikes, throwing punches.

"One on the right, that's Gonzales." Ross pointed.

Gonzales removed his mask. Even from where she was, with the red light spinning, she could see his facial scar. He threw a punch into the other man's gut. As the guy doubled over, Gonzales grabbed the top of his head and slammed it downward toward his rising knee. The faceplate cracked. Gonzales tore the mask off the man and flung it toward the giant pillar.

Two guards ran at the men who had now become entangled, had fallen to the cement, and were rolling around, still throwing punches.

Char strained to see. It was an awkward angle. The bikes and the people still on them blocked her view.

"Keep walking," Ross said.

She hadn't realized she'd stopped again.

The guards pulled the men apart. It looked like Kyle Newstead had Gonzales in a half nelson and struggled to gain control.

The other guard knelt on the back of the man he'd fought to restrain.

"They come around asking for a statement, you tell them you didn't see a thing," Ross said.

"I didn't."

"Doesn't matter. They won't believe you. You being new, they'll figure you'll be easiest to crack."

"I really didn't see anything until the siren started and you pointed it out to me," she said. She was willing to wager that Ross had seen it all, watched it unfold. It was why he didn't react when the siren started. He'd been waiting for it to blare.

Ross definitely knew what was what around here.

"What happens now, they get taken out of here?"

"No dinner for them, maybe no breakfast. Guards will separate them on the bike line."

"No solitary confinement?"

"Not here. The punishment is working through meals. Solitary in a place like this would be a vacation. You'd have non-stop anarchy," Ross said. "Hey. Look sharp."

Char had no clue what that meant.

Ross nodded forward.

Lou headed toward them. She knew it was him by his Carhartt. He stopped in front of their mills and raised his mask so it sat over the top of his head. "What did you guys see?" he said.

Char shook her head. She breathed in. Breathed out. The sucking noises made filled her ears. She wanted to raise her mask, too. She hated wearing it. It felt restrictive.

"Did I tell you to stop walking?" Lou said.

Char nearly stumbled as she clambered on the belt and walked a bit faster than she had been. She was not sure how much time had passed. She was thin and muscular. All she did the last three years is walk. This just felt different. It seemed more like extreme exercise, like something you completed in thirty to forty minutes, not kept at from early morning until late night. "Sorry."

"Ross, what happened over there?"

Ross shrugged. "I missed it, boss. I was orientating McKinney here. We were talking. I was telling her how we do things around here, how everything works. Next thing I know, lights and sirens are going off."

"You didn't catch anything going on, Mister-Know-It-All?"

"Sorry, boss. I didn't see anything."

"How about you, McKinney? I know you saw something."

"I was talking to Ross," Char said, careful to keep a steady pace on her mill. She wasn't sure if she'd just been warned. She didn't want to miss out on dinner.

"Who threw the first punch?" Lou said.

"They were punching each other?" she said. "I missed it. Are they okay?"

Lou stared at her. For the first time she was thankful for the mask. There was no way he could clearly see her eyes. Not with the plastic faceplate, and not with her bouncing up and down while she walked on the mill. He couldn't see her eyes, couldn't read her expression, and he wouldn't notice the extra sweat that dripped from her temples and rolled down the sides of her face.

Lou walked away from them and stopped in front of Chris.

The siren was silenced. The spinning red light stopped. The guards moved the men to bikes at opposite ends of the line of equipment.

"Look ahead, and keep walking," Ross said.

Chapter 28

"How are you holding up?" Frank sat down at the picnic table next to Chris, and across from Ross and Char. The same way they'd sat for breakfast. It was about repetition and consistency. She figured if she sat, say, in Chris' spot, it would throw the three of them off kilter.

"Me? How about you? I watch you work that wheel all day. I have no idea how you keep at it like that," Char said. She stared at the brown pouch on her tray. She was not in the mood for chicken fajita again, but was so hungry it didn't matter what was inside.

"Beef ravioli," Chris said.

Char tried to smile. "Cold?"

"They have heaters. You add water. It's a chemical reaction. It will heat the entree," Ross said. "Like this. Watch."

He laid his pouch over the side of the tray at an angle, and poured a small amount of his water into it.

She glanced around. Everyone was doing the same thing.

"Takes a few seconds, and in a minute or so, the ravioli will taste like it just came out of a microwave oven," Chris said.

"A weak microwave oven," Frank said. "When I was a kid, I'd open a can of Chef Boyardee, grab a fork, and sit in front of the television eating them cold, right out of the can. What? They're no different from this. Pre-cooked before being packaged."

Chris nodded his head from side to side, as if deciding whether to add something to the conversation. "I did the same thing, but with hotdogs. I'd cut open the package, take one in each hand, and just eat them raw."

Char touched the bag. It was pretty warm. She emptied the ravioli onto her tray. She didn't need to blow on it before eating it, but it was warm and tasted better than if she'd been forced to eat it cold. "This isn't so bad," she said.

While they ate, she waited for them to bring up the fight. Frank had practically been ringside for the entire thing. No one mentioned it. She left it alone. She glanced over at the table where Gonzales sat. He wasn't there. It was as Ross had suggested. He was forced to work through dinner as part of the punishment.

The idea of spending three years in prison was daunting, to say the least. If anything, these guys were teaching her how to behave. The lessons she picked up on would help her survive in the Cog.

"So where is this underground river?" Char said, hoping it sounded like a casual question.

"The Roanoke?" Frank said. "There's a few paths behind the cells that lead to it."

"That's so weird," Char said. "I never knew rivers could run underground."

"There are many places, on most continents, with underground rivers," Chris said, "and there are even a good handful of rivers that flow south to north."

"South to north?" Frank said. "That's ridiculous, not to mention impossible."

"It is so possible. You are thinking of north as up and south as down. Most people do that, but north and south are just directions. It's about the elevation. If it is higher elevation in the south, then naturally the water will flow north. Up in New York there's a river called the Genesee. It flows south to north," Chris said.

"I know that river. I'm from Rochester. Originally," Char said. "The Genesee was just a few miles from where I grew up."

"Small world," Chris said.

Some of the beef was cold in the next bite full. She cringed. "Got an undercooked piece," she said, taking a sip of water to wash it down. "Where does the Roanoke let out? I mean, it can't run forever underground can it?"

"The Albemarle Sound," Chris said.

"That's not where it comes out of the mountain, that's where it empties into," Frank said.

"What's an Albemarle Sound?" Char said.

"It's like an enclosed body of water. It's just before the Atlantic," Chris said.

"We're nowhere near the Atlantic," Char said.

"We're not. It's not where the Roanoke comes out of the mountain, like I was saying," Frank said.

Ross held up a hand. "Why are you so interested in the river?"

Char furrowed her brow. "Because it's interesting," she said.

Ross used his tongue to dig at food in his teeth while his hands tousled with a napkin. "Two things, kid. You listen, and you listen closely, okay? One, this is your first day here. Day one. Relax a little. Learn the ropes. It's important you get yourself as acclimated as possible. You got me on that? And two, whatever it is you're thinking, stop thinking it."

"You don't know what I'm thinking," she said.

"No, and I don't want to know. What I am saying is, stop thinking it. It's for your own good." He picked up his tray and dumped the wrappers into a garbage basket by a cart for empty trays. "Let's get back to work. Finish this shift up. Come on."

# # #

Of everything she had seen the last several years, enslaved infected might be the most disturbing. Harnessed monsters working to power a small town. It was ludicrous. If it caught on, though, it might change the way the world ran. She tried to picture Manhattan back to normal with the giant video displays and the hustle and bustle of people on the New York City streets, while beneath the subways, hundreds of thousands of infected ran on treadmills.

Ludicrous.

"You awake, kid?"

Char was in bed, under her blanket. The voice came from the wall. Ross.

She thought about ignoring him the way he'd ignored her the last leg of their shift on the mill.

She pulled back the blanket and carried it with her to the wall. She sat with her back against it, toward the front by the bars.

Lights had gone out nearly an hour ago.

6 A.M. would come fast. She couldn't sleep anyway. "I'm up."

"I'm sorry about earlier, at dinner."

"Nothing to be sorry for."

"I jumped to conclusions," he said.

She didn't respond to his statement. "What did you do up top?"

"Janitor. I sweep and mop floors, clean johns, empty trash," he said. "I took pride in the profession the mayor assigned. I have a high school education. Not a diploma, but I got close."

There was something in his tone of voice that contradicted what he'd just said. "What did you do to get in here, Ross?"

Silence followed. His turn not to respond.

She was about to ask him how long he'd been sentenced when he spoke up.

"I beat up my wife," he said.

She stared at the bars. She wanted to see his face. It couldn't have been easy for him to admit. Remorse dripped off the words. "Why?"

"She loved me," he said. It was not the answer she'd expected. It was by no means an explanation. "I was never good enough for her. That never stopped her, though. She never tried to make me feel stupid, or like less of a man. It was the exact opposite, actually. She bragged about me to her friends. The things she'd tell them were always true, it was just that she made the mundane sound spectacular." He changed his voice, made himself sound like a woman. "He mows the straightest lines when he cuts the lawn. He painted the trim around the shutters like Picasso."

Char just listened. He was talking. She wasn't going to interrupt.

His voice was normal once again. "She didn't do it to be mean, she wasn't trying to belittle me. I think she's just always been proud of me, but me, I didn't like it. Every time she bragged,

I took it personal, like a dig. You see, she went to college. Earned a teaching degree. What's the mayor do? The most logical thing. He gives her a job as a teacher. There aren't a ton of kids in Arcadia, but there's enough. She's teaching little kids, and elementary kids, and sometimes high school aged kids, and loving it. We'd get home from work at roughly the same time, and you know what killed me? I'd ask her how her day was. You know what she'd tell me? That it was good. That was about it. It was good. Then she would ask me about my day. I'd try the same thing, you know. I'd say it was good. She wouldn't let me off so easy. She'd ask specific things, like if I'd overheard any juicy gossip, or found any embarrassing letters in the wastebaskets. When I tried to get her to tell me about her day then, she might tell me a few things, downplaying what she did. She tried to anyway. What she didn't know was that the love for her job was in her eyes. It sparkled there. Glittered," he said.

She hoped his wife didn't take a beating for loving her job. She couldn't imagine a reason why a husband should ever hit his wife. There couldn't be one.

"I'll admit it, after a while, she had me convinced. She made me believe in me. That was when one day while I was sweeping up someone else's mess, I heard the rumors. I got home that night. I was first home, actually, and I went into our place and I sat at the kitchen table, and I waited. I didn't have to wait long. She walked in, saw me sitting there and knew —she just knew— something was wrong, so she asked me. I told her I'd heard she was having an affair. I was staring at her, watching her reaction. Figured if she lied I'd be able to see it in her face, or the way she moved her body, or something. She told me, though. She said straight out that she was. She did the strangest thing then, she sat down at the kitchen table across from me and began telling me everything about it. How it was another teacher at school; how they oftentimes combined their classrooms and taught together; how they spent so much time together outlining lessons, and that it just happened. Only, once it happened, they both realized that it felt right and didn't want to stop. While she's talking, while she's telling me all of this, I get up and walk over to her, and I just punch her in the face."

Char didn't know she was crying until a tear fell from her chin onto her wrist. She sat hugging her legs tight to her chest.

"I don't remember too much more. The only thing I know, is I hit her more than once. While I awaited my trial, she spent time in the hospital. Broken nose, split lip. She missed work. I don't think she wasn't able to go to school as much because she was too embarrassed to go. She told me she didn't want the kids seeing her all bruised up and swollen, and when she told me this, because she came to see me while I was in that holding cell at City Hall, when she told me about not wanting the kids to see her it was gone. In her eyes. That sparkle was gone. Her eyes were flat, dull. They were lifeless like anyone else who realized life was mediocre at best. I did more than beat her physically, I crushed her mentally. I stole her joy away."

He had to be punching the wall behind her; a steady thud of fists against solid walls. She heard his sobbing. She had no words to console him.

Her mother had cheated on her father.

Char's father never beat her mother.

Like her father, she never forgave her mother for ruining their family. "Do you have kids, Ross? You've not said."

The thuds against the wall stopped.

"No. No children."

"How long have you been down here, Ross?"

"Two and a half years," he said.

What was waiting for him in a month when he returned up top? A broom and a mop? Hopefully, not a wife. "I'm going to bed, Ross."

"Good night, kid."

She ignored him, climbed back into bed, and pulled the covers up to her chin. There was no way she'd fall asleep, she thought, as she closed her eyes, her breathing evened out, and she fell asleep.

Chapter 29

Char woke up before six. She had to use the bathroom. Holding it wasn't an option. She figured with everyone else still asleep, she'd have some privacy. That she'd waited this long amazed her. There were still lights on, but her cell was mostly in shadows. She sat on the toilet. Her urine came out like a waterfall. It sounded like a fire hose spraying into the bowl as she emptied her bladder.

Her body odor was raw. She had not heard mention of showers. There had to be a place to get cleaned up. She was surprised she hadn't been advised otherwise.

She put on her Carhartt and set her gloves and mask onto the bed next to where she sat.

When the lights came on inside the prison, she was ready. She stood by the door to her cell and waited for Kyle Newstead.

She heard his footfalls on the walk.

She listened as Ross greeted the guard.

At her cell, Kyle said good morning. His mask sat on top of his head. "You're up bright and early. Trouble sleeping?"

"Not at all." She appreciated the civility. The Cog was bad enough. There was no reason the guards had to be jerks, too.

"Stand outside your cell," he said.

"And wait for the nod," she said.

He smiled.

She'd comply, follow the rules, and fly under the radar. She figured in to time at all, the novelty of having a female prisoner would wear off. No one would notice her. She was counting on that.

Staring straight ahead, she swore she felt Ross' eyes on her. He had to be trying to gauge how she'd respond toward him based on the story he'd shared during the night. At this point, she wasn't sure how she felt. It changed things. That much she knew. Burning bridges was not the route she wanted to take.

Below, Gonzales Morales stepped out of his cell and stood with his hands folded passively in front of him.

Newstead gave the nod.

Char turned and followed Ross down the staircase. She passed the tables where Gonzales and his gang sat, and sat down in her spot on the bench, across from Frank and Chris.

The men talked, attempting to engage her in their conversation. She provided enough of an answer to questions asked, but mostly kept quiet. Her attention was on a guard leading Gonzales away from the tables toward the elevator that led down to the work area.

They were not going to feed him breakfast either, she realized.

She grabbed the granola bar from her M.R.E. and casually slid it up the sleeve of her Carhartt. Frank caught it. She saw it in his eyes, and knew it by the way he immediately looked away.

"How'd you sleep?" Chris asked. "Like a baby?"

"Pretty well," she said.

"How do your legs feel?" Ross said.

"A little sore," she said.

"Thing is, it seems to be the second morning that is the worst." Chris set his wrappers onto his food tray. "At least that's how it had been for me. Day two, painful."

"Same," Frank said, crunching into his granola bar. He chewed with his mouth open. Char was forced to look someplace else, otherwise, she might get sick watching him.

"You've been unnaturally quiet," Chris said to Ross.

"Did a lot of tossing and turning last night."

"You don't look too hot. Coming down with something?" Chris said.

"Need a flu shot?" Frank said, and let a burst of laughter erupt from his mouth, bits of granola generously scattered across the table.

"What's the deal with showers?" Char lifted her tray. "Want me to take yours?"

Chris shrugged and handed her his tray. "Thank you. I appreciate it."

"Welcome."

"Every other day. There's a locker room the guards use. We shower tonight in groups of four after the shift ends," Ross said.

She made her way around the table and knew it must appear obvious that she'd avoided interaction, and even eye contact, with Ross. When she returned to the table and said, "It's bad enough having a toilet on display. I'm not showering with everyone. If they think I am, they've got another thing coming."

# # #

Char hated the elevator rides. The shaft was just wide enough to fit the car. The men were so big that she felt trapped between them. Breathing inside the mask was unnatural. She kept gasping. The sound attracted attention. The others would turn toward her, and then turn away. It was just enough that it made her uncomfortable and self-conscious.

Stepping out of the car was a relief. It even helped her breathing. The Cog was so well lit, and the ceilings so high that a lot of her claustrophobia subsided in the work area of the prison. She preferred it to where her cell was. It felt more as if she was inside a factory and that beyond the walls might be a parking lot, and a Wal-Mart. She supposed thoughts like that would help her achieve a mental happy place, somewhere she could eventually escape to while passing time.

Three years' worth of time.

Lou Kilmer held a clipboard and directed each prisoner to a work station. "McKinney, you're on the mill again. Ross, you too."

Chris and Frank were already on this level, and working. Frank was at his wheel and Chris on a bike.

Gonzales was on a bike again. It was on an end. As she followed Ross toward the mills, she stopped and introduced herself to Gonzales.

He kept pedaling.

"I'm Char. I didn't get a chance to meet you yesterday."

He stared at her.

His head wobbled slightly side to side while he pedaled.

She held out her hand.

He stared at it.

She couldn't see his eyes. Char was confident they bore holes through her skull.

"McKinney, get to a mill!" Kilmer pointed the clipboard at her.

"I was just introducing myself," she said, risking further reprimand. She looked back at Gonzales, and then down at her still extended hand.

He shook her hand, but did not say a word.

"Mingling time is over, McKinney," Kilmer said.

Char lowered her head and walked away. She climbed onto the mill next to Ross and started walking.

"What the hell was that?"

"What was what?" Char said. She looked straight ahead. She power walked.

"Slow down."

She didn't.

"Why would you have gone over there? I'm trying to do you a favor, kid. You don't want to be interacting with Gonzales or any of his people."

She turned her head. "Why?"

"You just don't."

She concentrated on the walk.

After several awkward moments of silence, Ross said, "You did not do that. Tell me you did not bring him food?"

Char looked at Gonzales. He snuck bites of the granola bar she'd handed off.

"He missed two meals," Char said.

"Because he started a fight," Ross said. "You bring anything for the other guy? The victim?"

The victim would never be able to help her get what she needed. Gonzales was different. He was exactly what she wanted. Ross was getting out in a month. Gonzales, like her, might as well be serving a life sentence down here.

# # #

She stood under the nozzle. The water was not hot, but neither was it cold. She felt the dirt washing off her skin. It was never suggested that she would have to shower with the other prisoners. She just had to go last. Almost better than the shower, was the bathroom stall. She was allowed to go to the bathroom without anyone watching, it felt like freedom. There was no way she'd be able to wait two days to go to the bathroom. Newstead said as long as she was quick about it and ate her meals quickly, he'd let her use the bathroom after breakfast and dinner as well.

Civility.

After rinsing the suds out of her hair and the soap off her body, she toweled dry and dressed in fresh clothing. While she zipped up her jeans she thought she heard something. A howl. It was different from an infected moaning. She wasn't sure where it came from. She picked up the towel and continued to dry her hair as she walked around the small locker room. There were three rows of lockers. Some had Master combination locks on the handles.

The air vent was above a waist high cabinet. The sound she heard was wind.

She dropped her dirty clothes and her towel into a hamper, as instructed and left the sanctuary of the locker room.

Three years was two years and eleven months too long.

Chapter 30

Benjamin Forti took point. He held his rifle in both hands as he stepped over tree limbs and brush. The sky was cloudless. It was nearly a full moon, and stars filled space. They didn't need to use the flashlights clipped to their belts.

"You heard something?" Earl was behind Ben. He had a machete in his right hand, a long pole in his right.

"Shh," Benjamin said. He pointed forward.

Earl turned and rolled his eyes at Wayne. "Guess they're this way."

Benjamin stopped walking and stood up straight. "Are you kidding me?"

Earl winced.

"When I said, shhh, what did you think it meant?"

"That we should be quiet," Earl said.

"Then I pointed to over by those trees. Why do you think I did that?"

"Because the noise you think you heard came from over there."

"Over where?" Benjamin said.

"By those trees." Earl answered each question with confidence.

"Then what did you do?"

"I told Wayne."

"You turned around and told Wayne. You didn't even try to whisper."

"What if he didn't hear me?" Earl said.

Benjamin wanted to call it a night. Earl was an okay guy, he just sucked at Gathering. He was the sheriff's cousin. Huber didn't want him patrolling town and didn't trust him to uphold the law, but somehow managed to pull strings getting Earl a job on Gathering Patrol. Earl did not belong in a deputy uniform as a peacekeeper, but neither did he belong in a deputy uniform outside Arcadia walls hunting for zombies. Benjamin never complained about getting shafted by the sheriff. He knew because he was the mayor's son, people talked about him behind his back endlessly.

"When I tell you to be quiet, do me a favor, don't talk." Benjamin knew taking out his aggravation on Earl was somewhat uncalled for. Yes, Earl did this every time they went out, but it wasn't Earl he had the issue with. It was Huber and his father.

Charlene had been railroaded in court. She was used as a political pawn. His father had held the mayor's seat for the last three years. Rumor was, Gary Priestly planned to campaign and run against his father next year. To prove to the people of Arcadia that he was serious about maintaining a safe a peaceful community, someone had to be punished for the murders committed. Since everyone involved was either dead or in a coma at the hospital, Charlene was left to take the fall.

A three year sentence was absurd. While his testimony at her trial had been accurate, it did not allow for explanation. His father and Huber had told him that he needed only to answer questions asked and to not elaborate.

He'd had his chance to take a stand when he testified. He could have explained how events played out. A jury would have had to have found Charlene innocent and that her actions were purely self-defense. He hadn't. He'd crumbled to the pressure. He'd let his father intimidate him. The guilt from backing down crushed him. He had no one to blame for the sleepless nights but himself.

"No more talking. Earl, you got it?"

"Yes."

Benjamin cringed. "Wayne?"

Wayne nodded. He carried a pole like the one Earl held, and a handgun.

Benjamin walked toward the brush. Something was close by. He'd heard the rustling. The closer he got to the thicket, the more he could smell them. He held up his hand. The three of them stopped. Just to be sure his command was not misinterpreted, Benjamin pressed his finger to his lips. "Shhh."

He motioned for the others to stay put. He crept forward. He knew he was breathing fast, with quick and shallow breaths.

He stopped.

Listening, he could hear them grumble. They had to be on the opposite side of the bushes.

The moonlight was perfect. It was nearly as bright out as if the sun had been shining.

He knelt down beside the bushes and poked the barrel of his rifle through. In his scope he saw four zombies. He'd have to shoot and reload until they were all down. He panned left and right just to ensure more creatures weren't in the area. He did not see any.

The rifle sounded like a puff of air being released when he fired.

Through the scope he saw the tranquilizer dart stick the tallest zombie in the neck.

He loaded a second cartridge, aimed, and fired. The tranquilizer stuck in the female zombie's back.

Without putting hands out, the tall zombie fell forward, face first.

The third zombie got hit in the thigh, the fourth Benjamin hit in the triceps.

It took roughly four minutes for the other three zombies to collapse. Benjamin raised his arm and waved Earl and Wayne over. "String them up," Benjamin said, "and we'll head home."

# # #

The main gate closed and locked, as Ben followed behind Earl and Wayne.

Wayne had dropped lassos around two of the zombies' necks. The ropes from the opposite ends of the lassos fed through the six foot hollow pole. Earl controlled two with the pole he had, dog catcher style.

The zombies were slow, groggy from the tranquilizers. The drug didn't last long. It merely incapacitated the creatures long enough for the gatherers to secure them with the ropes.

Four was a pretty good haul considering there seemed to be less and less zombies in the area. The cold, wet weather didn't help. Winters were always tough. It was why it became important to store up on zombie while there were zombies to nab.

They led the zombies toward City Hall. They'd lock them in a holding cell until morning, and then Benjamin and Wayne would take them down to the Cog.

Normally, Earl and Wayne made the deliveries, but Benjamin had an ulterior motive for wanting to drop the zombies off to the warden.

# # #

Benjamin met his father at the Diner for breakfast. When he pushed open the door, a bell jingled.

"Morning, Mona," he said. His father was sitting at a booth by the window, staring out at the few people walking along the sidewalk.

"Coffee, hon?"

"When you have time, no rush," Benjamin said. He slid into the seat across from his father.

Victor Forti had both hands on his cup. "Good morning."

"Hey, dad."

"How'd it go last night?"

"Brought in four."

Victor nodded. "Not bad."

Mona came over with a spoon in one hand as she set a cup and saucer down in front of Benjamin. She dumped an ice cube off the spoon into his coffee. "Need a minute before ordering?"

Benjamin caught his father looking at him.

There were no menus on the table. The Forti's didn't need one.

"I'll just have some toast and scrambled eggs," Victor said.

"Of course, Mayor, and for you, Benny?"

"Same."

When Mona was gone, Benjamin watched his father. The man just continued to look out the window. He seemed older, his hair going more grey. "You okay, dad?"

"You've been on gathering how long now?"

"Two years."

"Two years. You know, there isn't a night that you go out that I don't lie awake in bed worrying."

"I can take care of myself." Benjamin wasn't sure he believed his father.

"I know you can. I do. Things happen. Plans go bad. There could be a horde of zombies that surprise you. You never know."

"If a horde of zombies surprised me, I'd be surprised. You can hear them, smell them—"

"You know what I mean, Ben. Please," he said.

"Sorry." Benjamin sipped his coffee. It was hot. It burned his tongue. It reminded him of a night by the fireplace with his mother drinking hot cocoa. He always wanted that chocolaty fill, and always sipped too much, too fast, too soon, burning not just his tongue, but also the roof of his mouth. From that point on, she always added a few ice cubes to the cocoa. He drank his coffee the same way, with an ice cube. "I am very cautious out there, I promise."

"The four at the jail?" The subject of safety forgotten, or was just ignored for the moment.

"Yeah. Dropped them there last night. In fact, after breakfast, I was going to meet up with Wayne and deliver them to the Cog." Benjamin stared into his coffee.

"Where's Earl?"

"Told him to sleep in. I'd handle it. I'm close to my wits end with that guy."

"He mess up out there?"

Benjamin shrugged. "Yes. Nothing I couldn't control, this time. Between you and me, father and son, okay? The guy's a liability."

Victor simply nodded, showing he understood but wasn't planning to comment, or for that matter, take any action. "I don't want you interacting with her."

"I'm dropping off zombies. In and out," Benjamin said.

"Your word?"

Benjamin held up two fingers. "I swear."

Chapter 31

Char sat on a stationary bike. Chris had been absolutely correct. Her legs felt like rubber. Kilmer let her switch from the mill to the bike when she told him she didn't think she could walk another mile. The boots she wore were heavy with cushion, but not meant for walking fifteen plus miles a day. Her feet ached. She'd rubbed them as best she could, but the backs of her ankles were chaffing. The bottoms of her feet felt blistered and calloused. With pedals she was able to position her feet in a way that delivered the least pain.

"You get used to it," Ross had told her, "and you will have muscles like marble in a month."

She was getting tired of his silver lining outlook.

She gripped the handlebars and leaned forward as she pedaled. She knew she was putting out close to ten miles an hour, just about the minimum requirement. There wasn't a single clock anywhere. It felt like she had been riding for hours and had gotten nowhere.

At the moment, all she could think about was music. She'd give almost anything for a headset with her own playlist downloaded. She could recall songs she'd loved. The lyrics, the beat. It was distant though, almost inaudible inside her head.

All those musicians. They were probably dead, or among the infected. She tried to imagine Ross Lynch from R5 stumbling around infected, pouncing on unsuspecting victims and tearing into their flesh with his teeth.

It was surreal.

She thought about celebrities, and politicians, police officers and factory workers. No one had been immune to the vaccination, and no one, as far as she knew, survived being bitten.

She'd made it.

The dark of the last three years should have gotten her somewhere. Instead, she was on a bicycle in the bowels of a mountain trying to out-pedal infected walking behind her on mills.

She laughed out loud.

The sound of her laughter startled her.

She looked around to see if anyone had noticed.

They hadn't.

The mask had kept the obscure sound mostly muffled and trapped behind the plastic faceplate.

To the right, by the elevator, she saw the guards stare up the shaft. It was far too loud inside the plant to hear anything over the hum and crackle of manufactured lightning of the generator. Something was coming, though.

The guards stepped back.

Char kept pedaling. She was getting used to how fast her heart beat inside her chest. Cardio was supposed to be the best exercise. Ross might have a point. Her thighs would be like marble, and she'd have the heart muscle of an ox if she stayed at this workout routine for long.

An elevator slowly descended.

She saw two infected in front of the car, and something behind them.

Benjamin Forti led the infected off, and handed a pole to one of the guards. That guard led the infected away. They reminded her of dogs on the end of an unbendable leash.

Char hated the way her heart betrayed her. She should not have nearly gasped when she saw Ben. He meant nothing to her. Nothing.

She looked down at the handle bars. She did not want him to see her like this. The prison garb made her look like a gang branch of the C.D.C. She was caked in sweat, and knew her body odor had marred the Carhartt material forever.

Her speedometer read 12 mph. There was no reward for putting out more energy than what was required. Her legs pumped fast and hard, not for recognition, but to keep busy, and preoccupied.

She saw two sets of boots by the front spinning tire of her bike, and looked up.

Lou Kilmer and Ben Forti.

She never stopped pedaling, and actually pedaled faster.

"We don't usually let visitors on the floor. Ben's different. He has two minutes. But you, McKinney, you keep working. Visitation is on the weekends. You're new. This is a different situation. It's the only reason I'm allowing it. Understood."

"Yes, boss." She hated that, calling him boss. The hate only multiplied because she had to say it in front of Ben.

Kilmer walked away.

Ben stood with his hands in front of him. His fingers kept moving, like he was about to say something. No words came out.

Behind the mask, Char rolled her eyes. "You make a delivery?"

Ben smiled and looked relieved. "Yeah. Four new zombies."

"Infected," she said.

"What?"

"I don't like calling them zombies. It's not what they are. They were people once, Ben. Real living people. They got sick. They changed. Because they were unlucky, they're damned. Look around. We've damned the dead," she said. "So I don't call them zombies."

"Infected," he said.

"Why are you here?"

"We just said, I brought new zo—infected."

"No. Why are you over here talking to me? I don't need the attention. I'm trying to fit in. If I have the mayor's kid schmoozing with me, how's that going to look? When you get on that elevator and ride back up top, guess what? I'll still be down here, only now I'm going to have to take shit from everyone for talking to you. I don't appreciate that, Ben. I'd prefer if you didn't come see me. Not on weekends, not ever again."

"Char—"

"Get lost, Ben. Go on, get out of here." She lowered her head. Her breath was fogging her mask. She closed her eyes, prayed he was walking away. After counting off sixty seconds in her head, she opened her eyes. Ben was gone.

"What was that about?" Ross said.

"I don't want to talk about it," she said. She just wanted to pedal her bike, do her work. She just wanted to get the day over and go back to her cell. She just wanted to be left alone.

"I feel like you're mad at me."

He sounded like kids she knew at school. Ross's feelings were hurt. That was too bad. She wasn't some kid. This wasn't school. "I have no respect for you as a man," she said. There was no reason to hold it in. He wanted to know why she was giving him the cold shoulder, she'd tell him. This wasn't a head game.

Char expected Ross to whine. That would have fit perfectly with his hurt feelings.

He didn't, but instead went in the exact opposite direction. "You don't respect me as a man? At least I didn't kill people. At least I didn't slaughter innocent people."

She stopped pedaling and sat up straight. "You son of a bitch."

"McKinney. McKinney!"

She ignored Kilmer as she climbed off her bike. She pushed Ross off his. Walking around the front of the bike, she watched him scramble to his feet. "Gonna hit me, Ross."

Someone tackled her.

She went down hard on her shoulder. Pain shot into her neck.

People were shouting. It could have just been the guard yelling by her ear. She couldn't differentiate sound. The hum. The static hiss. The spinning bicycle wheels. The infected were riled up, moaning and groaning liked they sensed the tension over the piece of dangling meat. It was pandemonium inside her head. She saw nothing but the color red. It tinted her vision. She closed her eyes as someone placed a knee on her back. She couldn't tell how many guards were on her. She knew she was struggling, could tell that her legs were kicking, and arms flailing.

Then they were off her.

A volt of current burned through her body. The pain started in her ass. It passed like electricity down her legs and up her spine. Her hands twitched.

She felt her eyeballs roll back as darkness enveloped her.

# # #

Char felt freaked out working through dinner alone. The infected walked on mills behind her. They were all around her. She knew they were watching her. She kept pedaling and tried to pretend she was alone and that she was appreciating the solitude.

Kilmer sat behind his desk. He didn't pretend not to stare at her. His ogling was blatant. He kicked his feet up, crossed his legs at the ankles and stared.

She didn't need a crystal ball.

The look in his eyes, even though the fogged face plate, even from a distance, was clear.

Part of her was surprised he wasn't making his way toward her, throwing advances around. The others had been gone nearly thirty minutes. They'd be gone only a little longer, and maybe his thoughts hadn't turned to assault until just now. She knew she was going to have to miss breakfast in the morning. If the evil thoughts weren't fleeting, the morning might prove more dangerous.

She shuddered and did the only thing she could do. She pedaled the bike and maintained thirteen miles an hour. She didn't want to give Lou Kilmer, her boss, any excuses to harass her.

Chapter 32

"I have a problem." Char was in the front corner of her cell, close to Ross. "Can you hear me?"

"Are you talking to me?"

"Don't be an ass," she said.

"You attacked me," he said.

The lights went out in the prison an hour ago. There was no movement below on the first level.

"Did I hurt you?"

No response.

"Did you get punished?"

"I didn't do anything."

"No harm, no foul," she said.

A silence fell between them. She was sure he wasn't going to talk anymore. She turned to walk back to her bed when he said, "What's the problem."

"Lou."

"What about him?"

"He's going to have me alone tomorrow morning, while you guys have breakfast."

"Alone?"

"I have a bad feeling," she said.

"Shit."

"Yeah. Shit." It was a no win situation. If he attacked her, and she defended herself, it wouldn't even be a he said, she said situation. It would be his word against hers. He was a foreman and she was a convict sentenced to prison for murder. No one was going to believe her. "What do I do?"

"Haven't been any women down here before. Not as prisoners. You're the first. I don't have a clue," he said.

She let out a despairing sigh. "Should I tell Kyle in the morning?"

"He seems to like you," Ross said.

"I'm not going to get raped. Not here. Not by him," she said. She wasn't talking to Ross. She was just speaking out loud.

Something hit the bars of her cell.

Char jumped.

"What was that?" Ross said.

"I have no idea," she said. She worried they were being too loud. She didn't want to wake a sleeping guard. Whatever struck the cell was on the walkway, just outside of her bars. She knelt and pressed her face against the bars. She saw what it was. She reached through the bars. The wrapper crinkled in her hand.

"What is it?" Ross said.

She looked toward his cell. His arm was sticking out from between the bars, and he held a small mirror in his hand. He was watching her.

Char stood up and walked back over toward the wall she shared with Ross. "A granola bar."

Ross didn't say anything. He didn't have to. They both knew the food came from Gonzales. "It's better to have friends," she said, speaking in a whisper. "You said it yourself. You are out of here in a month. Unless I find a way out of here, I'm looking at three long years. I can't be afraid all the time. Turns out my biggest problem wasn't going to be the scary gang down there."

She wanted to cry.

"The river," Ross said, "it isn't a safe way out of here."

"Do you know of any other way?"

"There isn't. The elevator is the only thing I've seen. There are some other tunnels around here, but they could lead anywhere. They could be blocked off. I saw them bring wrought iron sections of fence down here a while back. Lots of it. I never saw it again. If I had to guess, they used it to block off tunnels," Ross said.

"That's crazy. What if there is a collapse and they need to evacuate?"

"There were door sections, too. Warden, Kilmer, they must have keys. Probably the guards too. There's no way you're getting your hand on those. It's not like the old westerns where they left the giant key ring on a hook by the cells, and we string our belts together and knock them off and drag them to within reach," he said.

"Ross. Please, tell me about the river."

"It runs fast. It's cold. It's dangerous."

"I don't belong down here. The people of Arcadia might think they've re-established democracy, but they haven't. My trial was a joke. The public defender I was assigned, a joke. There are no appeals. The jurors are biased residents at best, because they sure as shit weren't peers of mine. I just want to leave. I get out of here, I won't look back. I'm not a danger to people. What I did was in self-defense," she said, and told Ross about what had happened, how Broadhurst kidnapped and tortured her friends.

"I'm sorry all of that happened."

"Ross, is the river accessible?"

"When I first got here, I spent months trying to map an escape. I know I have no wife or job to go back to. The mayor will find me work, I suppose, but I won't have anything as good as a janitor, if you can imagine that."

"And you found a way out?"

Again, there was silence from Ross' cell.

"Ross?"

"Yes. I'd found a way out." He reached an arm out. "Take this. You'll need it, but if things go south—"

"I didn't get it from you," she said.

# # #

Char found it difficult to sleep. Her mind was filled with too many thoughts. They jumbled inside her brain making it hard to concentrate on any one idea. Ross had given her an out. It was not a complete escape plan, but the potential was there. She had no idea what would happen if she was caught. She supposed time would be added to her sentence. She'd only been down in this hell hole for a few days. That was already far too long. Weighing the idea of freedom against the risk of more years tacked on seemed worth it.

If she had been in the wrong, she might respect the sentence. She'd do the time, whether she believed in this dystopian government or not. Her father was a dispatcher for 911. He had hung out with police officers and had been raised to respect the law. Given the situation of the world, she doubted he'd have been disappointed in her plan.

She wished he were still alive. She'd give anything to talk to him. Not just about whether it was right to carry out an escape plan, but just to hear his voice. He knew how to comfort her, and she never felt safer than when she was with him. They had some of their best talks fishing. Cash hated fishing. He'd stay home with their mom. The two of them would get up early, and they'd stop for coffee and doughnuts and head down to Charlotte. They sat in those sports chairs, side-by-side and cast into the Genesee River along the pier at the beach. He'd told her the best part about fishing together was that she was not squeamish about hooking her own worm, or wrangling a fish off the hook. Sometimes they would sit for hours and just quietly fish. The silence between them was never awkward.

"Got a boyfriend?" It was always one of his first questions. She always said no. She used to wonder how'd he react the time she said that she did. She would never know.

"I miss you, daddy," she said, and wiped tears from the corner of her eyes.

When the lights came on inside the prison, she climbed out of bed. She put on her Carhartt and retrieved her mask and gloves off the shelf over the toilet. She needed to be prepared, but without looking anxious. There was no way anyone, other than Ross, would suspect a thing. She was too new for them to know her personality. Part of her suspected no one cared about how she behaved. If the guards and the warden kept a close eye on anyone, it would be Gonzales and his men. They looked the dangerous part. The issue she face was that eyes were on her because she was the only female. It made her different. Different could be as unwanted as looking dangerous.

The routine was already stale.

She listened for Kyle, and heard him climbing the staircase. He walked so heavy. His boots fell hard on the metal walk. She didn't think he'd be able to sneak up on someone if he tried. She heard Ross's cell swing open. The hinge whined as it moved.

"We're going to have to get some oil on that thing," Kyle said.

"It's the moisture down here. Everything will rust up eventually."

Kyle appeared in front of her cell. He did not say good morning, or a single word as he opened her cell. She stepped onto the walk, and out of the way so he could close and lock it back up.

"You will not be joining the others for breakfast this morning," he said. "Follow MacNeil down the stairs, but not to the picnic tables. Understood?"

She nodded. "Sir?"

"What?"

"Can I have permission to use the restroom before we go down?"

"Use it. Wait for me outside the door when you finish. We clear?"

"Yes, sir. Thank you."

Kyle Newstead walked away. Char wanted to see if Ross was staring at her. It took mental strength not to move. She kept her eyes on the guard, anxiously waiting for the signal. The thought that she could be an hour from escaping filled her. The energy from the thoughts made her limbs tingle.

Following Ross down the stairs, he went toward the picnic tables. She went toward the locker room.

Her heart beat so fast that she felt it bang into her ribcage.

She breathed in. Breathed out. In. Out.

The temptation to look back and see if anyone watched her felt strong. She didn't. She stepped through the doorway. She ran to the air vent she'd seen the other day and she climbed onto the cabinet. She removed a screwdriver from her Carhartt. She had no idea where Ross got it from, but was thankful he had it.

Four screws secured the grill over the vent. It would be a tight fit, and she wasn't sure how she'd be able to move swiftly once inside, but didn't care. As long as she was making strides away from the Cog, she didn't care.

The first screw came loose easily. The second did as well. The third took some time.

"Let's go, McKinney!"

It sounded like Kyle was standing behind her. She almost dropped the screwdriver.

The fourth screw was tight. Rusted. She pushed the screwdriver in tight and tried twisting it loose. It was stubborn and it wouldn't budge.

"McKinney! We'll add extra time to end of shift if you don't step it up!"

She held the handle in both hands and pushed using all of her weight.

"McKinney, don't make me come in there for you! McKinney?"

"I'm just about done!"

That might buy her a minute or two. She needed to hurry. If he came in here, if he caught her, the plan to escape wouldn't just be thwarted, it would be crushed forever. She'd never get out.

Chapter 33

"McKinney! McKinney!" Kyle Newstead said.

Char emerged from the locker room. "It's my stomach. I'm sorry," she said.

She caught Ross' eye. He stared at her from the picnic table. Everyone was staring at her.

The screwdriver was in her pocket, the screws were mostly secured back in the vent cover, finger tight. She'd just managed to loosen the fourth one. She had run out of time. She'd never have gotten all four screws out, climbed into the vent, replaced it, and wiggled her way out the other end. Never. It was best not to rush an escape, but to wait for the best time.

Kyle nodded, thumbs jammed into his jeans pockets. "Come on. We've wasted enough time."

Char walked ahead of the guard. They reached the elevator shaft that would lower them to the work floor. It was nearly impossible not to feel depressed about failing. There was no point in masking the emotions. Newstead could assume she was depressed about being in prison, or missing breakfast, or on the rag. It didn't matter.

"I want to say something." She waited until she was alone with Newstead. "I have a bad feeling about Kilmer. I know saying this could put a target on my back with all of you, but the way he was looking at me, I don't trust him."

"I'm sorry to hear that, McKinney."

"So you believe me?"

Newstead laughed. "Fuck, no. Lou's good people. He comes to work every day. He stays late. He puts in six, sometimes seven days a week here making sure things run correctly. You guys, you come down and work until nine at night, but guess what? Kilmer don't go home at nine. He's even got a room down there. Sleeps here a lot of the time; the other foremen, they don't have his kind of dedication. You've been here all of what? Three or four days and you're going to throw around accusations because someone was looking at you funny? You're a girl. Don't tell me people haven't stared at you because of it in the past. This is prison, McKinney. Who started a fight yesterday? Was it Kilmer? No, it was you."

The lecture lasted until the elevator car stopped.

Kyle opened the gate. Char stepped off.

"Don't make waves, McKinney. Just go work. No one's going to bother you."

She put on her mask and turned away.

She hoped he was right. She might just feel apprehensive about Kilmer because of the life changes that are constantly thrust at her. A guy fantasizing about a woman was not uncommon, she knew. It was likely, actually, that all he had been doing was fantasizing. She might have been overreacting. In a way, she now wished she'd never said anything to Kyle. Kyle would always have that in the back of his head.

Always was relative. She still did not plan on remaining at the Cog long. She was going to get out. Eventually, this would be nothing but a part of her past.

Kilmer waved her over with his clipboard. He waved at Kyle.

She did not turn around, but heard the elevator gate close. The hum of the elevator motor chugged, and she knew Kyle was on his way back up. Her mouth and throat went dry. She felt cumbersome and ill equipped to handle herself in the gloves, jacket and mask. It was clumsy.

As she walked toward Kilmer, she saw behind the first row of mills that circled the pillar-generator, the infected. They lumbered ever forward on the belts. The meat that dangled on wire in front of them couldn't be that irresistible. She had no idea how long they survived down here. A part of her felt sorry for them. It was a small part. Killing them seemed more humane.

"Come with me," Kilmer said.

The stationary bikes were idle.

No one walked on the first row of mills.

Where was he taking her?

She followed behind him. Her gloved hand was stuffed in her jacket pocket. Even with her hand inside the glove she could feel the screwdriver's handle. If it came down to it, she'd kill him.

There was a doorway by the back west corner of the work floor. He unlocked and pushed it open. "Inside," he said.

She thought about stabbing him now. It made more sense just to get it over with.

Her intuition had not been wrong.

Kyle had been wrong.

There was no denying a hunger in a man's eyes. Women picked up on that kind of thing. She figured it was an instinct they were born with.

"What's in there?"

"Doesn't matter. It's where I told you to go."

Char knew her pulse was quickening. She felt her face grow hot, and knew behind the faceplate her cheeks were reddening. She grit her teeth, walked past Kilmer and into the room.

It was his room.

There was a bed and dresser, and another door that presumably led to either a closet or a bathroom.

"Take off the jacket," Kilmer said. He pulled his mask off and set it down on the dresser.

"It's cold in here," she said.

It wasn't. It felt like a sauna. With no mask on, with the smell of sulfur all around her, the odor that stood out most was his cologne. Sweat and Old Spice. Her grandfather always wore Old Spice. The scent used to give her wonderful memories. Now those would be forever charred.

"Take off the jacket. Now."

She pulled her hands out of her pockets. She took off one glove, and hid the screwdriver inside it, before she unzipped her jacket.

"Hurry. Get that jacket off," he said. He had on a polo shirt. He pulled it off. His undershirt was yellowed at the armpits. Chest hair protruded out of the top of the neck. He shoveled his fingers through his hair. "You know what this is. Get out of those jeans."

"You don't want to do this."

He moved fast. In a single, fluid motion, he stepped forward and open handed her across the face. It caught her hard on the cheek and chin. It caught her off guard and her head whipped to the side from the blow.

She dropped the glove, her weapon.

"Shut your mouth," he said. He grabbed her by the shoulders and yanked down on the jacket, pulling it off her. His breath stunk of coffee and fish.

She ran her tongue over her bottom lip. The blood tasted like licking a penny.

"The jeans," he said.

She fumbled with the button. Her eyes darted around the room. There was nothing she could use. She lowered the zipper.

He was breathing heavy. He couldn't contain his excitement.

"Get the fucking pants off now and get on the—"

Someone knocked at the door. Three fast, hard raps. "Mr. Kilmer, are you in there?"

Lou punched the air. He smoothed his hair with the palm of his hand. "Ah, just a moment," he said. Lou pointed at Char. His lip quivered as he mouthed the words, "Get dressed."

She zipped and buttoned her pants. She picked up her jacket, put it on, and carefully retrieved her gloves.

Lou opened the door. "Yes?"

It was Kyle. He peered over Lou, looking into the room. Char just stared at him. Her hair was wet with sweat. She knew her lip was still bleeding, and possibly swollen.

"I forgot I was supposed to get a new zombie count for the warden. I was wondering if you had the nu—am I interrupting something?"

"No. Not at all. She, ah, McKinney was just—what did you need?" Kilmer said.

"Latest zombie count. I know the mayor's kid brought two down yesterday."

"Four."

"Four? I thought it was two," Kyle said.

"Two at a time. Four total," Kilmer said.

"Should we do a walk-around? Get an accurate head count for Hermann? You know how them engineers are. He likes to have all the numbers in front of him so he can do all his math shit." Kyle laughed, but his eyes never stopped staring at Charlene.

She wanted to cry, and thought she might if he didn't look away soon.

"McKinney, we all set here?" Kilmer said. "Why don't you get back to work? First bike on the end. I'll be keeping my eye on you."

His authoritative voice trembled. He knew it. She knew it. They knew that Kyle caught it as well.

She walked out of the room, went directly toward the bike she'd been instructed to use. The infected on the mills along the end seemed to watch her as she passed. Was it possible that the milky and clouded-over eyeballs of the infected were filled with pity?

She climbed onto the bike and started pedaling.

She never looked up.

She never looked up until the other prisoners started showing up and were assigned bikes and mills.

She hoped Ross was next to her.

He wasn't.

Gonzales was. She knew that Kilmer put Gonzales there as a threat. The gangbanger didn't bother her, but Kilmer didn't know that.

"Thank you for the granola bar," she said, after a while. "I appreciate it."

"It was my way of thanking you first," he said.

That was it. Seventeen words only. The bond was there. Formed. It might not be unbreakable, but it was more than they'd had before.

When Kyle returned to escort them back up for dinner, Char was thankful. Although she was still upset, she knew that part of her belly ache came from hunger. She never thought she'd find herself looking forward to an M.R.E. In truth they weren't all that terrible. Some of it just tasted like flavored cardboard, but right now, even cardboard with a little salt and pepper sounded like a gourmet meal.

She climbed off her bike.

Kilmer dropped a heavy hand on her shoulder. "Not you."

She shuddered and knew that if she was forced to stay, the punishment would be worse.

"Lou," Kyle said, "can I see you for a second?"

"Keep riding," Kilmer said.

Char sat on the bike seat and placed her feet on the pedals.

She watched Kyle and Lou walk toward each other. They closed the distance fast. Kyle placed a hand on Lou's shoulder. Char could not see Kyle's eyes, but knew he was looking at her while he talked with the foreman.

After a moment, Lou turned around. "McKinney, go on. It's dinner time."

Char was apprehensive. She cautiously got off the bike again. Kyle waved her toward him. "Let's go, McKinney. Step to it."

She walked toward them.

Lou stared at her the entire time.

She wished her breath would fog up her faceplate. She did not think she could handle seeing him anymore, not ever again.

Kyle led her to the elevator shaft.

"What happened?" she said, when they had begun ascending.

"Told him you already missed your two meals," Kyle said.

"Thank you."

Kyle nodded. "I'm sorry I didn't listen earlier. Are you all right?"

"I'm looking forward to my shower tonight," she said. She felt dirty. She wasn't sure she'd be able to scrub away the filth. It was inside her. There was no way that she knew of to clean it.

"Don't tell anyone, but I'll give you a few extra minutes in there tonight. Okay?"

"Thank you, sir," she said.

"Not a word. Got it?"

"Mum." She said, and twisted an imaginary key in front of her faceplate and tossed the imaginary key over her shoulder.

# # #

Char tore into the M.R.E.

Ross sat next to her with his elbows up on the table, his hands in front of his mouth. He whispered, "I was surprised to see you this morning."

She ate the cheese tortellini with a thin plastic spork. "I had trouble with the screws on the vent."

"I don't want to bring it up, but Kilmer—"

"He didn't touch me. Almost," she said. "Kyle came back."

Ross nodded. "Now what?" he said.

"Now, let me eat. I'm starving," she said. She knew that Frank and Chris listened to what they said, but guessed they had no idea what they were talking about. It was better that way. They had never really gotten around to how long each of them was sentenced, and honestly, she didn't care. Not at this point.

Gonzales Morales and his men got up from their table. They walked toward Char and the people seated at hers.

The man stopped by her, holding his tray in lowered hands. "Take my granola bar. Save it for later."

She reached for it, looking up at him. "Thank you," she said.

They filed away, emptied the M.R.E. bags and wrappers into the trash and set down their trays.

"What just happened?" Frank said.

"He's not such a bad guy," Char said. He was though, and she knew it. He reminded her a lot of Antonio Velasquez. Gonzales was a dangerous man, and fearing him made sense. Keeping one's distance was best. All she'd ensured was a connection. It was there now. Once again offering her a granola bar proved the connection was soundly established.

They stood up with their trays. "Few more hours down there," Chris said, "and showers. I love shower day."

"Only time I can take a quick shit without anyone watching me," Frank said.

"That's never stopped you," Chris said.

"Didn't say it did. Just nice to have a little privacy, is all."

232

Char touched Ross's wrist. He stopped as the others left the table.

"I just want to say thank you, and goodbye."

"You're still going to try this? It's foolish, McKinney. Foolish and reckless. If you don't get caught, you could die," he said.

"I'll remember you."

Chapter 34

Kyle Newstead stood by the locker room doorway with Char, while another guard walked four men with wet hair back to their cells. A third guard was inside the locker room as the next four men cleaned up.

Char stood shoulder to shoulder with Kyle. She knew he was going to try to talk to her. She just wanted silence. A lot was on her mind. The time was essential to prepare mentally. She would need to move fast, every action flawless. Kyle had promised her a little extra time.

He had promised it to her because he knew that Kilmer had tried to rape her, because he felt guilty for not being there to protect her.

She started to cry.

The tears were real, but she wanted them. She didn't think she needed to remind Kyle about the extra time to shower, but it couldn't hurt to show him that she was still upset.

He shifted his weight from one foot to the other, clearly uncomfortable. If they had been having drinks at the Bent Elbow, he'd console her. He had no idea how to interact with a woman in the Cog. He was a decent enough guy. She did not feel guilty taking advantage of that fact. He might get some static once her escape was realized, but she didn't think anyone would be too harsh on him. Maybe she'd be doing him a favor, and he'd wind up with a new job up top. It's hard to believe anyone would choose to work down here voluntarily, except for maybe George Hermann, the warden.

"Sounds like they're using all of the hot water," Kyle said.

Here comes the uncomfortable and awkward small talk. She didn't reply, but sniffled and ran her forearm under her nose.

"It's never really hot, though. You're missing lukewarm water, at the most," he said.

It seemed like time had stopped moving. She just wanted her turn in the locker room. "I feel so dirty. I just feel …"

More tears came. They were a little forced this time, a little fake. She didn't want to over act this, but she wanted Kyle as sympathetic and understanding as possible before she was given her time in the locker room.

The next four men came out talking, their hair wet.

"Enough chit chat," Kyle said, his tone of voice gruff and commanding. Char saw who this man was, and gruff and commanding was not any part of his true colors.

The guard came out next. "Clear in there," he said.

Kyle nodded at the man, and turned to Char. "You're up. A few extra minutes to get yourself together, okay? Don't make me regret this."

"Thank you," she said.

# # #

Char McKinney entered the locker room, walking slow, knowing Kyle watched her every step with sympathetic eyes.

As soon as she rounded the corner, she changed gears. She ran to a shower stall and turned on the water. She went for the small cabinet, pulled herself up onto it, and used fingers on both hands to remove screws in the vent.

She set the vent cover down and crawled into the shaft. It was a tight fit. She wanted to try to replace the vent cover but would have had to back in. There would have been no room to turn around after, and she didn't want to back her way out of the prison. She knew if the vent cover was replaced, they would still realize had happened. No one was going to think she simply vanished. So replacing the cover didn't matter, and wouldn't really buy her much extra time.

The galvanized steel around her was thin. She had to crawl forward slowly. Every time her booted toe tapped the sheet metal it sounded like thunder. Ross told her he wasn't positive what was around below the air duct, but that he'd heard it was a large dry goods and weapons storage facility. If that was true, she hoped it was an unmanned facility. Otherwise, even with normal prison noise, a deaf man would know someone was scurrying around in the ducts.

She passed over mesh grill vents now and then. There was no light below. She figured she was over, or well past the storage area depending on how big it actually was. She knew she had maybe two, three more minutes before Kyle started yelling into the locker room for her to hurry up.

She hurried up all right. At this point, time was of the essence, and she felt like it was also her enemy, working against her.

She'd noticed the continued incline, though. It was slight, but it was apparent. That was a good thing.

Unnatural fears filled her. The duct was so dark. She couldn't turn around and look, but felt like something was back there, closing in on her.

An infected?

Kilmer?

She could not gauge how far she'd have traveled inside the duct. It felt like miles and miles; it was more like yards and yards.

She couldn't hear the shower running. It either meant she'd put some distance between herself and the locker room, or they'd discovered that she was missing.

She crawled faster. Her imagination now running her brain.

It was all irrational, but she was sure that the warden had set infected loose in the ducts.

She heard the sheet metal buckle and snap back into shape behind her.

They were coming.

Something was coming for her.

She was done being cautious, and moved on hands and knees. Her knees slid on the metal. Her palms gave her traction.

The one thing she noticed was that there had been no off chutes. Whoever was coming after her would never have to stop and wonder which way she had gone. There was just the one direction.

That brought up another concern.

There would only be one exit.

The duct continued to lead her upwards, only the incline was becoming more and more obvious. She worried that at some point she might just hit a forty-five or ninety degree angle and be royally screwed.

She crawled as fast possible. It wasn't easy. The space was cramped. The darkness was terrifying. She moved her arms and legs, knowing that whoever was behind her was closing the gap. She felt like she couldn't gain any momentum, that she did more slipping. The traction was terrible.

She breathed in nothing but sulfur. It was as if she was crawling over a spoiled egg storage area.

Char fell flat. A charlie-horse gripped her thigh. Dragging herself forward with her hands, and one leg, she cringed at the pain. She dropped her head, unable to continue. It was a great effort. She'd almost. . .

She heard it. Ahead of her. There was no mistaking the sound.

Behind her, the sheet metal banged.

The river was close.

She couldn't give up. Not now. Not being this close.

Char lifted her head and got onto all fours. The muscle in her leg spasmed. She ignored it. She pushed forward. Forward. There was no stopping. Not now. No giving up. Not ever.

She wished she could see something, anything, but there was some kind of light.

It wasn't far ahead.

She tried to ignore whoever was coming up behind her, tried to block out the fact they seemed to be getting closer, and closer.

The incline was steeper now, but the sound of the rushing water louder.

She braced her feet on the sides of the duct. It was an awkward angle, but it kept her from slipping backwards.

She scooted forward; climbing toward what she hoped was the end of the duct.

Escape was always the plan, but now that she felt so close actually to getting away, doubt filled her. She knew she needed to fight that. It could get her caught, or killed. Ignoring the doubt and remaining positive and confident was imperative.

Her boots lost their grip. She slid down the duct several feet. The thunder of wracking sheet metal was so close, she was afraid if she tried to see behind her that they would be almost on her.

She wanted to live.

She needed to get out of this place.

Char was not going to stop. She dug in with the toe of her boots, and kept on moving.

Her hands hit something. Her fingers raked across a grate. The end of the duct? A vent cover?

It was a way out.

She punched at the cover. If the screws at this end were rusted, she might be trapped. She punched hard, using the heels of her hands. The vent didn't seem to budge.

Time was running out.

She wasn't about to get caught. Not now.

Not this close.

There wasn't room enough to get much leverage. She wished she could turn around and kick the vent out. That wasn't possible.

She struck the vent over and over.

Over and over.

Something gave.

They were almost directly behind her. She knew it now. The sound was louder, different.

She slammed her heel of her hand into the vent, over and over. A rage filled her. She thought of Kilmer trying to rape her, of Tony, of Sam. . .of Grace, alone and in a coma in a hospital bed. She thought of Cash and her father.

An anger filled her, coursed through her, and exploded from her fists in a strike that knocked the vent free of the screws that secured it in place.

She reached her hands forward, and pulled her upper torso out of the duct.

She felt blindly around for some kind of hand hold. There was nothing. Her eyes never adjusted to the darkness. There just wasn't any light to assist.

She turned so she was sitting in the duct, and felt around for the top of the lip. She then pulled out her legs and dangled. She had no idea how far down the drop was. Looking down the duct she saw light. A flashlight beam played on the metal. They'd caught up to her.

She dropped. It felt like freefalling. Then her feet hit the ground. She relaxed her knees, fell, and shoulder rolled. Her left elbow crashed into something jagged, and sharp. Pain shot up her left arm. She cradled it as she struggled to get to her feet.

She thought the river would be right there, right in front of her. As best she could tell, it wasn't.

She heard the trampling of feet on crushed rock.

They pursued her from inside the duct, and knowing where the duct exited, must have sent a team to retrieve her.

She was a fugitive.

She saw several flashlight beams run across the walls of the cave she was now in. Their shadows danced across the walls as big as giants.

More light came from above, from the duct she'd just jumped out of.

She heard the river to her right.

There were no options left. She walked as carefully and as fast as she could toward the water.

She didn't want to look back. She didn't need to know how close they were.

The back of her neck became suddenly hot. She clapped a hand over the area. It almost felt like her skin was on fire under her clothing.

It was the tattoo. The burning feeling was circular.

She lost her footing.

She couldn't see a thing, and braced her arms out in front of her.

Her hands splashed through water. Her body followed. She was submerged in an icy river.

She fought to get back to the top. She'd swallowed water and choked on her way up, taking in more. Her head broke through the surface. She was all turned around in the darkness. She knew she was moving, and that the water was swift, but she felt lost and weightless. Her leg struck something under the water, and she went under with barely time to catch her breath . . .

Chapter 35

The knock at the door was insistent. Vincent Forti pulled his pillow out from under his head and stuffed it over his face.

"Coming!" No one could hear him. He was upstairs in his bedroom.

He threw off his blankets and slid his legs out of bed. His feet slid into slippers, he stood up and stretched while letting out a big, loud yawn. "This better be important."

He reached for his bathrobe on the back of his door and tied the belt around his waist as he shuffled down the short hallway to the staircase.

The knocking persisted.

Moonlight came in through the windows on either side of the door.

"Coming!" He took the stairs carefully, a hand on the railing. "Better be a fucking emergency."

He unfastened the chain, and disengaged the deadbolt. Arcadia might be pretty safe, but Vincent was never one to take unnecessary chances, and safety was a top priority, regardless.

He opened the door. "What is it?"

George Hermann's hair was unkempt. He shook his head. "We've got a problem."

# # #

She kept her hands up, and they scraped against low rock ceilings, but helped her keep from smacking her head. Her legs were out in front of her. She was trying to float with the current. Water splashed inside her mouth, up her nostrils. She gasped and coughed.

The river sounded like a locomotive. It picked up speed. She worried there might be a waterfall ahead. That's what she always recalled in any movie where someone used a river to get away. A treacherous waterfall.

The water was so cold, but did nothing to relieve the burning on the back of her neck. Rebecca Bowman had done something to her. She knew the sensation was somehow related to the powers the mystical woman had spoken of. What else could that woman do? What else did she know?

Then the ceiling disappeared above her hands.

She didn't lower her arms. She might just be in a. . .

Above was light.

Bright.

She saw the moon. Stars.

She was out of the mountain.

She put her legs behind her, swam with the current but angled for the bank. The water carried her quickly to it. She kept expecting to have her body slammed into a partially submerged boulder.

# # #

George Hermann was seated at Vincent's kitchen table when he came down the stairs fully dressed.

"Okay, so what do we have in place?" Vincent said.

"Team of guards went for the river, where the vent lets out."

"She hits the water and she'll be beyond our borders."

"True."

"Will they get her?" Vincent said.

"She's crawling through an air duct. They're running—it's a roundabout way to get there, but yeah, they should get to her before she gets to the end of the duct."

Vincent pursed his lips. A prison escape was the last thing he needed right now. Gary Priestly would exploit the hell out of this. Despite Vincent not having anything to do with a prison break, anything that happened in Arcadia, good or bad, reflected on him.

He wished he could think of a way to keep all of this secret. "So, what, only people in the Cog are aware of this?"

"So far, yes. You're the first person I came to tell when I found out." Hermann had his glasses in his hands. He used a paper napkin to wipe his lenses. "What do you want to do?"

"Your men can keep this quiet for now?"

Hermann shrugged. "They do what I tell them."

"Let's head back to the Cog. See if they've caught her. If they did, I don't want anyone outside of that place learning about the attempted escape," Vincent said. That was best case scenario. He mentally crossed his fingers.

"And on the off chance that she got away?"

"You said they would nab her where the duct exits."

"I said we should be able to get her. We are supposing though. Suppose they didn't catch her."

"I know a guy, someone I trust to find her and bring her back."

"If she's gone, there's no threat to Arcadia's people. Banishment is just as harsh as punishment during times like this, if you ask me." He fit his glasses back onto his face. The lenses made his eyeballs pop through the glass.

"We have three years to find her." Vincent Forti said. He'd win an election against Priestly without giving a race much pause, unless word of the escape went public. If he won another election, it would be essential in three years to have McKinney exit the Cog rehabilitated, and a free woman. "Come one, let's get a damage assessment, prepare for a debriefing, and see how confined we can keep this news."

Hermann got up from the table. "You're the boss."
I am, Vincent thought, but for how much longer?

Epilogue

Char stayed in the shadows of the woods and moved slowly, and cautiously around the fortress that protected Arcadia.

She figured if they came looking for her, they might assume she continued to follow the river. Hopefully, they would never think she was doubling back.

Guilt filled her heart. She hated leaving Grace alone inside that town.

There was nothing wrong with Arcadia, as long as laws weren't broken. Grace would be alone, all alone.

So am I, she thought. I'm all alone.

There were silver linings that could not be ignored. She was free. She had escaped from a prison built in the bowels of a mountain, and the moon and stars had never looked more glorious. She knew that her father was up in the heavens somewhere looking down on her, and smiling. She had no doubt that he'd taken the job as her guardian angel. He was still with her. Helping her wherever possible.

She knew she was weaponless. She stayed alert. The last thing she wanted to run into was a herd of infected.

The irony of dying that way would be too much to accept.

There was the Gathering Patrol, too. Running into them, into Ben, could prove a worse fate, if only because she had no idea how he might respond. Would he arrest her and bring her in with the infected he'd caught for the night, or would he let her go?

Would he choose to go with her?

She shook her head to knock that last thought free. She didn't want him tagging along.

# # #

Char knew the sun would be rising soon. She needed to hurry. On her knees in the forest of trees she dug up the earth with her hands. She shoveled away mounds of dirt, and kept thinking she was digging in the wrong spot. It was hard to tell if she was in the correct location. She was pretty sure she was.

For a few minutes, anyway.

Just about when she was going to stop and move to someplace else, her fingertips dragged across the bags.

She outlined them and removed them from the dirt.

Standing up, she secured the longsword's belt to her waist and the machete on her back. She strapped the knives and sheaths onto her thighs. She picked up Tony's bow and slung the quiver over her shoulder.

Relief flooded through her body, the tension spilling out of her pores.

She'd felt naked without her weapons.

She felt whole now.

She stayed inside the cover of the trees but followed the trail leading away from Arcadia, and back up the mountain. She figured the first place she'd go is back along the road to where they'd hidden the rig.

Something snapped branches.

Char stopped, knelt, and removed the machete from its sheath and listened, looking all around her. Two infected ambled between trees. They moved slow, sluggish. The guy's face looked shredded, as if someone had raked fingernails across his cheek peeling back the flesh. Black bags encircled milky eyeballs. The woman wore a tattered skirt showing off bruised, dirt-caked thighs and soiled panties. She was missing an arm, and walked on a broken ankle dragging a limp foot behind her. They were skeletons, starving. Putting them down would put them out of their misery.

She didn't have it in her. They weren't coming for her. They looked too weak to pose any threat. She ran around them, past them, and never looked back.

Char stopped when she heard a noise, not a snapping of branches. She walked toward the sound, her heart beating heavy in her chest. She could smell the dead leaves all around her. Each step crushed and crunched the crisp leaves on the ground.

She heard the sound again, a snort and a neigh.

The horse stood still, majestic and beautiful on the edge of the trail. "Dispatch?"

It shook its head. It neighed again.

She looked up. "I love you, dad. I love you."

She hugged Dispatch around his thick neck. She petted his mane.

She climbed up onto him, bareback. Before finding the rig, she'd retrieve the saddle she'd left behind. "Good boy," she said, "that's a good boy."

Char knew she was leaving, but thought it might not be for good. She had questions for Rebecca Bowman, the tattoo had been tingling since before she fell into the river, and only now as she was on Dispatch's back, did the sensation subside. . . Now armed, part of her wanted to storm Arcadia, launching an attack. It would be suicidal. It wasn't the town she was upset with. It was Lou Kilmer she wanted to kill. The time she'd spent in the river did nothing to rid her body of his filthy odor. As much as she wanted to have questions answered by Rebecca, and as desperately as she wanted to check up on Grace, Kilmer would be the main reason she'd ever return to to Arcadia; not curiosity, not concern, but *revenge*.

About the Author

Phillip Tomasso is an award-winning author of numerous novels and short stories. He works fulltime as a Fire/EMS Dispatcher for 911. As the father of three, he spends any spare time with his family, writing and playing guitar. He is hard at work on his next novel.

www.phillipytomasso.com
phillip@philliptomasso.com
@P_Tomasso (Twitter)

Special Thanks

No book writes itself. I have so many people to thank. I hope I do not leave anyone out. First, to my Beta Readers: Janice McFadden Mickolas, Amy Harps Rodwell, Amy Downs, Charles Vitale, Caroline Lee, Allen Gamboa, Dawn LaForce, Rosa Thomas-McBroom, Cathy Williams, Nikki Robbins, Kaaren Dziegiel, and Louis Schweigert. Next, I would like to thank my proofreader, Linda Tooch. She is by far one of the best out there, and I am lucky to have her in my corner, and as my friend. I would like to thank Gary, and everyone at Severed Press. They treat me well, respond to my countless emails, and answer my never ending list of questions. . .promptly! The constant love and support of family, friends, and readers is humbling. Thank you.

Novels

Mind Play
Tenth House
Third Ring
Johnny Blade
Adverse Impact
The Molech Prophecy (as Thomas Phillips)
Convicted
Pigeon Drop
Pulse of Evil
Sounds of Silence
Vaccination
Evacuation
Preservation
Treasure Island: A Zombie Novella
Blood River

Reading Groups / Book Clubs

I would like to extend an invitation to reading groups/book clubs across the country.

Invite me to your group and I'll be happy to participate in your discussion. I'm available to join your discussion either in person or via the telephone. (Reading groups should have a speakerphone.)

Looking for discussion questions? Let me know which book your group/club is scheduled to read, and I can assist with developing a list of questions. You may have your own. If your book club comes up with any interesting and provocative discussion questions, please e-mail them to me.

Also, to schedule book signings, speaking events, or arrange for interviews, feel free to contact me.

phillip@philliptomasso.com

CHECK OUT OTHER GREAT ZOMBIE NOVELS

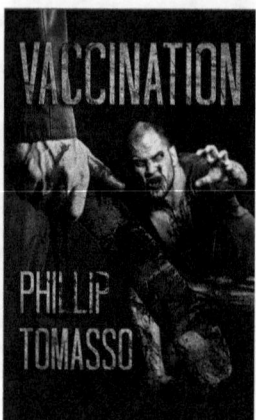

VACCINATION
by Phillip Tomasso

What if the H7N9 vaccination wasn't just a preventative measure against swine flu?

It seemed like the flu came out of nowhere and yet, in no time at all the government manufactured a vaccination. Were lab workers diligent, or could the virus itself have been man-made? Chase McKinney works as a dispatcher at 9-1-1. Taking emergency calls, it becomes immediately obvious that the entire city is infected with the walking dead. His first goal is to reach and save his two children.

Could the walls built by the U.S.A. to keep out illegal aliens, and the fact the Mexican government could not afford to vaccinate their citizens against the flu, make the southern border the only plausible destination for safety?

ZOMBIE, INC
by Chris Dougherty

"WELCOME! To Zombie, Inc. The United Five State Republic's leading manufacturer of zombie defense systems! In business since 2027, Zombie, Inc. puts YOU first. YOUR safety is our MAIN GOAL! Our many home defense options - from Ze Fence® to Ze Popper® to Ze Shed® - fit every need and every budget. Use Scan Code "TELL ME MORE!" for your FREE, in-home*, no obligation consultation! *Schedule your appointment with the confidence that you will NEVER HAVE TO LEAVE YOUR HOME! It isn't safe out there and we know it better than most! Our sales staff is FULLY TRAINED to handle any and all adversarial encounters with the living and the undead". Twenty-five years after the deadly plague, the United Five State Republic's most successful company, Zombie, Inc., is in trouble. Will a simple case of dwindling supply and lessening demand be the end of them or will Zombie, Inc. find a way, however unpalatable, to survive?

CHECK OUT OTHER GREAT ZOMBIE NOVELS

900 MILES
by S. Johnathan Davis

John is a killer, but that wasn't his day job before the Apocalypse.

In a harrowing 900 mile race against time to get to his wife just as the dead begin to rise, John, a business man trapped in New York, soon learns that the zombies are the least of his worries, as he sees first-hand the horror of what man is capable of with no rules, no consequences and death at every turn.

Teaming up with an ex-army pilot named Kyle, they escape New York only to stumble across a man who says that he has the key to a rumored underground stronghold called Avalon..... Will they find safety? Will they make it to Johns wife before it's too late?

Get ready to follow John and Kyle in this fast paced thriller that mixes zombie horror with gladiator style arena action!

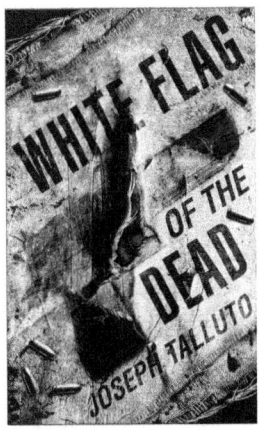

WHITE FLAG OF THE DEAD
by Joseph Talluto

Millions died when the Enillo Virus swept the earth. Millions more were lost when the victims of the plague refused to stay dead, instead rising to slaughter and feed on those left alive. For survivors like John Talon and his son Jake, they are faced with a choice: Do they submit to the dead, raising the white flag of surrender? Or do they find the will to fight, to try and hang on to the last shreds or humanity?

 SEVEREDPRESS

facebook.com/severedpress
twitter.com/severedpress

CHECK OUT OTHER GREAT ZOMBIE NOVELS

Z BURBIA
by Jake Bible

Whispering Pines is a classic, quiet, private American subdivision on the edge of Asheville, NC, set in the pristine Blue Ridge Mountains. Which is good since the zombie apocalypse has come to Western North Carolina and really put suburban living to the test!

Surrounded by a sea of the undead, the residents of Whispering Pines have adapted their bucolic life of block parties to scavenging parties, common area groundskeeping to immediate area warfare, neighborhood beautification to neighborhood fortification.

But, even in the best of times, suburban living has its ups and downs what with nosy neighbors, a strict Home Owners' Association, and a property management company that believes the words "strict interpretation" are holy words when applied to the HOA covenants. Now with the zombie apocalypse upon them even those innocuous, daily irritations quickly become dramatic struggles for personal identity, family security, and straight up survival.

ZOMBIE RULES
by David Achord

Zach Gunderson's life sucked and then the zombie apocalypse began.

Rick, an aging Vietnam veteran, alcoholic, and prepper, convinces Zach that the apocalypse is on the horizon. The two of them take refuge at a remote farm. As the zombie plague rages, they face a terrifying fight for survival.

They soon learn however that the walking dead are not the only monsters.